CLOSE QUARTER

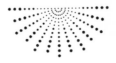

ANNA ZABO

CHAPTER ONE

*R*hys Matherton sipped his champagne, listened to the band play upbeat jazz on the deck of the ocean liner, and wondered what the hell he was doing. Taking a luxury cruise across the Atlantic wasn't at all his style, and it certainly wasn't what you were supposed to do right after you buried your mother.

Callous, one news site had said. Disrespectful. And those had been the kindest of the words thrown at him.

Maybe he was a coldhearted bastard, but he didn't want to face his life yet, not with all that had happened. Flying back to New York from Vienna would've given him only fifteen hours of peace before he plunged headlong into the morass of friends, colleagues, and reporters. Never mind the creeping mass of people who wanted to be his very best buddy now that he was worth millions.

He swallowed the knot in his throat and chased it with the rest of the champagne.

Amazing what money did. Everyone wanted a piece of him. Even galleries that had snubbed their noses at his work now wanted to display his sculptures. Friends and ex-lovers called his cell so often he let the damn thing run out of power and hadn't bothered to recharge it.

He didn't even want to think about his e-mail.

A waiter offered to take his empty flute as the ocean liner slid past the waterfront at Southampton and made its way toward the channel. A second waiter came and offered a second flute, but Rhys declined. He wasn't about to add another spate of drunkenness to his exploits bandied about in the press.

Taking the slow boat, literally, gave him an entire week to put himself back together, to have a little calm before he stepped back into his upturned life.

It wasn't his mother's death that had thrown him off. He'd known that was coming. They had mourned her stage IV brain cancer together, that last month.

No, it was the aftermath. The lies. Seeing his father again. Facing that man's anger and loathing was one thing—he'd done that most of his life. But witnessing the utter relief on Derrick Matherton's face during the reading of the will had broken every wall Rhys had built over the years. The contents of the will shattered what was left. After it was all over, his father—*Derrick*—spoke his first words to Rhys in fourteen years.

"I always knew you weren't my son."

Rhys pressed his lips together and stared out at the tourists waving from the round block fort they passed. At least that secret hadn't been leaked to the media. But then, the solicitor had been from a very highly regarded firm, and Derrick had been given a tidy sum with the stipulation that he, too, would never reveal the truth.

Not his son.

Rhys inhaled the damp June air. Fuck the champagne. What he really wanted was a beer. And a lump of clay to pound his fists into. The latter would have to wait until he was back in his studio. The former—well, the ocean liner had a wide variety of bars. He chose the one farthest away from the band and the mingling crowds watching the liner pull into the channel.

To his dismay, the lounge wasn't empty. Several men and women stood at the dark wooden bar, more around nearby tables. A particularly loud group hushed when one of the women at the table saw Rhys. She whispered to her neighbor and then giggled.

Great. Rhys looked down as he walked, his face warm. Which story had they read? The one where he was a womanizer who slept with two a night? *Derrick* would've greatly preferred that. It was so much better to have a son who went through women like tissue than a son who was single and gay.

"Sir!"

Rhys looked up in time to see the tray of glasses before he ran into it. Neither he nor the waiter could catch the tray as it tipped sideways. It fell, sending a shower of stemware and cocktails down onto a man sitting by the window.

Glasses shattered on the tile floor. One fell into the man's lap, spilling its contents and staining his dark trousers.

"Oh God, I'm sorry," Rhys said. "Oh hell." *Great, just great.* He half expected a camera flash to go off.

The waiter shot him an exasperated look before addressing the man in the chair. "Mr. Quint! Are you hurt?"

"I'm fine." Clipped words. The man stared at the glass in his hand for a moment. Then he set it down on the small table next to the chair. His movements were languid, but his knuckles were white.

Rhys wondered what the drink had been before something creamy had landed in it. Looked like shit now.

The man lifted a margarita glass off his lap and set that next to the other drink. The guy's suit was ruined too.

3

"I'll pay for it. For it all," Rhys said. He looked at the waiter. "I didn't see you. I... Shit."

Servers with towels descended on them like locusts, pushing Rhys away from the scene. He stepped back and tucked his hands into his pockets to keep them from shaking. He spied several people with their cell phones out.

Fucking fantastic. He didn't need this. He was supposed to be relaxing, not fucking up someone else's vacation. Not making the news again.

In short order, all the glass was picked up and removed. Towels sopped up much of the spilled alcohol from the tiles. Rhys heard the distinct sound of a cleaning bucket and mop clacking over the floor. In a few minutes, the results of his clumsy inattention would be a memory.

Except for the man he'd completely pissed off.

A woman handed that man a towel. He used it to dry his face and blot his lap before he stood. He turned and glared at Rhys.

Oh God. Even with cocktails dripping from his hair, the man was too close to perfection to be real. Beautiful, exquisite anger. High cheeks, long jaw. Dark hair and brows.

Rhys knew his mouth hung open a little. He took his hands from his pockets and stood straighter. "Dry cleaning." The words came out as a croak. "I'll pay."

"I have no need of your money." The man balled up the towel and whipped it at the leather chair. "Use it to buy yourself a brain."

Rhys felt the blood drain from his face. Well, he deserved that.

A moment later, a manager appeared. He ignored Rhys entirely and spoke to the dark-haired man. "Our most profound apologies. We'll take care of your laundry and the tab—"

The man held up a hand. "Yes. Thank you." There was less anger in his voice now. "This was not Vasil's fault."

The waiter who had been carrying the tray flinched.

Right. Rhys had no desire to ruin yet another person's day. He stepped forward. "It's my fault. I walked right into his tray."

The manager frowned.

Rhys patted his jacket pocket. Thank God the business cards were still there from his last gallery opening. He pulled them out, handed one to the manager. "Whatever compensation you need."

Rhys offered a second card to the dark-haired man. The guy stared at it as if it were a dead fish before he turned and stalked out of the lounge.

Hell. Rhys watched the man's back vanish through the lounge's entrance. "Wait a minute!"

The man didn't even slow down.

Gone. Perfect. Beautiful. Utterly angry, and now gone.

Damn it. He turned back to the lounge manager. "Honestly, I'm sorry. I'm good for it."

The manager raised an eyebrow in that very British fashion and studied the business card. His expression changed. Considerably.

Of course he would recognize the name. It had been in every paper. WORLD-RENOWNED CELLIST SAMANTHA MATHERTON DIES. ONLY SON RHYS INHERITS MILLIONS.

The manager tucked the business card into his shirt pocket. "We'll send you a bill, Mr. Matherton. Once we add up the expenses."

"Thanks." He lingered only until the manager turned his back. Then he fled the lounge. The stares had become too much. And if he left now, he might have a chance to catch up with that guy.

5

Short, loose black curls, like something out of ancient art. Those tanned features begged to be carved into stone. Or sculpted in clay. Or traced with fingers and lips...

Not a chance in the world, not after dumping a tray of drinks on him. But the least he could do was try to set things right.

Rhys saw his target not too far down the hall. He caught up with the man and grabbed the guy's arm. "Wait. Let me—"

The dark-haired man whirled about, pushed Rhys into a short hallway, and rammed him against the wall. Hard. "I said I don't need your money."

Rich, deep voice and eyes the color of honey. An accent Rhys couldn't place. The man wrapped his fingers around Rhys's throat. His other hand pinned Rhys against the wall. Strong. Fast.

A tick of apprehension traced down Rhys's spine. "How about an apology?" His voice was steadier than he felt.

Maybe it was the alcohol clinging to the man's hair and clothes. More likely it was the hot press of his body, but Rhys could barely draw a breath. Fear. Desire. God, he was hard already.

"I don't need your apology either."

That dismissive scorn unlocked anger in Rhys. He was so tired of people looking at him like he was nothing more than a simpering piece of shit. He pushed the man back but only managed inches of distance. "I'm trying to be nice here! What do you want? Should I get down on my knees and beg your forgiveness? Lick the drinks off your body?"

Oh, fucking brilliant. What a thing to say.

The man chuckled. That, too, was rich and dark. "Would you like that?" He shifted his body and pressed his thigh into Rhys's crotch, right against his very hard cock. Pinpricks of heat ran up Rhys's back and spread around his head.

Rhys let out a soft moan. *Damn it.*

"Ah, so you would." Mockery in the man's words. Lust too. One hand kept Rhys pinned, but the other released Rhys's throat. With those fingers, the man brushed Rhys's lips.

Pineapple. Cherry. Heady flavors. Rhys couldn't help it. He ran his tongue over the digit and then sucked it into his mouth. The man obliged him, feeding him one finger after another to clean.

Damn, this guy tasted good. It couldn't just be the drinks. *What the hell?*

When there were no more fingers, the man leaned in even closer. "That was very well done." Hot breath caressed Rhys's cheek. "Let's see what you can do with something else."

He kissed Rhys. No. Kissing would've been gentle. This man devoured Rhys's mouth.

Rhys answered back just as hard. If he was going to be felt up by a hot-ass stranger in a hallway, it damn well would be on his terms too. Rhys tangled his hands in the dark, sticky-wet curls of the man's hair and sucked at his tongue. Rhys pushed his cock into the hard muscles of the man's thigh and felt the answer against his leg.

God, it had been a long time since anyone had kissed him this way. Whatever had been on that tray smelled wicked on this guy. Sweet, then dark. Night descending on the jungle. Earth layered against the smell of mango and pineapple.

Rhys felt more alive than he had in weeks. Months, maybe. Every inch of his body hummed. He didn't want it to end.

The man shifted, moving his leg away from Rhys's cock.

Damn it!

There was a tugging at Rhys's belt, then at his pants. Oh shit, the guy wasn't going to—

Rhys moaned into the man's mouth. Yes, yes, he was.

The fingers Rhys had sucked encircled his cock, exploring his shaft and teasing at first. Then the man stroked his thumb over the tip and set up a rhythm that sent lust down into Rhys's feet and out to his fingertips.

Oh fuck. He didn't usually come from hand jobs, but the heat of the man, his mouth, and his damn hand set every nerve in Rhys's body on fire.

It didn't even take that long. Rhys tried to hold back—wanted to hold on to this moment forever—but the heat in his veins curled into his balls and then rose. Rhys rocked against the man and came, his shout swallowed by the other's mouth.

Once Rhys had come down a bit, the man broke the kiss. He trailed semen-covered fingers up from Rhys's crotch, leaving wetness behind on his stomach. He stroked those same fingers against Rhys's lips.

"Now you're as sticky as me," that velvet voice said. "An even exchange, don't you think?"

Rhys tasted himself. Little pinpricks, like cold mist after a rainstorm, traced down his arms, and he shivered, but before he could suck on the guy's fingers again, they were gone.

The man chuckled and let Rhys go.

"Wait." Rhys caught the man's arm. "Your name. You have to tell me your name."

"Do I?" The man broke from Rhys's grasp. Stepped back. He sucked a smear of semen from the tip of his index finger and then grinned. "Perhaps you should've asked for my name before you offered to lick my body." Still cleaning his fingers, the man stepped out of the alcove and strode down the hall.

Gone. Again.

Fucking hell. Rhys exhaled and leaned back against the wall.

That had to have been the single most erotic thing he'd ever experienced. It was the kind of encounter he'd envisioned happening on some tropical party cruise, not during a stuffy transatlantic crossing. On the first night, no less.

His body burned from the man's touch. And for it. That mouth, those hands. Just thinking about them had him hard again. *Shit.* That never happened, not after coming so damn fast.

From morose to horny as hell. He was supposed to be getting his head on straight, not getting his rocks off. He didn't even know the guy's name. Needed it, needed to find him again. Wanted to yell that name out loud when he came.

Rhys took a swallow of air. *Damn.*

The waiter in the lounge would know. Had even said his last name. Rhys racked his brain but couldn't remember.

Fuck.

Right. First things first. He needed to clean up. Sticky wasn't the half of it. He glanced down. Yeah, it wouldn't take a genius to figure out what had happened to him.

He zipped himself up, fastened his belt, and tucked his shirt in.

The long way back to his cabin was safer than the main hall. Wouldn't that make another interesting photo shoot? The newly minted millionaire with jizz-stained pants.

Rhys swallowed the lust in his throat. He had to find that guy again. It was irrational, but for the first time since the reading of his mother's will he felt like himself again.

Whole.

CHAPTER TWO

*S*ilas Quint licked semen from his fingers. Perhaps this damnable boat trip wouldn't be so bad after all.

That American had been downright delectable. Proud and arrogant, yes. But weren't they all? He'd expected to frighten the man, not turn him on. Oh, but that had been lovely, that hard cock, his unhindered moans. And the way he'd responded—not passive at all, despite being utterly at Silas's mercy. Wonderful. He'd been tempted to drag the man back to his cabin and see what else that hot mouth would suck on.

He'd nearly given the American his name too and started the dance that would lead to more encounters. But no. A distraction like that could get him killed. Hunting the soulless was hard enough. Tracking them down and fighting them in the middle of the ocean would use up every last bit of energy he had. Indulging in lust was a luxury he couldn't afford.

Eight soulless, the Messengers had said. Eight.

Juno's tits.

Why couldn't they have sent one of the water fae on this

journey? There were no damn trees in the middle of the ocean, no fields. Oh, there were potted plants here and there, little good they would do him. He needed true greenery. Meadows as lush as that American's eyes.

Now there was a body he wouldn't mind plowing a dozen or so times. Silas pulled out his key card, unlocked his door, and pushed it open. Auburn hair, tight muscles. Sloppy clothes. Silas preferred neat and trim. Still, he'd enjoy stripping an ill-fitting suit off that man all the same.

Would that he *could* indulge himself. He was still hard from his little bout of inventiveness in the hallway. The American had come so fast, squirmed so wonderfully under Silas's hands.

He tossed the key card on the side table. Sunlight streamed in through the panel of windows.

Good.

It would be some hours before it touched below that horribly wet horizon. He still had time to eat. And take care of his own erection.

Peeling his sticky and sweet-smelling clothes off wasn't at all pleasant. He dropped them to the floor of the bathroom and stepped into the shower.

Warm water washed the scent of rum, fruit, and coconut from his skin. Perhaps he should have brought the American back here to see if the man was truly willing to lick his body free of the drinks so carelessly spilled there. He'd certainly had a talented enough tongue.

Silas wrapped his hand about his cock and stroked. How would it look to see the American's proud mouth stretched around his shaft? To feel his tongue running over his glans, have those hands on his ass as Silas slid in and out between those lips? Gods, how he wanted to find out. His soap-slicked hand was a poor substitute for the velvet heat of a willing mouth. Still, sweet tension slid into Silas's belly and balls.

He leaned back against the wall of the shower and imagined what the American's moans would sound like when he slid his entire length down that throat. Warmth like the heat of the summer sun radiated out from his core, down his arms and legs, and his shaft hardened even more. He certainly could envision tangling his fingers in the American's soft hair. Holding that auburn head still while he shot his load down the man's throat.

Silas's balls tightened, and he came hard into his hand, gasping a low moan of his own.

Water cascaded against him for a bit before he straightened and set about washing himself off. The afterglow of orgasm relaxed him but didn't free his mind from thoughts of the American. He still envisioned those grass-green eyes looking up, that mouth quirked into a smile, a dribble of spunk sliding down the man's chin. Though Silas's cock flagged, liquid sunlight pooled in his belly. He needed more.

Silas shut the water off abruptly. No, what he needed was to stop thinking about that man. The soulless would take no pity on him, give him no quarter. It was only his sword and his wits against eight.

He stepped out of the shower, grabbed a towel, and paced out of the bathroom. Mooning over some damn human wouldn't keep him sharp. Fooling about with one always drained him of elemental power. He couldn't afford that right now.

It cost quite a bit to hold on to a glamour so close to another when passions were high. It wasn't an issue on land, where he could reach about and draw his element in. Sex in the middle of a field, for instance. But floating on water, he was cut off from his source.

He stared out the windows at the ocean.

Only he wasn't drained at all. The encounter had been

brief but intense enough that he should've depleted some energy. Instead, he brimmed with power, as if he'd drawn it right out of the ground.

He now held more than he'd carried aboard.

That wasn't right.

Silas sank into a chair close to the bed. Yes, land was close by, but it was harder to draw an element through another and took enough concentration that it wasn't worth the effort. The energy must have come from somewhere, though.

The American?

No. Impossible. Humans only had the most rudimentary elemental abilities and held only the smallest amount of the power themselves. The auburn-haired man, while quite delicious, was most certainly human. Had he been fae or half-fae, Silas still couldn't have tapped into his energy—not without losing his soul.

No creature had the ability to act as an elemental reservoir for a fae. Such beings were myths, something from the oldest of their tales.

Unless, of course, they weren't. Every myth had some basis in reality, after all. That thought chilled.

Silas tapped the armrest of his chair. He needed to find out more about the American and put his sudden notion to rest. Before the sun set and the soulless came out to feed.

———

AFTER A SHOWER and a change of clothes, Rhys found the waiter whose tray he'd knocked over. The man was still in the lounge but stationed behind the bar instead of serving tables. From the waiter's initial expression, he remembered Rhys quite clearly, but that smoothed over into a professional smile. "Can I help you, sir?"

Eastern European accent. His name tag read Vasil

Kutsera. "I hope so. The man who was here, the one I dumped the tray onto. Do you know his name?"

The frown returned. "We're not allowed to give out a guest's personal information to other passengers, sir."

"But I heard you say it. I just don't remember."

"I'm very sorry."

Exasperation made Rhys lean over the bar. "Look, I tried to give him my card, but he left before I could."

The waiter remained unfazed. "I was there, sir. He chose not to take it."

Goddamn it. Rhys reached into the pocket of his suit coat, pulled out a folded fifty-dollar bill, and placed it on the counter. He slid it toward the waiter. "Would this help?"

The waiter stared at the money, his whole body suddenly tense. "What do you take me for?"

"I—"

"Do you think me some country bumpkin?" He gripped the edge of the bar. "Poor former Soviet who'd break any rule at the sight of the almighty dollar?"

Rhys felt his face grow hot. "It's not that. I just thought—"

"You thought I could be bought." The waiter took a breath. "I speak four languages. Have two engineering degrees. I'm not a fool. Keep your damn money."

"I just wanted to know his name." The words came out as a whisper.

"My name," said a deep voice, far too close to Rhys's ear, "is Silas Quint."

Rhys felt a hand press into the small of his back as the dark-haired man stepped next to him. It took him a moment to remember to breathe.

"Rhys Matherton." It was the only thing he could say to the man who stood too close, the man Rhys wanted to stand even closer. If Rhys's name brought any recognition, Silas didn't show it.

Rhys wasn't sure whether he should be relieved or disappointed, but damn, the guy was hot. He had changed too, from dark gray to a black pinstripe suit that looked as if it had been tailored straight onto his trim form. A tie that swirled with the muted colors of sun and fire.

Silas nodded to the waiter. "Vasil."

"May I get you something, Mr. Quint?"

"More of that scotch I never had the chance to drink would be lovely." He slipped the fifty-dollar bill out from under Rhys's fingers. "Mr. Matherton has been so kind as to offer to pay for it."

The waiter, Rhys noted, was trying very hard not to laugh. "And for you, Mr. Matherton?"

"Nothing."

"He'll have the same," Silas said.

The waiter paused for a moment, then nodded. "Two scotches. Right away."

Rhys cleared his throat. "I don't really like scotch."

"You will after tonight." The smile that came after those words was wicked.

Rhys noted that Silas had yet to remove his hand from Rhys's back. Mostly because he felt Silas's thumb drawing little circles through his coat and shirt. He might as well have been naked, such was the effect.

God, this man was like a drug.

The waiter returned and placed two scotches in front of Silas. Only then did the hand at Rhys's back drop away. Silas took one glass and handed the other to him. "Cheers."

Rhys knew enough to swirl the glass slightly and sniff before sipping. The burnished liquid smelled of wood and sin. He drank and then waited for the burn, but it didn't come. This scotch slid down his tongue and vanished. He stared at the glass. "What is this?"

"A very good, very expensive single malt scotch," Silas said. "Someday I might even teach you to drink it properly."

Rhys felt the room sway, hoped it was the boat, knew it wasn't. "Someday" implied more than he wished to think about at the moment. He was more than a little surprised by the words that came out of his mouth. "I'd like that."

"Yes," Silas said. "I'm sure you would."

Would everything this man said set him on fire? He took a deep breath, then another sip of the scotch, and spoke. "Would you let me apologize for dumping a tray of drinks on you?"

A dark laugh. "You already have. I rather enjoyed that."

The mere thought of that encounter in the hall threatened to tent his pants. Rhys took another shaky sip of scotch.

Silas lifted his glass. "And now you've compensated me for my ruined scotch. I'd say that sets things aright."

An even playing field. Rhys licked his lips. "Now what?" The question came out as a whisper. He both hoped and feared the answer.

Silas set down his drink. Took Rhys's from his hand. "You take a break from the scotch while I fix your tie."

Fix his tie? Before Rhys could protest, Silas had loosened the knot below his throat and started tugging at it. In short order, he had it undone completely and set about retying it.

"You don't wear a suit often, do you?"

"No." How was it that no one else in the bar noticed what was happening? No one even looked their way. "Not that often."

"It shows." Silas straightened his collar and smoothed down the front of his jacket. "Better."

Except for his hard-on. If only Silas would run his hand over *that*. Rhys had to admit his neck felt less constricted.

Why was Silas doing this? What did he want? "Who are you?"

A flash of teeth. Amusement in that deep voice. "Have you forgotten my name already?"

Rhys swallowed. He eyed the glass on the bar counter but knew not to pick it up yet. Silas had been right. He did need a break from the scotch. The man was far more potent than alcohol.

Silas pressed close and spoke into Rhys's ear. "My name?"

Rhys shuddered at the command. "Silas." He doubted he'd ever forget. He certainly would remember the hand at his hip, Silas's fingers stroking his side beneath his suit coat, the quick nip of teeth against his ear.

Not a person in the place was watching them.

Rhys dropped his voice. "You're the most attractive man I've ever met. Stunning. I mean, every head in this place should get whiplash when you walk by."

Something shifted in Silas's expression. There was still a sense of amusement, but his smile slipped away. "I should be flattered."

"The thing is," Rhys said, "no one notices. Hell, you take off my tie, then feel me up, and not one person even looks this way."

"It is rather odd, isn't it?"

The whole thing was damn strange. The tone of Silas's response sent a trickle of fear down Rhys. "You know it's happening."

Silas said nothing, just picked up his scotch and sipped.

Well, theories begged to be tested. Rhys snatched the scotch out of Silas's hand and set it down on the bar counter. Then he took Silas's face in his hands and kissed him.

Rhys doubted he would ever get enough of this man's mouth on his, or their tongues twining about each other.

Not a tropical night this time, but some pine forest in the

height of summer, a hint of warm rock and damp earth. Rhys felt Silas's finger brush his throat; then the other man pulled away.

"You're exceedingly brash."

"You seem to enjoy it," Rhys said. "And I was right. Not a person in this room saw that."

Down the bar, Vasil chatted with other patrons. A few people glanced their way, but it was as if he and Silas didn't exist, rather than people pointedly not watching two men make out.

"So, who are you?"

Silas's amused smile returned. "You keep asking the wrong questions."

Damn it. Rhys picked up his scotch. "Then what the hell are the right questions?"

The other man chuckled. "I do like you, Rhys. That's a very dangerous thing for the both of us." Silas retrieved his own drink. "Would you care to join me for dinner?"

Dinner? "Why do I have the feeling you've already assumed I'd say yes?"

"Because I have. Because you will." Silas cupped his hand under Rhys's chin. "Because if you ask the right questions, you might get the answers you so desire."

Silas's grip was strong and his fingers warm. Rhys resisted the urge to lower his chin and lick them.

"Yes, I'll go to dinner with you."

CHAPTER THREE

S ilas stroked the side of Rhys's jaw with his thumb before letting Rhys go. The American was dangerous, indeed. He saw straight though Silas's glamour. More interesting, Rhys saw Silas's true appearance and he wasn't overwhelmed by it. Driven to lust, yes—that was easy enough to see. But he maintained control of himself.

Not exactly a human trait. But Rhys *was* human. Silas pushed aside his growing doubts. Rhys *had* to be human, despite the soft flow of energy that came with his kiss.

A bold move. Unexpected. Enticing. Silas still tasted him, even through the scotch. Apparently Rhys was the kind of man who gave as well as received. Silas's cock stiffened at that thought.

It had also been a test to gauge what was happening to the room about them. Smart move.

Bedding Rhys might be very interesting.

"Shall we, then?" Silas gestured toward the lounge entrance.

Rhys hesitated. "The scotch?"

"So you like it after all?" Silas guessed the answer but was rewarded by a touch of color in Rhys's cheeks.

"Yeah. I do." Rhys paused and leaned close. "You make everything taste better."

Even bolder.

Silas brushed his fingers against Rhys's throat and stole a quick taste of his lips. "We'll have to put that to the test sometime."

Oh, that flustered Rhys. Silas was tempted to skip dinner altogether, take Rhys to his cabin, and put that mouth to work. But the sunlight outside cast long shadows. He didn't need a clock to tell him night was approaching. After so many years, he felt sunset in his bones.

Rhys would be in danger then, if what Silas suspected was true. If such a thing could be true.

"As for the scotch, bring it along." Silas raised his glass and set off for the restaurant he'd chosen. Rhys fell in step next to him.

It was a short walk from the lounge to one of the smaller and more upscale dining establishments on the ship. Soft light, golden accents, and crisp white walls gave the room a Greco-Roman revival feel, though most Roman eateries had never had marble quite this polished.

Silas gave his name to the maître d', and they were seen to the table he'd reserved a scant hour and a half ago.

That had been the first item he'd attended to after his shower. The second had been to track down the manager of the lounge for Rhys's business card. His third stop had been the ship's library to access the Internet. The American came with an interesting personal history.

Rhys slid into the seat across from him.

A waitress took their order. Seafood Feuillantine for him, Chateaubriand steak for Rhys.

Once she'd left, Rhys looked around. "Wow."

Silas hazarded a comment about Rhys's past. "Surely you've been in elegant restaurants before? When your mother was on tour?"

That caused a reaction. Muscles tensed. Voice thick with accusation. "You knew who I was."

He was going to bolt.

"Rhys, don't." Silas put as much command into his voice as he dared, though he doubted it would work on Rhys. He added an honest, *"Please."*

It was the latter, he suspected, that stayed Rhys. He still trembled, but he remained in his seat.

"After I showered, I returned and asked the manager for your card. Then I looked you up."

Some of the tension in Rhys vanished. "After you showered?"

"When we...conversed...in the hall, you were a perfect stranger to me."

Rhys shifted in his chair. More anger abated, but not all. "I've been in the news for two weeks."

"I don't pay much attention to the news. Haven't for years."

"I'm not sure I believe that." Rhys sipped the scotch. "And I'm not sure I believe you about the business card. That waiter didn't want to give me *your* name."

"His name is Vasil."

Rhys stared at him.

"Names are important, Rhys. Notice them. Remember them." Silas lay his left hand on the table, palm up. He didn't know if Rhys would understand the gesture, the invitation. "The manager, Benjamin, gave me your card because he saw you offer it to me."

It didn't mollify Rhys. "So did the waiter."

He was too wrapped up in his indignation to see the difference. "Vasil saw you offer your information to me. He

21

didn't see the reverse. I left nothing for you."

That must have sunk in, because Rhys slumped back against his chair. "Oh."

Silas let the silence hang, content to wait. A moment later, Rhys nodded. "I should've left a message for you."

"Might have been wiser than bribery." He did so enjoy watching Rhys blush.

"Yeah." Rhys's gaze focused, traveled up, then along the table to where Silas's hand lay. He brought his own hand up and slid it into Silas's grasp. Warm flesh on flesh, a tiny trickle of elemental energy.

Rhys's pulse still beat wildly, but the tension was gone. Silas gave the hand a gentle squeeze.

Rhys cleared his throat. "Silas? What are you doing to me?"

He answered with the truth. "Nothing."

"Then what are you doing to everyone else?"

He couldn't help but smile. "Merely showing them what they wish to see."

Rhys laughed. "What are you, then? Some sort of magician?"

"No, not a magician." He picked up his glass and drained the last of his scotch. Set it back down. "I'm one of the fae."

Once more, Rhys went taut with shock. "Fae. You mean like a fairy?"

"Well, I don't have wings. Nor do I fly about trailing pixie dust." Silas stroked his thumb over the top of Rhys's hand. "And I am a bit longer than five inches."

Color drained from Rhys's cheeks. "You're serious."

"Very."

Rhys opened his mouth to speak again, disbelief clearly etched on his face. Fortunately the food arrived, providing Silas with a respite from questions.

He did have to give up Rhys's hand to eat. Pity, that. He

missed the touch of Rhys's skin. Best to leave him be, for a time. From having watched the man this past hour or so, he knew Rhys needed to work things through in his mind.

Dinner conversation was nonexistent until Rhys spoke again. "Um, I'm not your servant for the next seven years, am I?" There was a clip to Rhys's voice that was hard to interpret. Sarcasm, perhaps.

"Thomas the Rhymer. You know your classic tales." Impressive, though Silas suppressed a shudder. Seven years bound to another's will? He'd not wish that on anyone. He'd lived it, for far more years than seven.

Silas toyed with a shrimp on his plate. Rhys had gained back the color in his face, and splotches of red marred his neck. "No. I can't bend your will to mine. There's no Elfland beyond a river of blood to which I can take you. I'm as much of this world as you."

"I suppose that's good. I'm not ready to believe in magical worlds beyond this one." He looked up at Silas. "What do you really look like?"

There was that tone again. Silas set his fork down. "You see me as I truly am. You ask why no one else reacts to me? To everyone else, I'm not quite as arresting."

He mulled that. "So whatever you're doing doesn't work on me."

"It doesn't seem to, no."

"Why not?"

Silas studied Rhys. Oh, there was skepticism there, perhaps anger as well. And why not? But the creeping awareness of truth lurked deep inside Rhys. "That's what I'm trying to find out."

He has to be lying. Rhys repeated that over and over in his

23

head. Silas had to be lying, because the truth was impossible. *Fae?* Did Silas think he was a fool? Was he playing with the ignorant rich boy's mind for some kink? This had gone too far.

He latched on to anger. Fae? No way in hell. "That's a convenient dodge."

Silas shrugged. "It's the truth."

What an asshole. "You don't know what makes me so superspecial to see through your illusions?"

"Glamour." A touch of annoyance crept into Silas's voice. "I have an idea but no proof."

"You're so full of shit."

Finally, the anger Rhys had witnessed that afternoon spread over Silas's expression. "Am I?" It was every ounce a challenge.

"Yes." Rhys pushed back his chair. Kissing a guy was one thing; people could ignore that. He took a deep breath and then shouted as loudly as he could. "Hey! Everyone! This guy says he's a fucking fairy!"

The conversations in the room didn't even dip. No one turned. Dishes clinked; servers moved. It was as if nothing had happened at all.

Oh hell. Rhys's whole body grew warm. He looked down at Silas.

"Are you through?"

He sank to his chair. "Holy shit."

A quirk of a dark smile formed on the lips of the man—the fae—who sat at the other side of the table.

"That can't be real. You can't be…" *Oh fuck.* Silas's looks, his passion and strength, and that no one else on this entire ship wanted to jump him—as unbelievable as it sounded, the explanation fit. Except maybe—

"I'm not being punked, am I?"

Lines of consternation appeared on Silas's forehead. "I don't even know what that means."

Oh. "Tricked. Pranked."

"No." Silas rose and towered over the table. "Do you require more proof?"

He was afraid to say yes. Afraid to say no as well. "What are you going to do?"

"I haven't decided." He rounded the table and looked down at Rhys. "Truth is, I could lay you out on the table, strip you naked, and fuck you senseless, and no one would bat an eye. In the end, our waitress would simply come over and offer us dessert."

Rhys's mouth went dry and his whole body felt like fire. "You're not going to…"

Silas knelt. "No." He grasped the leg of Rhys's chair and pulled it sideways. "The china's too nice to simply push to the floor. I have another idea." He reached for Rhys's belt and unbuckled it.

His objective became blindingly obvious.

"Silas!" Rhys hissed his name. "You can't!"

"I can. I will." Silas looked up. "Unless you tell me to stop."

Rhys stared at those amber eyes. Oh God, Silas really was telling the truth. He should tell him to stop, voice that one simple word. More than anything else, he ached for this man. Fae. Whatever the hell he was.

A grin parted Silas's lips. He unbuttoned Rhys's pants, pulled the zipper apart, and then shoved his underwear down.

Cool air surrounded Rhys's erect cock. A blowjob in the middle of a restaurant. Talk about a wicked wet dream come true.

"Last chance." Whispered words, smooth as silk.

"Do it." His own voice was guttural.

A chuckle, then Silas's hot mouth engulfed the head of Rhys's cock as Silas wrapped his hand around the shaft.

The slick, soft warmth and the flick of Silas's velvet tongue over Rhys's crown caused every part of his body to tingle. Deep inside Rhys, a chasm formed that could only be filled by Silas's heat. "Oh fuck." He tangled his fingers in Silas's hair and bucked forward.

Silas obliged and took more of Rhys into his mouth, before pulling back. The cool touch of air on Rhys's shaft sent more fire into his veins, and to that aching place inside. Then Silas's mouth engulfed Rhys again.

Pulses like electricity zinged over Rhys's skin. *God.* Silas's tongue caressed the side of his shaft, flicked over his glans and the slit at the top. The air around them smelled like a rainy summer night, the windows open. Damp oak leaves and a warm, wet wind that carried just a hint of honeysuckle.

Oh hell, maybe Silas really was fae.

Rhys looked down. The sight of those perfect lips stretched open around his shaft caused that ache inside him to throb. Then Silas hummed, a gentle sound of pleasure that vibrated through every inch of Rhys's body. Fire rushed into the chasm inside Rhys, and his balls tightened.

"Silas, I—"

Rhys came, clenching Silas's hair and calling his name out loud in the middle of a five-star restaurant on a damn cruise ship.

Apparently Silas was the type of guy to swallow. Because he drank every drop of Rhys and licked his cock clean. Then Silas tucked Rhys back into his pants. Even zipped and belted them back together.

Rhys had gotten blowjobs before, but they'd never made him so damn…complete. He ran trembling fingers through those black curls. "God, Silas. That was fucking awesome."

"Look around the room." His voice sounded rough but cheerful.

Rhys did. Business as usual. Diners chatting and laughing. Servers moving with wine, drinks, dishes—both full and empty. No one looked their way at all.

"I believe you," Rhys said.

Silas rose and leaned over and kissed him. "You damn well better. It's not every day I go down on someone." He was breathless, and a flush colored his tan skin.

Rhys tasted himself in that hot mouth. "But you liked it." He'd heard that thrum of pleasure and spied the bliss in Silas's face.

"Very much so." Silas straightened, walked back around the table, and sat. He picked up a napkin and blotted his chin. "As I said before, I do like you."

He didn't know how to answer that. Couldn't sort through his thoughts fast enough.

He was saved by the waitress. "Would you gentlemen care for dessert?" She handed each a menu.

Silas waved his off. "Just a cappuccino for me."

Rhys handed the menu back. "The same, please."

She nodded and left.

Rhys chewed on the inside of his mouth. How could he explain his feelings when he didn't understand them himself? "Silas, I… How much did you read about me on the Internet?"

Silas folded his hands. "Not much. You're the son of a world-class cellist and an antiques dealer. You're an artist in your own right—a sculptor. Your mother died two weeks ago, and you inherited eleven million dollars no one knew she had. That's about it."

Rhys laughed. "I know there's more out there."

"Yes," Silas said. "But I stopped paying attention to the

media years ago. Ninety-nine percent chaff, one percent wheat. It's not worth the time to sift."

The waitress came back with their coffees and then retreated.

Rhys wrapped his hand around the cup. "My family was perfect for seventeen years. A mother who let me sing and dance, explore the arts until I found what I loved. A father who taught me to throw a baseball and went to every one of my football games." He tried to keep the bitterness out of his voice and failed.

"Then?" Silas's voice was soft.

That took Rhys by surprise, but then, so did everything about Silas.

He took a breath and plunged onward. "Dad caught me making out with another guy. Would've thrown me out of the house that day, but I was *seventeen*. Mom wouldn't let him. For my eighteenth birthday, he bought me cardboard boxes and told me to get the hell out. I did. Didn't speak to either of my parents for years."

Silas seemed to absorb all of this. He nodded slowly. "But you reconciled with your mother."

"Yeah. For as much as that's worth now. She and Dad divorced five years after I left. A month after that, she called me and begged me to forgive her." Rhys sipped his coffee. That had been an awkward, painful, and wonderful conversation. But now—all that honesty and openness for those scant few years—it was all worth shit.

"And your father?"

"Oh, Derrick." Rhys barked a bitter laugh. "He hates my guts. Blames me for the divorce. Probably for the cancer too." He paused. "Are you still doing that thing you do?"

"Glamour," Silas said. "You can assume I am, unless we're alone."

"Because"—Rhys lowered his voice—"I can't tell you

28

what I'm about to tell you. That was the deal. But you won't understand if I don't."

Silas tipped his head to one side, his expression changed to intense curiosity. "No, no one will hear."

"I mean, could another fae…?" Rhys waved his hand over the table.

"Another fae could see and hear through my glamour, yes. But there isn't another of my kind on this ship. I'd know if there were."

"What about someone like me?"

Silas stilled and spoke as if choosing his words carefully. Even his accent became more pronounced. "I believe you're fairly unique in the world."

Rhys chewed on that. Unique. He pushed the upwelling of questions aside. *One thing at a time.*

"Nine months before I was born, on the last night of a tour in Europe, Mom had an affair with some guy she met at the after-concert cocktails. Came home with me. Told no one."

"But she knew she was pregnant by him?"

"Yeah. And apparently that guy found out she had his kid and gave her a ton of money never to tell anyone. Not even her husband. Or her son."

Silas shifted in his seat and leaned over his coffee. "That's a very odd thing to do."

Understatement of the year. "It's a fucking hideous thing to do. At the reading of the will, not only did I have to face the contempt and hatred of the man I *thought* was my father, but I found out he wasn't my father at all. And the guy who *is* wants so little to do with me he's willing to fork over eleven million dollars so I never seek him out." Rhys drank the rest of his coffee. "In an hour, I learned everything I ever knew about my life was a lie. My dead mother lied to my face, and I have two fathers who'd rather see me planted in the ground."

Silas sat back and watched him but said nothing.

Rhys ran a hand through his hair and lowered his voice. "You know, most of the stuff in the papers is shit, but some of it isn't. I didn't handle the news well. Got drunk out of my gourd and smashed a car into a fountain in Vienna. Spent five days holed up in a hotel in my underwear. Punched a photographer."

Silas nodded. "Rage. Understandable."

"But that isn't me. I've been...shattered. Broken. For weeks." Rhys drew a breath. "And then I met you."

"And?" Honest curiosity in that voice.

"I felt whole again. Myself." Rhys laughed. "And now you're telling me you're fae, which pretty much destroys what I know about the entire fucking world."

"And?"

"I feel as though everything is exactly right. Like my whole life just snapped into place."

CHAPTER FOUR

Silas could've dealt with confusion, lust, or even anger. He understood those emotions. Not this. Not *this*.

Wholeness. Rightness. Those words rammed through him like a pike to the gut. Sharp. Fast.

His reaction surprised him far more. Warmth. Pleasure. A fierce protectiveness. If Rhys was what Silas thought he was...

Mercury's balls. His heart pounded.

Complete. Two edges to *that* blade. Companionship. Eventual *love?*

No. He couldn't afford love. That cursed emotion had nearly destroyed him once. Killed everyone he'd ever cared for instead. Never again. Fae loved too deeply, for far too long.

When Rhys's smile faltered into horror, Silas knew he hadn't schooled his expression.

"I shouldn't have said anything." He made to rise.

"Rhys, it's not what you think." Sunset. Ice in his bones.

Time was running out. Damn all the gods and their children to darkness. "Please...give me a moment."

Hurt in those eyes, but Rhys remained in his chair.

Words wouldn't come to Silas, at least not in any language Rhys would understand. Silas placed his hands on the table and stared at his fingers. He'd known English for centuries, used it more than any other language. But deep matters? They always brought him home.

He found the words and translated. "I would like you to be happy, Rhys. I'm finding I want to see that you are."

Rhys settled, surprise replacing the hurt.

"This is highly unusual behavior for me," Silas said.

"What, seducing mortals?" Rhys said. "I thought that's the sort of thing fae did?"

He had to chuckle at that. "*Et tu?*" He shook his head. "True, I suppose. Yes. But I don't take them to dinner."

"Or go down on them."

Damn that quirky grin of his. Silas still wanted to see those lips around his cock. Or anywhere else on his body. "Also true."

Rhys shifted in his seat. "So do I invite you back to my cabin, or should we go to yours?" He looked expectant.

Ah, this would be another delicate moment, but one for which he was better prepared. Silas stood and rounded the table once more. This time he held out his hand.

Rhys hesitated but took it.

Such warmth. Such energy. Silas wanted to swim in it. He tugged Rhys to his feet and pulled the other man against him. He found Rhys's sweet mouth with his own and cupped Rhys's ass, pulling him tight against his body. The gentle tugging of Rhys slipping his fingers into Silas's hair sent a shiver down his spine.

Silas was painfully hard and knew Rhys felt his length against him. After a minute he broke the kiss and relaxed his grip. He spoke low into Rhys's ear. "Do you know how much I want you?"

"Yes." A breathless reply. "Much more than five inches."

Silas nipped his earlobe. "I'd love to take you back to my cabin and have you feel every inch slide into you."

Rhys stiffened. He pulled back. "But you can't." Frustration in his voice.

Silas knew that emotion all too well and felt it as keenly. "I'm of the field and forest and meadow. A boat in the middle of the ocean is—quite literally—out of my element."

Understanding flickered in those green eyes. "You didn't choose to take this trip."

"No. I was sent. And I have business to attend to tonight."

"And it can't wait until tomorrow?"

"No."

Questions obviously warred within Rhys. His brow furrowed, then his expression snapped into determination. "Tell me why you're here."

Rhys was learning. Command rather than question. Harder to dodge. "It'd be better if you didn't know."

"Either you don't trust me, or you're dealing with something really dangerous. I don't like either option."

"I trust you."

"Oh great. Danger."

Silas chuckled. "Yes. But I'm very good at what I do." He drew back from Rhys. Took his hand and kissed it. "Come. I have some time yet."

Rhys tugged him forward. "I'll lead."

Now that was intriguing. Silas let Rhys set the pace and direction, a flicker of delight growing inside him. So often he was the actor. This—this was *different*. But not unpleasant at all.

They took the elevator down two decks and walked the

length of the ocean liner. "I read about this place when I booked the cruise," Rhys said.

Wisps of energy—of Silas's element—flowed down the hall and wrapped themselves into...

Rhys. Not him, but Rhys. Sweet Diana. Humans didn't pull element like that.

Up ahead, beyond double glass doors, shone a wall of green. Plants.

"It's a mini botanical garden. Orchids. Ferns. Tropicals." Rhys led them through the doors. "And, of course, the requisite bar at the other end."

Greenery everywhere. Tall palms and the scent of citrus. Glass all around, letting in the reds and oranges of the fading sunlight.

Life surrounded Silas, slid through and into him. He took three steps down the path and touched a fern. "I should've known this was here. Should've felt it."

"Well, we are on a big metal boat." Rhys cocked his head. "Isn't iron supposed to poison you?"

"No. That's a misconception. Iron doesn't hurt us." Silas turned. "It—" Words died in his mouth.

Rhys glowed. Long strands of element licked from the trees and the ferns and every other plant and the energy twined and plunged into Rhys's body.

"Silas, what's wrong?"

This time he couldn't find words in any language to speak. Finally one thought surfaced.

Quarter.

Quarter-fae weren't supposed to exist. A myth—ancient legend that spanned back millennia, longer than humans had recorded history. The impossible explanation Silas kept avoiding, yet here Rhys was, draped in verdant power.

"Silas?" Rhys took him by the elbow and dragged him

34

down a side path to a bench and sat next to him. "I didn't hurt you, bringing you here?"

Hurt? Laughter bubbled up, followed by language. "Oh Gods, no. A place like this could never harm me." He looked at Rhys again. "It was just a bit much to take in at once."

The glow, Silas realized, was the sheer amount of energy Rhys drew into himself. No, not drew in. Circulated through. Renewed.

The air around them smelled of honey and tasted like the crisp edge of a spring morning.

"Do you enjoy gardens like this?" Silas ran his fingers down Rhys's jawline. Touching him felt no different from before, though now he saw his reserve of element lick off his skin and fall into Rhys. More poured back, fresh and new.

"Yeah. All this life. It's pretty amazing." Rhys slid closer, hip to hip. "I like gardens. Parks. Used to sit in Central Park and read for hours. Got more of a buzz from that than I did running, you know?"

"I do know, yes."

Even in the garden, deep fear found Silas. Ancient fae legends spoke of wars waged over a single Quarter. He understood those stories now. They—other fae—would want Rhys if they knew. And what of his own intentions? Did *he* have any true affection for Rhys, or was it the desire to *possess* a Quarter?

Games of lust and pleasure were one thing, but to entrap another? Never. But he wouldn't let any other fae claim Rhys, so what did that make him?

Rhys touched Silas's thigh, moved his hand upward. "How much time do you have left?" His fingers brushed against fabric made taut by Silas's hard cock.

Silas's heart hammered as need coiled like a snake around his core. Blood pulsed in his fingertips. He took a sharp breath and looked up at the glass roof. "Until true dark. Another hour?"

"Plenty of time, then." Rhys stood and straddled Silas's legs. He pulled Silas's mouth to his and opened it with his tongue, taking what he wanted, demanding a response.

Energy whipped through Silas and set every nerve alight. A craving awakened in him, a need for more than the fulfillment of lust.

Gods. He'd fucked in the middle of ancient forests, and none of those times had left him aching like this. Rhys was merely kissing him.

Who possessed whom?

Silas trailed his fingers down Rhys's throat and found the knot of the tie he'd so carefully fixed. He worked it free and set about unbuttoning Rhys's shirt. He wanted flesh under his hands. Warmth. When he found Rhys's nipple, he rolled it between his fingers.

Rhys broke their kiss and gasped.

Silas looked up at him. "Sensitive?"

"I'll show you sensitive." Rhys's voice was low and rough. He slid off Silas's lap and pushed his legs apart. Belt. Button. Zipper. A shift of fabric, then his cock was in Rhys's hand. "An hour, huh?"

The roughness and authority in Rhys left Silas breathless. He wasn't used to being the passive partner. Didn't have much choice in the matter at the moment.

Rhys flicked his tongue over the top of Silas's cock and branded a wet path over Silas's crown. Slowly Rhys circled the head. Little touches, no more than a tease. Each time that silky tongue caressed Silas's glans, tension curled into Silas.

He hissed and tangled his hands in Rhys's hair. He tried to urge that mouth forward and failed. He was strong. Resistant. "Damn it, Rhys. Don't."

The incredible velvet heat vanished, replaced by the chill of damp air. "Don't what?"

"Don't go so slow!"

"Oh, okay." He grinned and started again at an even more leisurely pace. Rhys's hot tongue—tasting here, touching there—wound Silas like a watch until he was ready to snap. Rhys lingered at the tip of Silas's cock and dipped his tongue into the slit. When Rhys withdrew, cool air followed, releasing enough pressure to keep Silas balanced on the precipice, steps from ecstasy. Again and again.

Silas gave in to the guttural moan in his throat. Every moment was agonizing. Wonderful. He'd do anything in the world to keep Rhys.

Rhys stopped again. "I want you to scream, Silas."

Brazen. But gods, he liked that. "I don't tend to." He stroked Rhys's cheeks with his thumbs. "But you're welcome to try to make me."

"I'm sorry. I misspoke." Rhys tugged Silas's pants down and around his legs. "I'm *going* to make you scream." He pulled Silas's hips forward, almost pulled Silas from the bench entirely when he slid his hands under his ass.

Rhys took Silas in again. Being surrounded by that unbelievable soft mouth was far better than he'd imagined. The reality of Rhys was going to kill him.

Rhys licked down Silas's shaft, nipping as he went. He mouthed Silas's sac and swirled his tongue around Silas's balls before taking each one between his hot lips.

Elemental energy wrapped Silas's body and pushed into every fiber of his being. He bit the inside of his mouth to keep from moaning too loudly. Release from this exquisite torture hovered just beyond his reach.

Rhys paused and chuckled low. "Having issues, Silas? Too much for you?" He mouthed the base of Silas's cock. Too gently.

ANNA ZABO

Silas groaned in frustration.

Rhys was everywhere. Nipping at the head, stroking his shaft, licking or gently scraping teeth across Silas's sensitive flesh. Never fully engulfing Silas's cock. Silas hovered on the edge, but every time he crept close to release, Rhys backed down. Changed the rhythm. Then started over.

Lightning lived in Silas's veins and he felt like glass about to shatter. Only the final blow, the one to break him to pieces, never came.

Had there not been so much damn energy flying through him, Silas would've lost his glamour ages ago. But Rhys was a focus, a well and Silas drowned in power.

Damn that mouth and those hands. "Gods, Rhys. Will you please suck me already?"

Rhys laughed. Then finally—finally—Rhys's sweet, hot mouth took him in. At first Rhys worked his way up and down achingly slowly, but then faster and deeper.

Silas cupped a hand around the back of Rhys's neck and urged the tempo to increase. The coil inside Silas wound tighter and every nerve ached.

At last Rhys complied, shifting and loosening his throat and giving over control. Now Silas set the rhythm, the depth. "All of me."

The vibrations from Rhys's moan pulsed through Silas's cock.

He tightened his grip in Rhys's hair and savored the sight of those lips splayed wide around the root of his cock.

His. All his. Damn anyone else.

Rhys shifted his hands. They still cupped Silas's ass, but one finger slipped into his crack and pressed against his anus. *Oh fuck!* Fire burned down every nerve as Silas fell off the edge. He threw back his head and screamed as he came in Rhys's mouth.

38

FAE CUM DIDN'T TASTE of pixie sticks; that was for sure. But Rhys enjoyed it anyway, nearly as much as he'd relished the raw cry of ecstasy that had come from Silas. He gave the fae's softening cock another kiss before looking up.

Silas had his eyes closed, his head tipped back. He took a breath and spoke. *"O di!"*

Latin? He thought he'd heard Silas speak another piece earlier. He rested his arms on Silas's thighs. "I said I would make you scream."

Silas looked down, then grabbed the sides of Rhys's shirt and jacket and hauled him up and kissed him. Hard.

He'd forgotten how strong Silas was. Rhys wasn't a slight man, not after slinging clay, stone, and metal around a studio, but Silas pulled him off the floor with ease.

And God, could he kiss. He had vague memories of the colored fairy books as a kid, the glossed-over sensuality of the good folk. None ever mentioned male fairies seducing men or sucking cock.

Truth was better than fiction.

Silas finished attacking his mouth and slid him onto the bench. "Let me put myself back together." He stood and tugged up his underwear and pants.

Fae, it seemed, preferred boxers. Or at least this one did. Rhys licked his lips, tasting Silas. Oh, part of him rebelled against the notion of Silas being anything other than human. Impossible, the logical side of his brain said.

Damn logic. Silas was the picture of a fantasy brought to life—tall, slim but with enough muscle to give a sense of his strength. He wanted to carve the man into marble—a modern-day *David*. He didn't even like the classical forms. Abstract was more his thing. But if he could get Silas into his studio, he'd do it.

Rhys never took any of his lovers there. Art was his alone. But for Silas, he'd share. Rhys cleared his throat. "What are your plans in New York?"

Silas sat. "I haven't thought that far ahead."

He had to be kidding. "You must have some idea. I mean, you don't just get on a cruise and not think about—"

Silas smiled, whether from amusement or sadness, Rhys couldn't tell. "I live day to day."

"Carpe diem, huh? Is that just you or all fae?"

"Just me." Silas brushed his hand against Rhys's cheek. "Do you know the rest of the saying?"

There was more? "No."

"It's the last line of an ode by Horace. '*Carpe diem, quam minimum credula postero.*' Seize the day, trust as little as possible in the future."

That was definitely Latin. It rolled off Silas's tongue as if he'd been born to it. "That's how you live life?" Would he lose Silas as soon as they docked in New York? "No thoughts of tomorrow?"

Silas fell silent. His gaze drifted upward to the darkening sky beyond the glass ceiling. "Oh, I have thoughts. I only consider them after I've seen the sun rise."

Fear rippled through Rhys. "You think you're going to die. Every night."

"No," Silas said, "but I know one of these nights, I will."

Compelled to be on this boat. Sent, he'd said. Dangerous business. "Why? What are you, some sort of fairy special agent?"

"Fae." Silas took Rhys's hand, drew it up to his mouth, and nipped at the ends of his fingers. "I work for the Messengers," he said between nibbles.

The sensation traveled straight to Rhys's balls. He tried to focus on Silas's words, rather than the wet and silky mouth around his index finger. "Messengers?"

"Hmm-mmm." Silas mouthed his ring finger.

Wrong question, apparently. He tried another. "What do you do?"

Silas stopped sucking on his fingers but didn't let go. "Whatever they wish me to do." He stood, still holding Rhys's hand. "I've run out of time."

Almost a whisper, that last bit. Rhys rose and kissed Silas's knuckles. "Will I... You..." Desperation threatened to close his throat. "I want to see you tomorrow."

Silence hung between them, longer—much longer than Rhys liked—until Silas exhaled. His slight smile offered a glint of hope. "You move me, Rhys, in wild and wonderful ways. That's very rare. If the Fates grant, you'll see me again."

"I don't like leaving my life up to fate." Rhys kissed Silas's hand again and inhaled the spicy scent of his flesh. "What can I do to help you?"

Silas looked up at the glass roof. Creases marred his forehead. "You said there was a bar here? In this garden?"

Rhys pointed through the palm trees. "Far end."

"If you wish to help me, remain there until I return." Silas released Rhys's hand. Traced a finger down his throat. "Please."

Though the garden was warm and moist, Rhys felt a chill work down his back. "How long? What if you don't come back?"

"Until first light."

A stone formed in Rhys's stomach. Business during the dark hours. Something that could kill Silas.

"God, are you hunting—"

Silas pressed two fingers against his lips, cutting off the final word.

"Stay here until first light." A sharp expression accented the long lines of Silas's face. It wasn't desire, though. Rhys

41

had seen that often enough tonight to know. "I *will* come for you."

The fierceness of those words made Rhys's cheeks warm. Silas removed his fingers.

"Promise?" He whispered the word.

"On my honor." Silas stepped back. "Don't leave the garden."

"You damn well better explain all this."

Silas took another step away. "Over coffee." He placed his hand over his heart. "Another pledge."

"I'll hold you to that, if I have to tie you down to get the truth."

A flash of teeth. "I have something to look forward to, then."

"Your pal Horace would be horrified. Looking forward."

Silas laughed. "Probably. He could be *such* an ass sometimes."

Rhys froze. Did Silas just say—

Another wicked grin from Silas. "Tomorrow," he said. Then he turned and strode down the path and disappeared from sight.

Gone.

Damn, he hated the emptiness that took hold and fought the instinct to follow Silas.

Bar. He could use a drink. Rhys set about buttoning his shirt, retying his tie. The fall of his jacket covered his partial erection for the most part.

The Tropics Bar was quite the happening place, it turned out. Most of the tables were occupied. All the discreet nooks under the palms were taken, not surprisingly, by couples.

The burble of a water fountain underscored the playing of a jazz pianist. The air smelled sweet, sensual, but not as vibrant as it had when Silas had been in his arms. Or in his mouth.

Rhys took a seat at the bar. He even knew the waiter who stepped over to serve him.

"Mr. Matherton."

What was the man's name? A cloth thrown over the waiter's shoulder obscured his name tag, damn it all. Names were important, Silas had said. *"Remember them."*

"Vasil."

The waiter nodded. "May I get something for you?"

The beer list was disappointingly short. "I'd been thinking about a beer." Rhys tapped the list. "But I'm open to suggestions."

Vasil looked at the menu. "Too warm in here for most of those." He looked up. "But you don't strike me as a fruit cocktail man."

"Yeah, I'm more of a beer or Jack kind of guy."

"Whiskey Manhattan, then."

Rhys nodded and handed his key card over. He had no idea what was in that drink, but the least he could do was trust the waiter he'd treated so poorly earlier.

The drink came in a martini glass, with a cherry and a twirl of orange peel. But it had the sting of Jack and something sweet and bitter. "It's good."

The waiter nodded again and shifted to move down the bar.

"Vasil," Rhys said. "I'm sorry. About earlier."

The waiter paused. "Think nothing of it." Light words. "That was quite a tip Mr. Quint had you leave for two scotches." He moved on.

Rhys chuckled to himself. Punishment. Payment. Silas had so many layers to him. Amusement dropped away. *Silas.* He looked back at the waiter. Did he know? No, of course not. Silas had said there were no other fae aboard this ship.

Fae. Rhys took a sip of his drink and then exhaled. If he'd understood their last exchange, Silas wasn't just inhuman; he was old. Really old. Rhys had no idea when Horace had lived, but he knew when Rome fell.

Rhys slid off the bar stool. Three unoccupied chairs sat near what seemed to be a bookcase. He took one. He needed some space, some time to think.

What had he gotten himself into?

CHAPTER FIVE

*S*ilas didn't bother to keep his sword sheathed in the Aether. One benefit of Rhys having gone down on him—he had more than enough power to keep a glamour around the blade. Crafted items were harder to hide from mortal eyes. This particular blade—a Roman gladius—had been forged from silver and diamond by a phoenix in her own fire. His sword was one of the very few objects that could damage the soulless. Only the Messengers' own swords were more dangerous. To glamour such a work was difficult, even when his feet touched earth.

Rhys's power in Silas's blood made the act as easy as breathing.

Not that the blade mattered one whit at the moment. If there were soulless on the ocean liner, Silas couldn't find them. They must be here, for the Messengers were never wrong.

Silas sauntered down the grand staircase that led into the most elegant of the ship's many lounges. The soulless were vain and drawn to crowds, to the elemental energy humans possessed, and to their souls. The more humans in one location, the greater those little flares of elements burned. The soulless would seek the taste of energy and follow it until they found their prize.

Fae were even more tempting to the soulless, with their great stores of energy and immortal bodies. Had Silas not wrapped a glamour about himself to tamp down his flare of energy, they would've come for him first. He didn't want to give away the advantage of surprise by drawing them to him. Later, perhaps, he'd use that trick.

Only a few of the eight would emerge tonight, to scout and report. Usually the younger ones were put to that task. The first night of the hunt was always the easiest. Once the elders emerged, things would get more interesting.

If only he could find the cursed beings. If they weren't going to bother to prey, he could've spent the night with Rhys.

Just the thought of Rhys sent a spike of desire straight through him. That fire of lust was followed by a cold slice of fear. Quarter-fae. Rhys shone like the moon on a cloudless night. No soulless could resist that. With the amount of energy and a touch of fae blood, he'd last the soulless quite some time. Years, perhaps, before they turned him into a husk.

A different fire ignited in Silas. He'd kill every last soulless before that happened, or die trying. That pain he'd never allow Rhys to feel. Thank the gods Rhys had stayed in the garden. That mass of life was brighter than even a quarter-fae. It would keep him safe.

He walked through the lounge, scanning the crowd. Nothing. Perhaps the dance hall. Or maybe they'd chosen to prey in the dark confines of one of the theaters.

He took a moment to pause and search for the garden. Even now that he knew of its existence, it was barely noticeable, as potent as a single African violet half a mile away. Troubling. He should've sensed it before and certainly should've been able to pull on it now. Hell, he should've known Rhys for what he was, even back before he'd spilled drinks on him.

Unless Rhys wore a glamour, one Silas couldn't see through from a distance.

He chewed on that thought. A glamour *would* explain why Rhys walked alone, why another fae hadn't discovered him. So much of the legend of Quarters was draped in mystery and lore. They could have defenses of their own.

"Do you require anything, sir?" A waiter peered at him.

How long had he been standing in the middle of the lounge?

"No, I'm fine." Silas moved toward the door. He needed to focus. Find the soulless. Dispatch them. Once the sun rose above the sea, he could return to Rhys and finally drag him back to one of their cabins and fuck him until neither of them could think. Maybe that would sate the desperate desire that kept his mind wandering and his cock half-hard.

Dangerous to be so distracted. Young soulless were less trouble but still deadly enough. Silas slipped from the lounge and found the dance hall. Nothing but humans there. He tried the theaters next.

The first two were half-full of humans—and only humans. In the third, a woman gasped for air in the back corner as she rocked on the lap of her partner. Their moans barely registered over the soundtrack of the action movie they were ignoring.

He forced himself to scan the theater carefully, despite the growing heat of his desire. It was one thing to go down on Rhys while covered with a glamour, quite another to fuck in public as the humans were doing.

Silas had never done so. Never wanted to, until that instant. What would it be like to sit in a place like this and jack Rhys off without the safety of a glamour, where anyone could notice?

Fire raked across Silas's back. A clawed hand covered his mouth. "Looking for someone, pixie?" Putrid breath against his face.

Oh fuck. Orcus take him down under the earth.

The soulless bit into his shoulder, and pain exploded through Silas's nerves. Centuries of discipline took over. He lurched forward, throwing the creature over him. Clothing and flesh ripped as Silas launched the soulless through the air and down the darkened ramp of the theater. Thin lines of icy fire burned across his shoulder.

Silas didn't bother to watch the creature land. He ran for the exit. A strategic move, rather than one born from fear. More space, more light in the lobby. Less chance he would slice a human with his sword. The Messengers forgave many things, but not accidental human death on the tip of a phoenix-made blade.

None of the theatergoers noticed the fight. The soulless wove their own kind of glamour over human senses.

Silas stumbled into the foyer. Gods, how he'd forgotten the pain of their bite, the numbness.

Careless and stupid to be caught so.

Poison raged through his limbs, slowing him. No time to heal.

Footsteps behind him. *Damn it all!* He turned and swung his blade at the soulless on his trail—and missed.

Missed. For the first time in five centuries. He couldn't help pulling back in shock.

That was all it took. The soulless caught his shoulders as he turned, dug in its claws, and slammed him face-first against the wall. The bridge of his nose shattered, and blood flowed down his face. The grate of the wallpaper against Silas's ruined face felt like acid burning through his flesh. Pinpricks of light danced in his vision. His throat ached to scream, but he wouldn't give the creature that satisfaction.

Everything smelled of blood.

"So, the great Silvanus." A male voice, dark and cold, spoke into his ear. "I thought the forest god was supposed to be a challenge."

Again, teeth sank into Silas's flesh, deeper than before. Agony flooded his senses, but this time fury rather than shame followed. Silas reversed the grip on his sword and plunged it backward into the gut of the soulless. It howled and released him. The creature must have backed itself off his blade, for the weight on the sword vanished.

So much for the element of surprise. Silas turned, letting the wall support him.

The soulless had been a man once and still held that form, but for a bloodied maw of jagged teeth and long birdlike claws for hands. Brown hair, black eyes, and a face that would've been handsome had it been human.

It spit at Silas and backed away, one clawed hand over the wound in its belly. The wound festered and smoked. Bits of flesh fell away and turned to ash. A young one, then. Had it been older, the blow would've merely slowed it down.

"Not so easy." Silas shifted his grip on the gladius and wiped blood away from his mouth with his coat sleeve. "And enough of a challenge to send you into oblivion."

It bared its fangs. "But at what price, Silvanus? The sea is no friend to you."

His name again. *How did it know?* Silas pushed himself off the wall and stalked toward the soulless. Blood from the wounds in his shoulder ran down his neck and soaked his shirt.

The soulless tried to back away but stumbled to the floor.

"Slowly or quickly," Silas said. "Either way, the gods will

take your body." He stopped when he reached the fallen creature.

"And the master will take your soul." It lunged for Silas's leg. Sank fangs and claws into his left calf.

Silas swore and swung at the creature's neck. His muscles bunched against the impact, but the blade slid through cleanly. The body dissolved into ash. The head bounced once and then did the same.

Silence, except for his ragged breathing. Silas hazarded a glance around the foyer. No one, thank Fortuna. His glamour was in tatters, much like his body.

Thousands of knives slashed in his blood. That had gone badly, indeed. Pride alone kept him upright. He'd survived far worse, just not in a very long time.

And never floating in the middle of the ocean.

Silas limped away from the piles of ash on the floor. Oh, that would confuse the humans, but they would clean it up and be none the wiser. His formal wear soaked up blood well. He wasn't trailing much of it. Dark red carpet too. *Good.*

He paused and sheathed his sword into the dark void of the Aether. He'd very little elemental power left and needed it to hide himself. Stop the bleeding, if he could.

The soulless had drunk deep when it pierced Silas's skin. All the strength he'd gained from Rhys was gone, along with much of his own energy. He'd barely enough to cast a glamour. Healing would have to wait.

Mercury's balls! Wait until what? He returned to the garden? He fucked Rhys, *used* him to gain strength, like some fae version of the soulless? Silas caught himself as he fell against the hallway wall. A deep craving for the quarter-fae shook his body.

The things he wanted to do to Rhys—the things he needed to do...

No.

He'd not turn into one of *them*. Not ever. His unbridled lust, his uncontrolled desire for Rhys had nearly gotten him killed. The garden would have to do for a source of energy. A day ago it would've been more than enough. He'd make it that far, crawl into a corner, and heal.

Seven soulless left. Already he was bloodied and poisoned, all because he couldn't keep his cock in his pants. Silas punched the wall. Pain radiated up his arm, and he regretted the move instantly.

Better for Silas to break his pledge to return to Rhys than entrap and use him as some damn battery or as a slave to desire.

Silas had been both, once.

He pushed himself off the wall. No, he'd rather die an honest death than become that which he most despised.

He took a shuddering breath and continued toward the garden. It would be enough. It *had* to be. He just had to stay out of the bar. Keep away from Rhys.

———

RHYS FLIPPED through a coffee-table book on New York City that contained beautiful photographs of places that looked more real on glossy paper than they did in life. Battery Park, with pristine blue water in the background. The Brooklyn Bridge in golden light, with no cars or people. Times Square, with not a drop of trash in sight. He'd been to most of them, knew their true colors and the bits the photographers had cleverly edited out.

Had Silas been to New York before? Probably, if he was as old as Rhys suspected. Hell, he might have been there back before they built the skyscrapers. The thought of Silas dressed as a colonial in tight breaches and a long coat coiled heat in Rhys's belly.

ANNA ZABO

He reached for his drink, his third this evening, thanks to Vasil. He'd been here two hours and had been through nearly every book in the scrawny bookcase. Most were like the book on New York, large and full of color photography. A few were dog-eared paperbacks, probably leftovers from past travelers —King, Patterson, Roberts.

Every single book he'd flipped through so far made him think of Silas in various costumes or in various states of undress.

He needed something to take his mind off the fae.

Fae.

The longer he sat, the more of a fool he felt. Would Silas even come back? He rubbed his forehead. Was any of this real? Was there truly danger, or had that been a convenient way to dump him? He could've gone to a movie. Or learned ballroom dance. Or smoked cigars and drunk brandy—whatever it was they did on cruises like this. Something more interesting than paging through picture books.

The memory of Silas's kiss intruded on his growing frustration, the pull of Silas's hands tangled in his hair, the taste of his jizz. His cry of abandonment and pleasure.

Rhys sighed and pushed those thoughts from his mind. Flipped a page. Central Park. All that greenery. What would it be like to fuck there? Or in real woods? Naked, his back pressed into the dark earth and Silas holding Rhys's legs apart as he entered him.

The tightness in his belly spread down to his cock. Damn, Silas better return soon. He wasn't sure how much longer he could put his fantasies on hold and it was getting more difficult to hide his erection, even under the large book in his lap.

"Are these seats taken?"

Rhys nearly jumped out of his skin when the woman

spoke. He hadn't noticed her approach. For a moment, all he could do was stare up at her.

"N-no."

Her laugh was bell-like. "Oh, I am so sorry. I didn't mean to startle you. All the other tables are occupied. You seem like you might enjoy some company." She smiled, baring a flash of white between her immaculate ruby lips.

Rhys exhaled a breath. "You're welcome to them." He gestured at the other two chairs and attempted a smile of his own.

"That's very sweet of you." She offered her hand, palm down. "Radmila." Her voice held a trace of an accent, different from Silas's. Closer to Vasil's.

He took her hand and gave it a gentle squeeze before letting go. "Rhys." Though her skin was soft, her hand felt like ice. Cold. Hard underneath. His heart rate kicked up. People shouldn't feel like sculpture.

"Charmed." Same smile. She settled into the closest chair.

Rarely did he pay that much attention to the physical attractiveness of women, but this one—she was different. Chocolate-colored hair that moved like water fell to her shoulders. Rich brown eyes set into a round face. Her skin was almost luminescent, like mother-of-pearl. If she'd been a man, he would've had a very hard time saying no to anything she asked.

Radmila frowned ever so slightly before her features smoothed over. "Are you alone, Rhys?" Soft words.

He shivered. Something about that question made his hair stand on end. He shouldn't answer, but the response tumbled out of his mouth anyway. "I'm waiting for a friend."

"We're waiting for someone too." She glanced back at the bar. "Perhaps we can idle the time together."

We. Rhys followed the path her gaze had taken. A blond man walked toward them, right hand in his pocket. His blue eyes took Rhys's breath away, even from halfway across the room—pale as a summer's morning. He was thin—thinner than Silas—and he had the same marble-like skin as Radmila.

She took the man's left hand as he joined her. "Has the waiter seen our friend?"

"Earlier, but not recently."

God, the man's voice. It dipped and rolled like the sound of an oboe. Rhys curled his hands about the book in his lap. Instinct told him to flee these two, but when the man's gaze shifted and lingered on him, he couldn't look away.

"I see you've found a new friend."

More so than Radmila's, this man's smile froze Rhys's blood. He'd do anything to touch the man, to be touched by him. The thought repulsed Rhys, even as it made him hard.

"Rhys, this is Jarek."

Jarek took a step forward and offered his right hand.

He tried not to take it. Failed. Cold skin. Iron grip. Rhys couldn't let go.

"I'm very pleased to meet you, Rhys."

The way Jarek said his name, the desire that lingered in the blond man's eyes, set Rhys's bones on fire.

"He's waiting for a friend too," Radmila said. She released her partner's hand.

"So I see."

Those words and the sudden chill of his own skin made Rhys pull away. Or at least think about it. His hand stayed in Jarek's grip.

"No, Rhys. That won't do at all." Jarek lifted the book from Rhys's lap and placed it on the table. "Why don't you sit between Radmila and me? Let us have a little chat?"

Rhys stood, though his mind shouted not to. *Oh, God.* Where the hell was Silas? He had to get away from these —people?

All he could do was what Jarek instructed. They

rearranged the chairs so they sat close together, with Rhys between the two.

"Now." Jarek stroked his thumb over the top of Rhys's hand. "Who are you waiting for?"

Sharp spikes rattled against Rhys's lungs when he tried not to inhale and struggled not to speak. Still, it came out. "Silas."

"Silas?"

"Quint." Speaking the word felt as though he'd been crushed into and then dragged over broken glass.

Radmila's laugh rang out. "He's rearranged his name."

Jarek smiled, displaying a mouth full of teeth that were *wrong*. Every last one was pointed, like a saw blade. "And do you know where Silas is?"

That question, at least, Rhys was willing to answer. "No."

"When will he return?"

"By first light." Because vampires—that must be what these two were—couldn't stand sunlight. But it was dark now, and Silas wasn't here.

Why wasn't Silas here?

"Of course," Jarek murmured. He brought Rhys's hand to his mouth and licked it. "You're absolutely delightful. So full of fear." He turned Rhys's hand over, scraped those razor teeth over his wrist, and then bit.

Jarek's mouth felt like acid burning through his flesh. Rhys couldn't even scream. An instant later, the pain diminished. Jarek pulled away.

Bite marks and blood, but a wound so small it looked like a kitten's nip. If that was what a small bite felt like, Rhys would never survive a real one.

"Now," Jarek said. "Give your other hand to Radmila."

God no. But he did as he was told.

Radmila bit him as Jarek had, to the same effect. By the end, he took air in short gasps. When she released his hand, she said something to Jarek in a language Rhys didn't understand. He laughed in response.

Jarek ran a finger down Rhys's neck. "Do you know what your friend Silas Quint is?"

The answer tore its way out of Rhys's throat even as he tried to pull away from Jarek's touch. "Fae."

"And did the fae tell you what you are?"

"I don't—" What he was? Dredges of dinner conversation surfaced. "He said I was fairly unique in the world."

Radmila snorted.

Jarek clicked his tongue. "Now, now. The pixie told him the truth."

"As far as that goes." Her hand encircled his wrist. "I want more of him."

"Yes," Jarek said. "But not here." He rose and pulled Rhys up as well. "Don't worry. Your fae will join you soon enough."

Radmila stood and snaked her arm around Rhys's. "It's a lovely night for a stroll on the deck."

They walked him toward the dark glass of the outer door, which slid open as they approached. The night air was breezy and cool, heavy with the smell of the ocean. A sliver of moon hung over the water, casting white onto the inky black of the water. It would have been beautiful had he not been strung between two vampires. Where was Silas? He was supposed to be hunting these things!

"I almost want to let you run," Jarek whispered into his ear. "Just to taste your hope die."

Sound escaped his throat then, but it was only a whimper.

Radmila licked Rhys's neck. "Oh, but it just did, didn't it?"

They walked him down to a table nestled close to the bulkhead and draped in shadow. Jarek pushed him hard against the metal wall. Cloth ripped, and his tie was stripped from his neck. His shirt followed, buttons clacking to the wooden deck. Cold lips skimmed his shoulder blade. Jarek's teeth ripped into Rhys's skin and muscle.

Flaming spikes pierced his flesh. Rhys's throat ached as though he screamed, but only whimpers came out. Those small sounds seemed to drive Jarek on. Fingers dug into his other shoulder and tore into that flesh as well.

Rhys was going to die. God, he wanted to die. Then the torment, the burning fire in his blood would stop.

It didn't. When Radmila yanked Jarek away, it lessened for a moment. She spoke, but the words made no sense. Again Jarek laughed and backed away. Radmila closed in.

Rhys burned as if someone had set fire to the marrow in his bones. When she pulled back, he would've cried out in relief had he been able to make any sound at all. *This isn't happening. This can't be happening.*

They ripped off the rest of his clothes, the fabric screeching as it tore. The only other sound in the night was the hum of the ship and the slap of the water against the hull. No footsteps. No one to save him.

Jarek lifted Rhys and laid him out on the table, the cold open-weave metal scraped against Rhys's bare back, an almost pleasant touch compared to what had come before.

The respite didn't last. Radmila hovered in his vision, teeth fully bared. She drew a claw down his cheek, a parody of a lover's caress. The wound stung as if sand had been rubbed into it. The sharp metallic smell of blood filled his nose. He tasted the tang in his mouth.

Then the vampires tore into his body. Ice sliced through his legs. Fire pulsed up in waves. He felt the tug and rip of his flesh and the acid burn after, when sea spray covered them. Teeth pierced Rhys's chest like glass daggers. Radmila's hair fell against the ruin of his face and shoulder. The fine strands slithered like maggots, then buried into his flesh. Rhys's nerves screamed and seemed to rip out of his body. A buzzing filled his ears, and lightning flashed over his vision. But he didn't—couldn't—pass out. Something close to a wail finally escaped his lips.

Rhys shouted a single name over and over in his head.
Silas!

CHAPTER SIX

Twice while Silas limped toward the garden, he nearly lost his glamour. Both times he propped himself up against the closest wall and reached through the ship for any traces of green life. Potted plants. Algae. Anything from which he could draw his element.

There was so very little. Frustrating and infuriating. He should sense the garden, be able to draw on it, but it was hidden from him.

One slow step at a time, he descended the metal stairs to the deck that contained the garden. The elevators were too public to attempt, not when he had trouble wrapping a glamour around his bleeding and broken form.

The ship itself shouldn't be the reason the garden remained distant. Metal wasn't useful to Silas, but it didn't affect him more than any other nonliving material did. While it wasn't easy to do, he'd drawn power from the green while in the middle of skyscrapers, surrounded by concrete, iron, and steel. A ship should be no different. He certainly could—and did—draw on those tiny sparks of element he did manage to find.

Whatever protected the garden must have been placed there to hamper him. Fear crept into Silas. The soulless knew his name. They'd been waiting for him. Knew his weaknesses.

How? He'd destroyed all the soulless he'd ever met, save for a handful very early in his life.

Silas reached out to steady himself against the stairwell wall. One more deck. He pushed off, gripped the railing, and tried not to fall down the stairs.

It was a near thing. His leg, the one the soulless had bitten, was numb from the knee down.

So he wasn't just the hunter but prey as well. This didn't bode well, but he'd deal with that tomorrow.

Once in the garden, Silas dragged himself to the farthest corner from the bar, crawled up into the plant beds, and collapsed among the ferns. Here was the life he needed. He drew on it as hard as he could without killing the plants around him, then set about dispelling the poison the soulless had sent into his body. That was the hardest bit. The cuts, the bites, and claw wounds were wounds of the flesh. Some bone and cartilage, like his nose, but all issues of sculpting matter.

Poison—at least for fae—was entirely different. What flooded his body was the *absence* of life.

He'd been touched by decay, the rot of the endless death.

Silas wrapped the spirit of the garden around the corrosion inside himself and vomited noiselessly onto the mulched bed.

Ah, the beautiful life of a fae. If Rhys could see him now.

He crawled a few feet away from the mess, sank to the ground, and closed his eyes.

Silas!

The plea—the scream—ripped through his soul.

He was on his feet and running toward the bar before his

thoughts caught up. He'd already pulled his sword from the Aether, wrapped himself in glamour, and killed two palm trees for their energy.

They had Rhys. There was no other agony quite like that of the soulless feeding. Silas knew it too well, felt it in the incoherent screams that sliced through his mind.

If the creatures had set a trap for him in the garden and then found Rhys...

The bar was quiet but held quite a number of people coupled off into nooks and tables. No Rhys. No soulless.

One face he recognized, though.

Silas stopped in front of the bar. "Vasil, where's Rhys?"

The waiter started and stared at him. "Mr. Quint?" His look turned vacant. "I...haven't seen Mr. Matherton."

Silas swore under his breath. So they'd touched Vasil too. Not fed, but influenced his mind. One remedy.

Silas clamped his hand down on Vasil's wrist and pressed against the man's mind with his own.

"Vasil."

The waiter gasped and tried to pull away. Silas had some idea what Vasil saw—for he now saw true—a bloodied fae with a silver sword, half-wild with someone else's pain. There was no time for explanations, however. He repeated the question. "Where is Rhys?"

Vasil's attention slid toward a small grouping of chairs by a bookshelf. "He's..."

But he wasn't. Three martini glasses, but no Rhys.

"Where?" He liked the waiter well enough, but gods, he would rip the thoughts from the man's mind if he had to.

There was no need. "They took him," Vasil said. "Outside." He took a deep breath and spoke a word in his mother tongue. "*Upyr.*"

Vampire. "Yes," Silas said.

Vasil looked back. "*Leshii?*"

Slavic woodland spirits. Close enough. He nodded. "Though I was born much farther south." He let go of Vasil's wrist and walked to the doors leading to the deck.

Once outside, Silas made his way up the starboard side of the ship. Rhys's screams had quieted, but the pain hadn't. Halfway down, tucked into the darkness of both the night and the veil of the soulless, a body lay spread out on a table—Rhys. Two soulless fed from him.

Silas knew only fury as he burst into a run.

The closest was female, its back to Silas and it never saw him coming. The other soulless did. It raised a bloody maw from Rhys's chest and hissed a warning.

Too late.

Silas brandished his sword and sent the female's head flying. It burst into a trail of flame and ash and the body slumped to the deck, burning to dust. Another young one.

The male stepped away from Rhys's body. "Quintus Silvanus."

So. This one knew his name as well. Silas kept silent and stepped closer to Rhys. He was alive—that much Silas knew—but in pain. He didn't let himself look at the extent—or type—of Rhys's wounds.

The male wiped blood from his mouth, then spoke. "You've not fared well tonight." Rich voice, full of amusement. "Your masters will not be pleased."

This one was older. Cautious. "Two of your kind are ash." He kicked at the pile that had been the female, sending what was left of the soulless swirling into the night air. "You soon will be, too. I think they'll be pleased enough."

"So confident for one so—" The soulless lunged, faster than Silas expected.

He parried, but the creature caught the blade with one clawed hand while raking the other down Silas's chest. The jacket caught some of the blow, but not all. This one's claws cut like razors, parting Silas's flesh with a cool touch. Then came the sharp fire of nerves fraying and flesh tearing. Poison burned in his blood again. Silas bit back a scream when all his other wounds flared to life.

The soulless clutched the blade and bared its teeth. Only a faint smell of burning came from where the metal touched its flesh.

Silas shoved the creature away and then stabbed after him. Every move kept Silas between the soulless and Rhys.

That hadn't gone unnoticed. "Protecting your prey, Silvanus? Don't want another tasting what you've laid claim to?" The soulless stepped out of range and licked the wound on its hand. "He's awake, you know."

Again Silas chose silence. He didn't recognize this one, nor the female. They were from Eastern Europe—perhaps Hungary. Silas had hunted there before. But those he hunted, he'd destroyed. Few soulless knew his old name, let alone the new.

Unease settled into his bones.

"You didn't tell him what he was, did you? Just took him."

The soulless circled. If Silas didn't step away from Rhys, he'd be pushed into a corner.

"Anaxandros will be pleased to see how much you learned from his hand."

With those words, two thousand years fell away and wrath exploded in Silas.

The soulless had been expecting the wild attack, of course. The rational part of Silas's mind screamed at him to stop, to control his anger.

Too late.

Once more, the soulless caught Silas's blade. This time it wrenched the sword sideways and punched Silas in the chest. Air rushed out of his lungs, and something—a rib or two, probably—snapped inside. The stabbing that radiated out swept nausea through Silas. Dizzy and breathless, he staggered back against the table and clutched his midriff with his free hand.

He had enough presence of mind to push the gladius back into the Aether. If he dropped it, he couldn't call it to himself. That would mean a mad scramble to regain it from the deck.

Good thing too. The soulless slammed a fist into him again. The pain in his chest turned into a lance of molten fire and robbed him of the ability to think. He toppled onto Rhys.

Energy flew from Silas unbidden, sucked into Rhys and returned laced with fire and death. Silas gasped for air and tried to pry himself free from the quarter-fae. Failed.

Beneath him, Rhys moaned and thrashed.

It was the soulless who broke their contact. It picked Silas up and hurled him against the ship's railing. The blow sent fire up his spine. Agony burst into Silas's skull, and sparks danced in his vision before he crumpled to the deck. His lungs burned with every breath.

The soulless wouldn't be able to resist taking him. Once the creature bit he'd perhaps a moment before it drained him to unconsciousness. One chance left.

"The master said you were soft." The soulless hauled Silas to his feet. "Nothing but a slave. How is it that you have survived so long?" Teeth plunged into flesh.

This one's bite was far worse than the young soulless. It seared through his heart, ripped through nerves like the barbed tongues of a whip. The creature drew on every last spark of energy Silas held, down to the one that kept his soul attached to his body. But he'd been here before with a much older vampire.

Anaxandros.

Silas reached through the miasma of pain and called the

gladius back to his hand. He plunged it straight though the soulless, where its heart would have been, had it had one.

"By not being afraid to die," Silas said.

Fire flickered behind the soulless's eyes. "Imposs—" And then it burst into flame.

The heat scorched Silas too and sent him stumbling back against the railing. This time he did drop the sword. It clattered to the deck amid a flurry of ash and smoke.

Silas slid down to the wood planks, utterly spent. There would be no glamour. No healing. He might live, if he could make it back to the garden. The gentle fall of the sea spray against his wounds made every inch of his body pulse with torment.

Five more soulless to kill. He didn't know whether to laugh or cry.

And Anaxandros was their master. *Merciful gods!*

Only Silas's gods weren't. Had never been, not to him. The Messengers? Righteousness was not mercy.

On the table, Rhys stirred. Cursed. Stood.

Silas made out only the silhouette of his form, backlit by the faint light from the ship. Rhys stumbled once but steadied. "Silas?"

He wanted to crawl away, but he couldn't move. He was, he realized, dying. Slowly, but yes. The poison had taken root. No escape. Fortuna had finally caught him.

Took her long enough.

Rhys called his name a second time.

"Here." It came out like crushed leaves in autumn. All dust and pieces.

Rhys stumbled toward him and caught himself against the railing. "Oh my God. You're—" He reached out.

Silas tried to pull away. "No!"

Too late again. Rhys's fingers brushed against the side of his face, and they both screamed.

65

All the elemental energy Rhys still held within him, Silas took. He couldn't stop the desperate act of his body. The flow also carried with it Rhys's torment and fear, scalding Silas's nerves and soul.

When it was over, Silas could move again. Rhys, however, had fallen—dead weight against Silas's legs.

Not truly dead, though. Rhys still breathed. But for how long?

Silas extracted himself from beneath Rhys, bent to take a pulse, but hesitated. He still wanted—desired—more energy. The poison of the soulless still lurked within him. What would happen when he touched Rhys again?

Well, he couldn't leave him here. Silas closed his mind, his emotions as best he could and laid two fingers against Rhys's throat. A pulse—quick but regular. Also a tiny trickle of energy.

Rhys's breathing turned to gasping; his pulse fluttered too fast. Silas snatched his hand away.

Gods, he couldn't control himself. The soulless was right —there was very little difference between him and them.

Silas crawled down the deck and reclaimed his sword, then sheathed it back into the Aether. He clutched the railing and, after a few attempts, managed to pull himself up.

He couldn't leave Rhys here, not naked and bloodied— misused by the soulless. Nor could he pick Rhys up, not without violating him anew, stealing the last bits of energy he had.

How far was the garden? He looked down the deck, judged distance, his own strength.

Damn all the gods. Silas bent, picked Rhys up, and fought not to drop the unconscious man. Pulses like stabbing knives cut through Silas's chest. Silas staggered to the garden as fast as he could manage. As the doors slid open, he reached for the garden's energy and wrapped a glamour about Rhys and himself.

There were fewer patrons in the bar, and those who remained were too intent on each other to notice anything more than a weary man walking in from the deck.

Silas threaded down a side path and laid Rhys down on a bench. He stepped away and forced himself to draw from the nearest plants, not from Rhys.

That was a struggle. Even with all the energy about him, he still wanted to take it from—and through—Rhys.

Silas rubbed at his forehead. What had the tales said about Quarters? Endless energy. Wars for control. Fae dying when their Quarter was killed. Or was it the other way around?

Silas's fingers shook. Oh, the gods truly were not merciful at all. He tucked his hands under his arms.

Bonded.

He truly had taken Rhys—as the soulless had said— without any thought and without any regard to Rhys's will. Silas doubled over and bit down on his tongue to keep from screaming.

Monster. Evil.

Silas called the gladius back to his hand and inverted it.

Rhys moaned and whispered Silas's name.

If he killed himself, what would become of Rhys? Would he live? Die? Be claimed by another?

Silas pointed the sword at the floor. Now *that* would be utterly unfair, to condemn another to death for his mistake.

No. He sheathed the sword.

There had to be some way out of this. Some way to give Rhys his freedom back.

WHEN RHYS WOKE, he wished he hadn't. The light in the room—even with the blinds drawn—made his head hurt like he'd spent the night inside a bottle of whiskey.

Where the fuck was he, anyway? Vienna? Amsterdam?

He sat up. No. On a ship, heading to New York. Only this vast room—with too many windows, a balcony, and more space than his first apartment—wasn't his cabin.

What the hell?

Then the memories came. Radmila's perfect lips. Jarek's jagged teeth. A shudder ran through his body. They had eaten him—his flesh and blood. His soul.

He didn't hurt at all, at least physically. He examined his arms. Smooth, unblemished skin over his wrists, chest unmarred by claws or teeth. He ran his hands over his neck. No scars. Nothing.

No clothes either. Naked in someone else's bed.

Silas. He'd come, a sword-wielding angel, out of the night. Fought the vampires. Killed them.

The cabin had to be his. But Silas was nowhere to be seen. Rhys scrubbed his face with his hand and took a better look at the room.

In the far corner of the cabin, a pile of crumpled and bloody clothing had been heaped around a dead potted tree. Dried leaves had fallen on top of the clothing and lay near the hands clutching the pot.

Hands. Rhys sucked in a breath.

Silas had wrapped himself around the plant. The heap of clothing was his, still worn, in tatters and stained rust-red with blood. Every inch of skin not covered by cloth bore cuts and bruises.

Rhys couldn't tell if he was dead or sleeping.

"Silas?"

The lump stirred and cursed in a language Rhys didn't

understand. Silas uncurled from the tree. Sitting up took him far too long.

"Holy shit!" The words slipped from Rhys's mouth.

Silas was far from the same man Rhys had accompanied to dinner—gaunt and so pale he looked blue. The rags of his clothes hung from his frame. Bloody gashes covered his neck and his shoulders, and he clutched his left side. His nose was a mass of bulging purple. "I didn't mean to fall asleep."

Even his voice had lost its fullness and life.

Rhys slipped out of the bed. God. He wanted to pick Silas up off the floor and hold him. "What did they do to you?"

Silas held up a hand and scooted backward several inches. "Don't!"

Rhys froze in his tracks. There was terror in Silas's eyes. Fear of him. "Don't what?"

"Don't come near me." Silas scrambled away until his back hit a set of dresser drawers.

The words were a knife to Rhys's stomach. "I want to help you. You're injured."

"How very observant you are."

The bitter sarcasm brought an unexpected stinging to Rhys's eyes. Not again. Not *this* man. He clenched his fists until his nails bit into his palms.

Silas swayed, even though he sat. He placed a hand on the floor, probably to keep himself from toppling over.

Rhys took another step forward.

Silas lifted his head and growled a single unintelligible word. He bared his teeth and tensed every muscle. Feral. Like a trapped wolf.

Rhys stopped. "Why won't you let me help you?"

"If you want to help me," Silas said, "go away."

Go away. Rhys's father had said those words—both his fathers, really. Five different lovers had spoken the same three syllables. A tightness grew in his chest.

Now Silas, who made him feel more true than he'd ever felt, who'd set the world aright by turning it upside down. Now those words came from his mouth. Discarded.

Rhys stepped back. Whispered two words of his own. "You promised."

"Promised?"

"That you'd explain. Tell me what this was all about."

Silas's sharp laugh cut the air. "I lied." He raised his head and stared at Rhys. "Get out."

Rhys hadn't realized how far he'd backed up until he clipped the frame of the bed with his shin. Pain flared up his leg, and he caught himself before he fell.

Fucking hell!

But the sharp stabbing cleared his head. This wasn't right. Terror lurked in Silas behind those harsh words. Pain too. He hadn't lied in the garden. If anything, he was lying now.

Rhys watched Silas. All those wounds. What had the vampires done to him?

A flash of memory—hands and teeth ripping clothing from his body—sent another tremor through Rhys.

Rhys straightened. "I'm not leaving. Not until I've had my coffee and my answers." Not until he found out what happened on the deck of the ship.

"I don't want you here. Leave me alone." There was hesitancy in Silas's beautiful voice.

Got you. "You're a horrible liar, you know."

The wild fury in Silas shattered. He swayed again and placed his other hand on the floor. Silence filled the room, punctuated only by Silas's rough breathing. Then he whispered a plea. "Rhys, please."

His name. The knot loosened in Rhys's stomach. "I'm not leaving. Besides, I can't just walk back to my cabin like this." Buck naked was certainly not part of the ship's dress code. "I can't glamour clothes onto myself. I'm not fae."

Silas sat back on his heels and stared at the tan carpet. "There're clothes in the closet. We're close enough in size."

"And coffee?"

Silas raised his head at that. Terror still lurked in him, but the blue tinge to his flesh had left. He gestured over to the side of the room. "There's a machine at the bar."

Rhys opted for the closet first. He took the only pair of jeans. They were an inch longer than he liked, but he did share the same waist size with Silas. Same shirt size too. Rhys quickly buttoned up one of Silas's white shirts. Then he inspected the bar. The creeping start of a headache lurked at the base of his skull, but he ignored it. Coffee would help.

The coffeemaker was a pod-style that brewed by the cup. Impressive. In Rhys's cabin there was an old drip machine. He poked a finger at the coffee selections. "Hazelnut, mocha, bold, or French roast?"

"I don't want coffee."

Rhys gripped the marble bar countertop, glad he no longer faced Silas. The thrum of his headache kicked to full force, stretching his patience thin. "If you don't choose, you're getting French. And you're going to drink it, even if I have to sit on you and pour it down your damn throat."

Nothing but the hum of the fridge, then something that might have been a laugh or a sob. "Bold, then. I can't stand French."

Of course not. He set the pod into the machine and pressed Start. "Pity there's no Italian roast."

A longer pause this time. "I'm not Italian."

Rhys faced Silas while the coffee brewed. "No. You're Roman."

Silas huffed a breath. "Well, aren't you clever?"

"Not really. You dropped enough hints."

A faint smile, the first Rhys had seen that morning, pulled Silas's lips upward. No doubt about it; he looked better.

Fuller somehow, even with the myriad scabs, scars, and bruises.

Rhys rubbed his forehead and leaned back against the counter. He would be happy enough to sit for a while.

Silas's good humor fled. "Rhys, you should go."

No anger this time, only concern laced with that ever-present hint of fear.

"Why?"

"Because I'm hurting you."

The coffee machine behind Rhys beeped, and he turned as he tried to make sense of Silas's words. He retrieved the cup and set the next one brewing. "I'm going to put this on the table. Can you make it there yourself?"

The table sat perhaps six feet from Silas.

"I believe so, yes."

Rhys crossed the room, set the cup down, and then retreated to the bar. His legs buckled, and he grabbed the counter to keep from falling. Good thing there was coffee. The events of the evening were catching up fast.

"Rhys?"

"I'm fine. I'm just tired."

"I know." Guilt laced Silas's words. "I'm sorry."

The coffee machine beeped again. "It's not your fault." Rhys took his cup and turned.

Silas stood, took the few steps he needed to reach the table, and sat. "But it is." Silas pointed to a couch against the far wall. "Sit. I'll explain."

Rhys walked to the couch and sat. Sipped his coffee.

"What flavor?"

"Hazelnut."

Silas grunted. "I would've thought mocha."

"I guess you don't know me as well as you think." Rhys took another taste. "After a day." Let Silas taste a bit of his own caustic medicine.

Silas finally took a mouthful of coffee. "You're a constant surprise to me." Warmth in those words. "Will you let me tell my tale without interruption?"

Rhys squirmed. Perhaps Silas did know him. "May I ask questions?"

"A few. I'll only answer if I care to."

Some concession. "I don't like those rules."

Silas shrugged. He looked more like himself than he had all morning, arrogant and proud. "You're free to leave."

"Oh, fuck you." Rhys leaned back. "Fine."

Silas nearly hid a smile before he spoke. "We're creatures of passion, fae. Of the elements. Field and forest, stream and sea, breeze and sky, rock and earth."

"Fire?"

"No. That's the purview of the phoenix."

Phoenix? Rhys opened his mouth, but Silas held up a hand. *Damn it all.* But he'd agreed. He nodded for Silas to continue.

"As you might have gathered, we're fond of humans." Silas toyed with his cup. "Occasionally those unions produce children."

Rhys sat forward. "I'm half-fae?"

"No." Silas took another gulp of coffee. "Half-fae have the same skills as the full-blooded. More. They require no glamour to walk among humans. They simply switch their state of being."

Rhys turned the information over. Sorted through it. "I'd know, then, if I were one."

"You'd see what I see. Have talents like my own. And you'd either be in one of the courts"—he paused, distaste twisting his features—"or dead."

"Dead?"

"Half-fae are seen as dangerous. If they live long enough, they eclipse full-blooded fae in power, all without the need of

73

glamour to be human. Glamour's not easy to maintain, especially under stress."

"But you can do it."

"When I have to, yes."

"But when we..." Rhys remembered the feel of Silas's hands tangled in his hair as Silas's cock slid through his lips. The taste of Silas's skin, his semen, his mouth. Silas's hands on his body, encircling his cock. The scent of pine and earth—

Silas banged his cup on the table. "Rhys!"

He started awake.

What the hell? His cup of coffee lay on the carpet, the contents staining the tan pile even darker. "I..." He glanced at Silas.

Silas's nose was better. Bruised but no longer horribly misshapen. And even the dark purple had faded to greenish yellow.

Silas exhaled. "Please don't think about sex right now."

Rhys tried to stand, but his legs wouldn't hold him. He tried again and managed, but it was all he could do to remain upright. White haze ringed his vision. A half cup of coffee and he was ready to pass out? Something was very wrong. "What the fuck is going on?"

"I'm trying to tell you." Silas's accent grew stronger and his grip on his coffee mug tighter. "But you keep interrupting me. Now sit!"

Rhys's face went hot, but he sank to the couch, obedient. For now.

Silas tapped a finger against his cup and started again. "Half-fae. They're hybrids. In all but very rare cases, they're sterile."

A coolness washed over Rhys. Something unique in the world. "Shit."

Silas nodded. "You were close in your guess. Your father is half-fae."

Rhys flattened his hands on his thighs to keep them from shaking. "Is?"

"I suspect he's still alive, since he bribed you."

Too many questions. Why would his father do that? Why was he only discovering this now? He voiced one. "What does that make me?"

"Quarter-fae." Silas picked up his mug. Drank.

"And what does that mean?" God, he wanted another coffee. Now. If only his legs would support him.

Silas ran a finger around the top of his mug. His next words were softer. "Quarters are extraordinarily rare. Millennia have passed without the hint of one. Much of what I know is dressed in myth. The rest I'm only discovering."

Rhys toed the mug on the floor. *Quarter.* A label to go with what he was. "Nothing in my life has been all that magical."

"There's only one skill ever talked about. It's not something you'd discover on your own." Silas pushed his mug away. "Quarters are elemental reservoirs. They store vast quantities of whatever element they have an affinity for."

Realization hit like a slap to the face. Silas's fear, his desire for Rhys to go. The dead tree in the corner of the room. Silas had killed it, drawn all of its life—its element. His expression must have been utterly readable.

"You're brighter than old forest," Silas said. "And I'm wounded in the middle of the ocean. I've been trying not to, but I can't always..." He looked away. "You really should leave, Rhys."

Something didn't add up. Rhys glanced down at his unmarked wrists. Another memory broke free. Of pain and the chill of the ocean. Dying leaves. Stumbling toward Silas. "Last night I touched you. After you killed the vampires. I felt—" Rhys sat up. "You were dying."

"I nearly killed you." Silas laid his hands on the table. Stared at them. "I couldn't stop myself. Took nearly all of your element to save my life."

Another memory stirred in the back of Rhys's mind. Silas standing with his sword pressed to his gut. There was more —much more—that Silas wasn't telling him. Later he would pry it from Silas.

"You healed me."

Silas nodded. "It was your energy anyway and you couldn't do it yourself."

From the way Silas had looked earlier, he'd drained himself. Kept nothing when he should've healed himself enough to survive. *Stubborn fool.* Rhys stared at the dead ficus and recalled broken bits of the vampire's conversation with Silas. Jarek had taunted him, said Silas had learned well. A glimmer of understanding grew. "You're not like them."

A tremor ran through Silas. "Are you so very sure of that?"

"You didn't kill me while we slept."

"I had the tree to drain, and we were far enough apart. And you weren't..."

Damn it! Every time Silas got close to explaining, he backed away. "I wasn't what?" A spike of anger gave Rhys strength enough to stand. He picked up the fallen mug and returned to the bar.

"You weren't awake."

There was no more hazelnut coffee. Rhys chose mocha and shoved it into the machine. "You're a piss-poor storyteller for someone who didn't want any questions."

Rhys didn't dare turn around during the cold stillness that followed.

"You're more than welcome to go."

Rhys could've made iced coffee from that sentence. "Not

yet." He enunciated each word clearly. Once his coffee had brewed, he took it and returned to the couch. "Continue."

The bruising on Silas's nose had gone from greenish yellow to a pale yellow. His expression was unreadable. Or perhaps not. Silas had looked like that moments before going down on him—defiance mixed with audacity and control.

Rhys felt his cock stir.

"Stop that!" Silas shifted in his chair. Shuddered once. "Gods, whatever am I going to do with you?"

"Anything you'd like." The answer slipped out without thought.

"This isn't a game!" Silas rose, retreated to the dresser. "Whenever we speak, when we touch, we form a connection —a bond, if you will. The stronger the emotion, the greater the link."

So thoughts of sex made Silas slip up. Broke his concentration. Rhys almost smiled. Would have, had Silas's gaze not been so severe.

"I heard you call my name," Silas said.

Last night. "And you came to save me."

"Did I?" Silas spoke low. "Or did I come merely to keep you for myself?"

Rhys met Silas's cold stare. "You're not like them. You're no monster."

"How do you know?" Silas stalked forward, a blush blotting his face. "You know nothing of me." His voice rose. "You know nothing of what I feel, what I want, what I need." He reached the table and gripped the chair back.

"But I do know."

"Get out." This time those words were laced with malice, not fear.

"Silas—"

"Get out!" The shout seemed to echo about the room.

Rhys shook, his anger rising to match Silas's. Then he felt

77

a trickle of something—like a breeze through sun-dappled leaves in the summer—flow into him.

Silas swayed.

So the connection worked in both directions. Did Silas know? Did he even think beyond the tip of that now-healed nose? Rhys tempered his anger. Stood. "I'll leave." He marched back to the closet. Earlier he'd spied Silas's key card on the dresser by the closet. He took the card and held it up for Silas to see. "But I'm coming back."

Silas said nothing, just leaned on the chair.

"Don't get the room rekeyed, either," Rhys said. "I'll find another way in if you do. Or I'll find you, wherever you go."

"It's a big boat." Insolence in Silas's voice.

"And you're the only fae on it." He tapped his head. "This is a two-way street." Rhys shoved the key card into his back pocket and walked through the short foyer and out the door.

Once in the hallway, Rhys took a deep breath. He hated to leave, especially like that, but he doubted Silas could be reasoned with right now.

Anyway, he had his own head to sort through. Quarter-fae? A bond? Vampires and a sword-wielding Silas? This certainly was no fairy tale. Rhys ran his hands through his hair. *Shit.*

As fucked up as his life had become in a day, it all made a bizarre kind of sense. That alone should've had him running for the hills—so to speak. But it didn't.

He'd found Silas.

Rhys glanced at the cabin number. His room was two decks below.

Well, that was a good place to start. A shower would clear his head. After that? Well, he knew the vampires had talked to one other person last night.

But would Vasil talk to him?

CHAPTER SEVEN

*E*ven after Rhys left, Silas clung to the back of the chair and stared at his coffee mug. Studying the dregs helped him ignore the tremble in his arms and the wild beating of his heart. Or so he told himself.

Gods, he *was* a horrible liar.

Rhys. Brash, young, and ignorant. He should change key cards, just to spite him. See exactly how he'd follow through on his threat.

Now that was something new. He'd never had a lover threaten to chase him down before. *Lover.* Anger slipped away from Silas's grasp, leaving a sudden longing in its wake. That couldn't be. He had to let Rhys go.

He enjoyed Rhys, their verbal sparring, and the teasing. The wrestle for control. But how much, truly, did his desire for Rhys come from the delight—and need—of the element he possessed? Would he put up with Rhys's flippant remarks —his *orders*—if he were simply human?

Probably not. He shouldn't put up with them now, Quarter or no. He only did because he wanted Rhys, needed the feel of that mouth and the taste of that skin and every drop of forest life he held. All his for the taking.

Silas pushed off the chair. He was *exactly* the monster Rhys said he wasn't. He limped to the closet and found one of the complimentary robes hanging there. He stripped off his bloody clothes before wrapping the robe around himself, then hobbled to the bed.

He sank down onto the soft surface and his bones cried out in relief. The floor had been hard and his dreams haunted by the past. Sleep would do him some good. He stretched out and buried his head in a pillow.

The cover smelled of Rhys. The sheets too. Silas groaned and inhaled deeply in spite of himself.

Curse the Fates, cruel mistresses that they were. He loosened his hold on the pillow. The Fates weren't the reason Silas was here. The Messengers had sent him.

He jerked upright.

The Messengers knew the past, the now, and the future. They knew Rhys would be here and knew what he was. Silas pounded his fist against the mattress. Damn them to their own fiery hell!

They'd sent him to kill Anaxandros. Of all the soulless, they should have named Anaxandros to him. If he'd known…

If.

If was the reason. This wasn't the first time the Messengers had neglected to inform him of some important piece of information just to see what he would do, what path he would take. Free will, they said.

After all this time, he didn't need one around to hear their words. *Would you have gone, had you known it was Anaxandros you faced?*

And Rhys?

Would you have avoided him or sought him out? Should we have kept him from meeting you? Or encouraged it?

He didn't have answers. He never did.

Quam minimum credula postero. Trust not the future.

Silas forced himself to his feet. The Messengers could take their free will, carve it into a phallus, and shove it in their assholes. If they even had assholes.

Oh, he'd pay for that thought later, because they *always* knew.

His nose itched, and he rubbed at it. The brief interaction with Rhys had healed the bridge and some of the wounds on his chest. Good thing he'd forced Rhys to leave when he did. He was too much temptation. Time would heal his other wounds.

The best medicine now would be to take a shower and then a nap.

After that, he'd sit in the garden and figure out how not to die when Anaxandros's soulless came for him.

And how to keep Rhys safe from the soulless. *And from me.*

RHYS SCANNED ANOTHER LOUNGE, the third he'd checked so far. Still no Vasil. Maybe he hadn't survived the night? But then, the ship would be in an uproar, wouldn't it? He resisted the urge to shudder. Maybe not. No one seemed to care that three passengers had been turned into piles of ash.

The artificial sound of a digital camera's shutter clicked nearby. A woman in a bright yellow sundress tucked a phone back into her purse. He caught several other people watching him, whispering.

Right. He'd forgotten about that. No one noticed him when he was next to Silas. But now? He was Rhys Matherton, newly minted shit-for-brains millionaire, rather than quarter-fae and tasty vampire snack.

Damn it all, where was that waiter? Rhys slipped out of the lounge. Too bad Silas's clothes didn't come with fae glamour.

He'd put Silas's jeans and shirt back on, added a pair of sandals. Casual clothes were fine for the day, and he felt better carrying a bit of Silas with him.

His throat tightened. When this was over, would that be all he had left? Clothing?

Shit. Not what he wanted.

Time to look for Vasil in the one place he'd been avoiding —the garden. He stalked down the hallway toward the elevators.

He wasn't going to let Silas go that easily. Not over something as stupid as him thinking he was anything like a vampire.

He wasn't. Rhys could turn over every moment of the time he'd spent with Silas. Nothing Silas had ever done had made Rhys uncomfortable. Fucking horny? Yes. Last night had been the only time Silas's touch had caused pain, but they'd both been badly hurt. And he, not Silas, had been the one to reach out. Because Silas needed him.

A memory of Radmila's pale face hovering over Rhys flashed through his mind and set his heart racing, and a rock of cold fear sank into his stomach. The vampires had loved his pain, and encouraged his fear. Drunk his blood.

He'd touch Silas again—if the stubborn fae would let him.

The vampires? He would rather die.

Rhys exited the elevator with three other people. None of them paid him much mind. Good. The sooner his fifteen minutes of fame were up, the better.

Rather than take the inside path to the garden, he chose to walk the deck, a route that took him past the table he'd lain across last night. The table was still there, exactly where it had been. A family sat in those chairs now—a mother, father, and young daughter, eating ice cream. No ashes on the deck. No sign of violence.

A cold chill rose up Rhys's back, along with the memory of being pressed against that metal top. He'd screamed and screamed, but no sound had come out.

Rhys gripped the railing and stared at the knuckles of his hand.

Silas had slumped here against these bars. Dying. And Rhys had risen from that table and crossed that short span of deck to be with Silas, to save him.

Rhys touched his shoulder where it met his neck. Radmila had bitten him there. It had been Jarek who'd moved lower.

Rhys exhaled and took a deep breath of the ocean air. No more memories came. Beyond the hull, the ocean swelled and fell, little caps of white forming and disappearing into the deep blue water. Salt water dotted his face.

He'd wanted to run from Jarek. He remembered the steel grip of the vampire's hand, his whispered words.

Damn it, why couldn't he remember more?

He let go of the railing and turned his back on the sea. The ocean wouldn't help him—nor help Silas. The garden might.

One foot in front of the other, then.

The glass doors slid open as he approached. Across the threshold, the scent of mulch, fruit, and crushed leaves wove into his body. Rhys stumbled but caught his balance a moment later. Everything smelled of summer. Or spring. A forest. A field on a hot August night.

Silas.

The garden felt like Silas. Rhys drifted to the closest empty table and lowered himself into a chair. Or perhaps Silas felt like the garden.

A mass of green towered above him, though two palm trees had turned brown. Dead, like the tree in Silas's cabin.

Drained.

How had that happened? What had Silas done? Why had the vampires taken Rhys in the first place? *Damn it!* He'd burst from all these questions!

Rhys scanned the bar and caught sight of Vasil. The waiter gave him a quick nod before he turned back to his patrons.

Well, hell. Now that he had him, how would he ask?

A few moments later, Vasil hurried across the tile floor, menus in hand.

"Mr. Matherton!" He placed a drink and a lunch menu on the table. "You're...well? Yes?"

"Yes."

The waiter dropped his voice. "And Mr. Quint?"

Rhys chewed on his tongue. Truth? Yes. "Not nearly as well. But he's alive."

Vasil spoke under his breath. It sounded very much like a curse. "If there's anything..." A waitress passed the table and nodded at Vasil.

"You can tell me what happened last night."

Vasil took a pad from his apron. "Order something. Anything."

Rhys spied the same waitress watching them. "Coffee." He glanced through the lunch menu. "And a Reuben."

"Fries or coleslaw?"

"Coleslaw. Will you tell me?"

"What I know. But I can't now. I'll be off shift in an hour and a half."

He handed the menus back to Vasil. "Thank you."

Vasil retreated to the bar under the gaze of the waitress. Probably a supervisor.

A few minutes later, Vasil returned with a large mug of coffee. "Here you are, sir."

"You're not in trouble, are you?"

He dumped five creamers onto the table. "Reprimanded. I closed the bar too early last night."

"I'm sorry." Rhys wrapped his hands around the mug.

"Nothing to worry about. Sweetener? Anything else?"

"No, I'm good."

Vasil gave a little bow before returning to the bar.

The Reuben arrived in the hands of the waitress—Erin, her tag read. She also cleared his table once he finished, took his key card, and brought the receipt. "And how was everything?"

"Excellent." It had been. He left a reasonable tip and pocketed his card.

Vasil still served at the bar. A check of his watch told Rhys it would be another hour before he got off shift. With the supervisor hovering around, Rhys wasn't about to go up and speak to him.

He chose to meander slowly into the garden, toward the inner door to the rest of the ship. Hopefully Vasil would see and follow when he came off shift.

Rhys ducked down the first side path and sat on the nearest bench. The location gave him a reasonable view of the main path, but no one could see him from the bar.

Unfortunately the spot also reminded him of the bench he and Silas had used the previous night, and he hardened at the memories.

Silas's fingers tightening in his hair as he urged Rhys on. The hard length of Silas's dick sliding between his lips, the scent of his balls, and Silas's sublime shout of abandonment.

That cry he wanted to hear again, preferably with his cock as deep into Silas as he could drive it. With that thought, the scent of the garden grew more intense. His pulse thudded in his hands, his ears and his dick strained against his jeans.

Silas's jeans.

Rhys wrapped his hands around the edge of the bench and shifted forward. Had he a glamour like a fae's, he'd slip farther into the garden and jack off to the fantasy of Silas mouthing his balls or to Silas sucking the head of Rhys's dick into his hot mouth.

A rush, like pricks of static electricity, passed through his body. A fern swayed and bent toward him. Leaves rustled as if in a breeze, though the air around him barely moved. A plant to his left that hadn't had any blossoms on it now had lush white blooms. Their sweet scent washed over Rhys. Ivy snaked over the edge of the bed, straining toward him.

Holy shit.

Rhys sat back. That had never happened before. He'd run off into the woods to masturbate as a teen but he'd never made plants grow. Or bloom.

Quarter-fae. Being with Silas must have unlocked something in him. God only knew what. When he cornered Silas again, there would be a long conversation, this time with his rules.

He touched the nearest plant and felt that same buzz of tiny shocks. An elemental reservoir, Silas had said. What did that mean? Silas had said Rhys couldn't use the energy, just collect it. Except his collecting of energy—and that must have been what had happened—hadn't caused any of the plants around him to die, as they had when Silas had taken their element.

Every green thing around him had grown, increased in health.

Each time they'd been together, he hadn't drained Silas. Nor had Silas drained him. Far from it. Every encounter but the one after the vampires had left him spinning with energy and feeling more alive than he ever had before.

Silas implied he was a battery, something to be tapped and drained. But the plants, leaning toward him as they were, suggested something else. Amplifier? Transformer?

For the first time in his life, he regretted sleeping through physics in college. Not that science would help much with magic.

Magic. Rhys raked his hands through his hair. That was worse than physics. Magic wasn't real. *This can't be real.*

Except it was. Silas, the vampires, and the flower-laden plant next to him. All real.

So now what? He still had forty-five minutes before he could speak to Vasil. Daydreaming about a certain fae was out, unless he wanted to cause the whole damn garden to overgrow. Too bad Silas wasn't here. With all his element floating about, Silas's wounds would heal up pretty much instantly, he bet.

Rhys touched the striped leaf of some kind of vine. Now there was a thought. He had a connection to Silas, one that worked across a room. But across a ship?

A tingling flowed up his arm. The scent of sweet blossoms filled the air.

Worth a try. Rhys closed his eyes and thought of Silas—his voice, the color of his eyes. The feather touch of Silas's hand against his own. The warmth of Silas's body next to his as they stood at the bar. The bell-like sound of Silas's laugh.

Silas. I want you to be well. The buzz in his body increased, stretched, flowed out. Two things existed in the world. The garden. Silas. Nothing else.

"Mr. Matherton?"

Rhys started and opened his eyes. *Shit!* How long had he been out?

Vasil peered at him from a few feet away. Rhys followed

the waiter's gaze to his own wrist. The vine he'd been touching had wrapped itself around his hand and trailed up his arm. "Oh. Um…"

"You're like him, aren't you? Like Mr. Quint?" The waiter's accent made him sound calm—at least a damn lot calmer than Rhys felt.

"No. Yes." Rhys swallowed. "Sort of?" He unwrapped the vine from his arm and tried to still the wild beating of his heart. "You're taking this in stride."

The waiter glanced back at the main path and edged closer. "I grew up in the mountains, in the forest. Near old places. I know."

"Then you're ahead of me." Rhys stared at his hand and wiggled his fingers. Everything worked, despite the tight wrap of the vine. "This is all new."

"Mr. Quint. I saw him last night. He asked for you. Touched me, and I"—Vasil stumbled over his words—"I saw *him*."

As fae. Rhys wet his lips. "What about the others? A man and woman?"

Vasil paled, and his mouth pressed into a thin line before he spoke. "Upyr. Of darkness and death." His hands trembled before he clasped them behind his back. "The man asked after Mr. Quint, though not by name." Vasil looked away. "I sent him to you. My deepest apologies."

"If it was anything like what happened to me, you had no choice."

The waiter stared deeper into the garden. "It was nothing like what happened to you."

The waiter's words opened a yawning chasm inside Rhys. Icy threads of fear washed through him and tightened his throat. An attempt to speak only resulted in a croak of sound.

"But as you say, I had no choice. Not until Mr. Quint came."

Rhys tried again. "What happened to me?"

A distant and haunted expression transformed Vasil's face. For a moment he looked far older than Rhys would've guessed. "I didn't see, but when Mr. Quint brought you back...there was flesh missing. Bites." He shuddered. "I saw a dog maul a man's leg in my village. Awful. Never healed quite right. You looked far worse." His gaze finally settled on Rhys. "That you are alive—it's a bit of a miracle."

For a moment, Rhys couldn't breathe. Eaten. Literally. He drew a breath and spoke. "I don't remember most of it. I woke like this." He held out his arm, palm up. No bites, no marks.

"Mr. Quint's doing." Not a question.

Rhys nodded anyway. "Healed me. Didn't heal himself, though."

Vasil's smile was thin and strained. "Last night his only thought was for you."

"That make you uncomfortable?"

Vasil huffed. "Far from it."

Oh. Warmth touched Rhys's face. It was—it seemed—true what they said about assumptions.

"But a leshii on the sea? I can't imagine what brought him, but had he not been here, the upyr would've killed us all."

Rhys ran a hand through his hair. Could he trust Vasil? Silly question, really. He already had. Too late to second-guess now. He plunged ahead. "Silas knew the vampires were here. Called them soulless. Said he was sent to hunt them."

"Sent?"

"By the Messengers. But I can't think of what they are." Rhys hiccupped a laugh and glanced down the path. "I mean, who could send a fae after vampires, anyway?"

Vasil had lost several shades of color in his face by the time Rhys returned his gaze to him.

"Messengers?" Vasil whispered.

"Yeah," Rhys said. "You know who they are?"

Vasil opened his mouth, but no sound came out at first. Then he spoke a single, heavily accented word.

Rhys understood. Then he *understood*. Blood drained from his face as well.

Of course. Messengers.

Angels.

CHAPTER EIGHT

*S*ilas woke when his door lock whirred and unlatched. A moment later, someone entered. Tendrils of energy slid around the bed, brushed against and into him.

Rhys. Footsteps sounded in the foyer but not enough for Rhys to fully enter the room.

Mercury's balls, how long had he been asleep? Silas peered at the clock on the nightstand: 4:27. Too long. He braced himself for the pain and rolled over to face Rhys.

No ache. Not even a twinge. Silas didn't know which was more shocking, that or the sight of Rhys.

He leaned against the wall closest to the foyer entrance, his hair more copper than it should've been, face too lean. Fae-like. Stunning.

Silas sat up. "What have you done?"

"I don't know." Rhys's mouth quirked upward. "But I see it worked."

Quite. Legs, arms, chest—any part of Silas's skin not covered by his robe—were pristine. Healed. Probably all the skin underneath too. He wasn't about to disrobe to discover whether he was correct.

Gods above and below. Even he couldn't manipulate the element like that. Silas balled up the bedclothes beneath his hands. "It more than worked."

Rhys's expression turned sharp. "I thought you'd be happy."

That wasn't one of the emotions churning through him. He clung to anger, because fear and awe would do neither of them any good. "Go look at yourself in the mirror."

Rhys pushed himself off the wall, strode toward the dresser, and came to an abrupt halt. "Oh shit."

Silas snorted. "Indeed."

"But I'm not fae." Rhys touched his face. "What the hell?"

"Enough of you is." The half-fae could change at will—a trick of breeding and power. But a Quarter doing it? Silas had never heard of such a thing.

"I don't underst—" Rhys looked away from the mirror. "Can you fix it?"

"Fix it?" Silas couldn't quite keep the scorn from his voice. "Not I."

Rhys's stricken look and reddening face tempered Silas's wry and dark humor. Impulsive though Rhys might be, he'd —somehow—healed all of Silas's wounds, and pushed so much element into him that he could last for weeks in the middle of the ocean even if he decided to glamour the whole damn ship into a giant squid.

Silas exhaled. His next words were soft. "Did you kill the plants in the garden?"

"No," Rhys said. "If anything, they're better than they were. I even fixed the palm trees."

All amusement fled Silas. He craned around to examine the ficus he'd drained. Lush green leaves sprouted from every limb. It had grown taller as well. *Dea Dia.*

"I guess I healed that too," Rhys said.

No fae had that kind of ability. Yes, they could draw life. Take, manipulate, and use the power their element gave them, but nothing like this. Silas could coax a plant to health over days and weeks, not regrow a whole damn tree in hours.

Wars had been fought over a single Quarter. Silas's mouth turned to sand. "I was wrong about you."

Rhys barked a sharp laugh. "Wrong? You? Has that ever happened before?" Sarcasm coated each word. "The great Silas?"

Silas flinched, despite himself. Wrong, oh yes. He'd followed his heart rather than his head. How many lives were lost last time?

So much power flowed from Rhys, but Silas's desperate need for it was gone. Probably because so much now flowed through him too.

When they reached land, other fae would come for Rhys, drawn to that firebrand of energy, just like the vampires. Just like he'd been.

Would they treat Rhys well? Would he even let another fae touch Rhys?

Silas shook himself out of his reverie. This had to end. He needed to warn Rhys. "I've made a mess of things with you. Come. Sit. We should to talk." He patted the bed next to him.

"Last time we tried to talk, you threw me out of your room."

"I didn't exactly throw you out."

Energy licked off Rhys like tongues of flame and coalesced around his closed fists. "Close enough."

Truth. Silas ignored it. "Then why did you come back?"

Rhys pushed himself off the wall and joined him by the bedside. He didn't sit. "You need me."

Not at all the answer Silas expected. He stared up at Rhys.

Rhys brushed the back of his hand against Silas's cheek. Blazing hot, full of life. It took all of Silas's resolve not to pull Rhys down on top of him.

"You're going to run from me again, aren't you?" Rhys said.

Run? That made no sense. "This isn't about me." Silas ran a hand through his hair, pushing errant locks out of his eyes so he could see better. "And what do you mean, again?"

"This *is* about you." Rhys finally sat. "Every time we meet, you leave me, and I have to chase you down."

Chase him down? "I found you."

"No," Rhys said. "I found *you*."

That wasn't correct. Silas opened his mouth to argue, but then Rhys's mouth was against his, and his tongue tangled around Silas's before he could think of the words to say. Rhys pushed him backward onto the bed and laid the length of his body down, his legs between Silas's own. Rhys pressed his bulging package against Silas's cock.

Presumptuous. So very American. But the feel of Rhys's body and the thrust of his tongue sent heat curling into Silas's stomach. He moaned against Rhys and tugged the back of his shirt up. Silas slipped his hands under the waistband of Rhys's jeans, wanting to feel the hot flesh of his ass.

Rhys ground against him.

He'd not let another fae touch Rhys. Not now.

Rhys broke the kiss, touched his face. "*I* found you."

"You spilled drinks on me," Silas said. He slid his hands around and worked the button and fly of the jeans open. The room smelled of sea grass and he wanted more of Rhys's skin against his own. "You weren't even looking where you were going. That's not finding."

"Doesn't matter," Rhys said. He slid his mouth down Silas's neck, nipped at his shoulder. "You left. Didn't even give me a second glance. I came after you. Chose you."

Pricks of heat blazed along Silas's skin, and he arched underneath Rhys, momentarily losing focus. In the time it took him to recover, Rhys had undone the tie to his robe and pushed it open. He sucked on Silas's right nipple.

That set his whole body aflame. No breath left to cry out, he bucked Rhys off him.

Rhys laughed and pressed a hand against Silas's stomach, achingly close to Silas's erection. "And you complained about me being sensitive?"

It took Silas a moment to catch his breath. He propped himself up on an elbow. "That wasn't a complaint, merely an observation." He'd—somehow—lost the upper hand in this conversation, and he was damn well going to get it back. He tugged at Rhys's shirt. "You're wearing too many clothes."

"Is *that* a complaint?"

"Yes."

Rhys sat up, stripped his shirt off. He peeled the jeans off his body. No underwear.

Glorious.

Silas had seen Rhys naked when he'd healed him. That had been clinical and necessary. The sight of Rhys's body aroused was magnificent, all his muscles taut, his breath rippling his stomach, his cock thick and flush.

Silas shrugged out of the arms of his robe and tossed it off the bed. "Much better."

Rhys crawled over and straddled Silas, his balls rubbing against Silas's cock, and effectively trapped Silas's legs against the bed. "Good. God forbid you have any complaints."

No human—and very few fae—had ever had the audacity

to control Silas in bed. Yet here he was, letting Rhys do just that. More than that. Silas's skin tingled.

Rhys gripped Silas's arms and pinned the rest of his body to the bed. He found himself looking up into Rhys's face, which held a wild beauty that stopped his breath. Desire and lust in those green eyes. Hope as well.

Hope. *Ah gods.*

Silas had no idea what Rhys saw in his face, but it caused Rhys to loosen his grip, lean down, and capture Silas's mouth with his own.

Amid the tangle of their limbs and tongues and the rush of blood to his dick, Silas's mind finally registered Rhys's earlier words. He broke their kiss. "What did you say?"

"God forbid you have complaints?"

"Before that." He knew, or thought he did. He needed to hear it again to be sure.

A sly smile touched Rhys's lush mouth. "What, that I chose your arrogant ass? Came after you?"

Yes. That. "What?"

"See? Arrogant." Rhys rubbed his thumb over Silas's lips, leaving behind the taste of sun-warmed ivy. "If I hadn't stopped you in the hall, would you have looked for me?"

He sought the memory—it had been only yesterday, for Juno's sake—and turned it over in his head.

Rhys's breath caressed his cheek. "Well?"

"No. You were just..." The stunning quarter-fae who lay atop him and the human who had spilled drinks on him were the same being, but not in his memory. "You were just another human."

"You were the most beautiful man I'd ever seen," Rhys said. "And I caught you."

Somewhere, Silas imagined, the Messengers were laughing at him. Or perhaps not.

What would you have done, had you known?

Run? Left the ship to the soulless?

Rhys had followed him of his own free will. "You did find me." He sounded stupefied, even to his own ears.

"Fool." Rhys kissed his way down Silas's neck, heading straight toward his nipple again.

Oh no. He'd had enough of that particular torture for the night. Silas pulled their bodies together. His cock slid against the hard length of Rhys's erection, with delightful results. Rhys twisted against him and gasped.

Silas trailed one hand down Rhys's spine and stroked his lower back. He tangled his other in Rhys's hair, neatly trapping the man against his body. Then he rocked his hips.

Rhys answered back, thrusting down. Insistent. Needy. He moaned into Silas's shoulder. "You damn well better have condoms and lube somewhere in this room."

He couldn't help the chuckle. "Black duffel in the closet. Front pocket." He let go of Rhys's hair and ran his knuckles over Rhys's cheek. "But you don't need the condoms."

Snakes might as well have slithered out of Silas's ears for the way Rhys looked at him.

"I'm not human."

"What?"

"Rhys, I'm not human. I neither catch nor carry any diseases."

Silas watched Rhys struggle against that thought, even with all he'd seen. "Not human," he murmured.

"I'm immortal. I don't get sick. I don't grow old."

"You can die. You almost did."

He stroked Rhys's hair. "All creatures born can die. Even fae." He paused. Then he spoke the words he hadn't wanted to admit to himself. "I would've last night, but for you."

Rhys kissed his neck, and once more Silas rose against the pleasure of it, pulling Rhys into a tight embrace.

"See," Rhys said. "You do need me."

"Very much so." Silas cupped Rhys's ass with one hand and pulled Rhys up his body, then slid a finger down the cleft between the cheeks, grazing Rhys's hole. Rhys squirmed against him, dick hard against his thigh. "Right now, in fact," Silas said.

Rhys took Silas's earlobe between his lips and sucked.

For a moment, the entirety of Silas's world tunneled down to the warmth and tug of Rhys's lips. Damn that mouth. Silas loosened his grip, only realizing his mistake when Rhys captured Silas's other nipple with his hand.

With Rhys's full weight against him, Silas couldn't throw him off. Gods, he was stronger than he looked. When Rhys rolled the sensitive nub of flesh between his fingers, bolts of pleasure slid down Silas. He moaned despite himself and twisted, just as Rhys had done.

Neatly caught.

When Rhys finally relented his torture, Silas devoured his mouth. Between breaths, he spoke three words into Rhys's mouth. "Even more now."

"Good." Rhys shifted, opening enough space between them to encircle Silas's cock with his hand. Strong grip. Excruciatingly slow strokes. Silas closed his eyes to keep the world from spinning. Rhys spoke into his ear. "I want to come inside you."

Fucked by Rhys? Oh, how he wanted that. Silas trembled and opened his eyes. "*Di,*" he murmured, more surprised at his reaction than Rhys's statement.

Rhys trailed kisses down Silas's chest. "That's not 'yes,' is it?" He paused and slid his hands underneath Silas's ass. "In Latin?"

"It's 'gods.'" Silas pushed Rhys's head farther down his body, wanting to feel those lips elsewhere. He shivered. "'Yes' is… There's no single word for 'yes.'"

98

"That explains a lot about you, you know," Rhys said. Then he sucked the head of Silas's cock into his mouth.

Silas tightened his hold on Rhys's head as lightning shot through his veins. Impudent, arrogant, beautiful man. "Yes."

He felt Rhys chuckle around his dick, but Rhys didn't stop, not right away. He slowed, though, until every stroke was wonderfully agonizing. The texture of Rhys's lips, the slight graze of his teeth as he pulled Silas's foreskin up over the head, then pushed it back down. Ripples of heat twined through Silas and set his veins throbbing. The delicate scent of sweet violets drifted around them. Flowers from the fields of his youth.

He would die from this. The first of his kind to be slaughtered by too much pleasure. "Rhys, please. Just—"

Rhys engulfed him completely, stealing breath and words.

No one had ever done this to him, taken away his thought, his complete control. Then again, he'd never let anyone try. Silas wanted more.

Rhys pulled off before Silas could get any rhythm started, licked the head of Silas's cock, and then his own fingers. "Yes?" Rhys said.

Wicked amusement in those green eyes. Rhys's wet fingers delved into the cleft of Silas's ass and teased the ring of his hole. Energy twined about the both of them and Silas fought against the tightening in his balls. "Black bag. Closet. Front pocket." Strange to hear himself panting those words.

"Is that a yes?"

He grabbed Rhys by the shoulders, pulled him up, and shook him. "Gods alive, man! Yes, that's a yes!" He let go. "What do you want from me?"

Rhys grinned down at him, full of mirth and triumph. "You to tell me, in plain English, what you want."

"You infuriating, insufferable—"

"Sexy?"

Silas laughed. In the absurdity of the moment, he could do nothing more. He ran his hands down Rhys's sides, and cupped his balls. "Yes, that too."

Rhys's arms trembled as Silas explored his length. He stroked Rhys slowly, tracing veins, the scar where he'd been cut. "I want you to come inside me." He'd never thought to say those words to any man. His entire body felt flush.

Rhys leaned down, kissed him, and rolled off the bed.

Silas tried to catch his breath and his mind, because surely he'd lost that somewhere. He'd intended to put Rhys off, explain why they couldn't be lovers. Now he was begging Rhys to fuck him?

Moments later, Rhys was back, towering over him. "You're terrified, aren't you?"

Terrified? Of a Quarter who slipped past every defense he had, made him lose all discipline, all thought? "Hardly."

Rhys lay down on him and placed his hands to either side of Silas's face. "Horrible liar." Then Rhys's mouth was on his, pulling at his bottom lip. And Rhys's hips—ah, they ground Rhys in slow circles against Silas's cock and balls.

Silas caught the flesh of Rhys's ass and spread his cheeks apart. "Are you nothing but talk and tease?"

Rhys's chuckle was dark and sensuous. He sat up, dislodging Silas's grip. "You hate being out of control."

He stroked Rhys's arms, well aware that his were trembling. Yes. That frightened him. Not the games they were playing right now, but his life tumbling into the unknown. Rhys—not he—had chosen the path they walked along. There wasn't any turning back. Not anymore.

His fate. Rhys's will. Silas's heart felt as though it would beat out of his chest. "'Hate' isn't quite the right word for it."

Rhys pushed him down. "What happened to carpe diem?"

He didn't wait for an answer before kissing his way down Silas's body.

"'Carpe' implies"—the warmth of Rhys's mouth on the shaft of his cock robbed Silas of most of his breath—"action." The last word was no more than a moan.

"Carpe Silas, then." A snap of a lid, then Rhys slid a lubed finger around the outside of his hole. Warm air surrounded his balls before Rhys sucked one into his mouth.

Silas's cock ached with the need to be in that hot, tight embrace. He thrust upward, seeking some release. But there was no relief to be found in air. Elemental energy wound up him and blossomed at the back of his skull. He crushed the sheets in his fists.

Rhys slid a finger into Silas, then a second, grazing against that spot inside that sent the whole world spinning into oblivion. Again and again Rhys thrust his fingers, working his hole. Silas moaned, wanting to be filled more, pounded deeper.

Though Rhys licked and sucked Silas's sac, never once did he touch Silas's cock. Maddening. Silas's balls ached from Rhys's torment, his cock hard with need. Seize, indeed. He reached to stroke himself, find the sweet bliss he craved.

Rhys caught his hand before he got near his cock, grabbed his other hand, and forced both above his head, pinning them against the mattress.

"No."

No? Silas stilled for a moment, then fought to break free of Rhys's grip. Failed. Apparently cords of muscle lurked beneath Rhys's frame. He twisted under Rhys in another attempt to break his hold. "Do you have any idea what you're doing to me?"

"Yeah." That brash grin lit up his face. "I'm driving you mad."

Every one of Silas's nerves sang with a chorus of desire. Mad? Insane. He stopped struggling.

"That's better." Rhys leaned down and kissed the tip of his nose. "Now let me finish."

"You damn well better." Oh, the things he wanted to do to Rhys. Recompense would be sweet.

Rhys let him go, dragged his fingers down Silas's arms and across his stomach. Every place Rhys touched tingled. Silas trembled as Rhys worked his way lower. This time Rhys did touch his cock, but only tapped a tantalizing rhythm down his shaft.

Not enough. Never enough. Breath hissed out between his teeth. Resisting the urge to stroke himself was excruciating, but he wanted to see what Rhys would do to him. He wanted Rhys to fill him, stretch him wide. Again. And again.

Ah, gods. He was lost. Completely. He arched back against the pillow and stared at the ceiling.

Silas heard the sound of the lube bottle snap open, then close. Rhys pulled Silas's legs up and his fingers slid inside Silas, twisting and stretching. Then the fingers were gone, even as Silas bucked his hips up.

"Silas, look at me."

He did as told. How could he not, trapped as he was? *If you had known, what would you have done?*

Sweat glistened on Rhys's skin, dampened his hair. His eyes shone with need. The warm, thick head of Rhys's cock pressed against Silas's asshole.

"Thank you," Rhys murmured and pushed forward.

Rhys was in him, spreading him open, filling him deeply. Touching every part inside him that craved to be touched. Complete. It was the end of the world when Rhys withdrew. And the beginning of another when Rhys drove in again. And again.

He hadn't expected to cry out. Certainly he'd been fucked before. Those years—centuries—of experience mattered very little. Rhys was too much, too fast.

And not nearly enough. He wanted—needed more. He moved, matching Rhys's thrusts, urging him deeper. Silas caught Rhys's arms and pulled him down.

And Rhys obliged, nails scraping against Silas's scalp when he tangled his hands in Silas's hair. Rhys kissed him, forcing his tongue past Silas's lips, devouring his mouth.

The world faded down to Rhys relentlessly pounding into him, setting his veins alight. Liquid sunlight pooled inside him and spilled out into his limbs. Just when Silas thought he couldn't be driven any higher, Rhys quickened his strokes. Staccato strikes of flesh on flesh resounded as Rhys hit his sweet spot over and over. Elemental energy wrapped around Silas and sank to his base. Jolts of heat shot up to his skull, and his balls tightened, and Silas gave himself over to the coming orgasm.

Only Silas didn't come. The element consumed Silas—and Rhys was *inside* him.

And he was with Rhys, walking every piece of land Rhys had ever trod. Around him rose the smell of salt grass and seawater from the dunes of a barrier island, then the crush of fall leaves and the last blooming of goldenrod. The taste of mulberries in the height of summer. The familiar scent of the Alpine foothills as Rhys climbed up a path to a castle. Countless moments filled with the tang of cut grass, the sudden expanse of green surrounded by concrete.

Amid the jumble of Rhys's life, Silas spied glimpses of other fae that never—quite—touched Rhys. Water. Field. Mountain. Air. Energy from those fae brushed against Rhys, but no one with Rhys's element ever lingered long enough to awaken what lay in Rhys.

Exquisite agony as twenty-eight years of collected life slammed through Silas's body.

Then he was there, in Rhys's memory, throwing a towel at a chair and turning away. Rhys ran after those thin traces of element, and caught him by the arm.

Here and now, Silas moaned and buried his face in Rhys's shoulder and came hard, thrusting his cock against Rhys's stomach.

Rhys cried out and drove into him, mercilessly hard as he came. When Rhys's thrusts slowed, he gasped for air, trembled against Silas. His low groan turned to a sob, and his nails bit into Silas's arms, hard enough to draw blood.

This—this was Silas's fault. He'd been alive a very long time, far longer than Rhys, and had walked the length and breadth of the Earth. There were more than just a few glimpses of fae in his past. Lovers, enemies, a precious few friends.

He prayed that was all Rhys saw—all Rhys felt in the long tale of his life. He held on to Rhys and sang snatches of old songs into his ear.

There was nothing else he *could* do.

After a time, Rhys stopped shaking, though his breathing, rough and ragged, rattled next to Silas's ear. Then words came. "What the hell was that?"

"Me," Silas said. "My life."

Rhys was silent. He shifted, slipping his cock from Silas. He rested his head on Silas's chest. "Well, shit."

"If I hurt you—"

"No, it wasn't painful, not really…" He looked at the hand he was about to shove into his hair. "You're bleeding?"

"It's nothing." It took only a moment to heal the scrapes.

Rhys sat up, examined Silas's arms, and touched the drying blood on them. "I hope that doesn't happen next time."

Next time. Silas rolled those two words about in his head for a while and decided he liked the sound of them. What was that English phrase? In for a penny, in for a pound? "I should think not. Though it wasn't bad for me." Silas wiped away the moisture at the corner of Rhys's right eye. "I *am* sorry."

"It didn't hurt. It was just...very intense." He peered down at Silas. "Exactly how old are you, anyway?"

He should've expected that question and knew better than to attempt a lie. "Two thousand four hundred thirty-six."

He watched as Rhys struggled against the truth. He sagged when the truth won. "Fuck me."

"Later," Silas murmured. He pulled Rhys into a tight embrace. "Later."

That produced a croak of laughter from Rhys and he stilled. "No more running?"

That choice was long gone for Silas. "No. You have me." He paused and added, "If you want me."

"Of course I do." Rhys spoke into Silas's chest. "I'd give my life for you."

That froze Silas's blood, chased every warm thought from his head. In the corner of the room, the *lemur*—the shade—of a long-dead fae lurked. "Please don't. Don't ever."

Rhys lifted his head, confusion written in the lines of his expression.

"I don't want to live through that again."

RHYS SEARCHED SILAS'S FACE, then sat up fully. Terror hid behind that soft expression, those low tones. *What happened to you?* A memory—not his own—stirred. He sucked in air and exhaled. "Tell me about the soulless."

Silas's lips twitched, and for a moment Rhys thought he might refuse, but he wilted into the mattress and looked away. "I was young, by fae standards, when I fell in love." There was a distance to his voice Rhys had heard before, in his own voice when he'd recounted the tale of his father—tales of *Derrick*.

"He broke your heart?"

Silas chuckled, a bitter and hollow sound. "Oh no. He loved me back. Passionately. We were of an age when we didn't know any better. He was..." Silas furrowed his brow. "I've never told anyone this story before."

"You don't have to."

Silas sat up. "No, it's important. You were right. This"— he waved his hand to encompass the room—"is about me, at least in part." Silas found his robe, pulled it on, and wrapped it closed.

"Most fae live in courts—groups of families led by one fae. A king or a queen."

"The summer court and the winter court," Rhys said. "That's in the fairy tales."

"Those are Scottish. I was born in Campania—south of Rome."

"What was his name?"

The question carved Silas's mouth into a deep frown. He shook his head once and then spoke. "*Vel Calavius Isatis.*"

It hurt to hear the pain in Silas's voice. How long had it been since he'd said that name? "Go on," Rhys said.

Silas rubbed his brow. "Life was idyllic. Blissful. Until Phyrrhus of Epirus waged war on the Romans in the region. It shouldn't have been an issue. Wars washed over us like heavy rain. We held on, dug in deep, then cleaned up the mess once the humans were through with killing each other."

"But not that time."

"No. Phyrrhus brought more than just humans with him from Greece, though I doubt he knew it. The soulless are always looking for an opportunity to take life, and what better place than in war?" Silas pulled his legs in and rested his chin on his knees. "Fae are more appealing to the soulless than humans. Full of the energy they crave. Humans die easily. We don't."

Rhys touched his neck. Just how attractive was he to the vampires? A battery—transformer—whatever the hell he was? He shook that thought away. "What happened?"

"A soulless found Isatis and me one night while we lay in a field together. We were far from the battles, but it must have felt the court, scented us out. It surprised us and dragged me away. Isatis attempted to rescue me but failed."

"Died?"

"He was slaughtered. Eaten in front of me." Silas ground his mouth closed and shook his head. "I...went mad. Tore the soulless to pieces with my bare hands." He frowned. "I don't know how I managed that, except it must have been very young. They're not easy to destroy."

Rhys wiped a hand over his mouth. One glimpse of the feral side of Silas was enough. "After that?"

"I went home. We mourned. That should've been the end of it. Except the one I killed was one from a pack ruled by an ancient soulless named Anaxandros."

He'd heard that name before. Dread dripped down Rhys. "Ancient when you were young?"

"Yes." Silence filled the room. Long minutes passed until Silas spoke again. "Anaxandros hunted me down, found me, and then slaughtered everyone I knew before my eyes. My parents. My sister. Cousins. Our king."

Rhys's tongue cleaved to the roof of his mouth. No wonder he hunted them. Hated them.

"Then he kept me as a toy for him and his. A never-ending snack, never *quite* doing enough damage to kill me."

Rhys fought to keep the bile in, swallowing against its rising. Those moments with the vampires feasting on him had been the worst pain of his life. When he could speak again, he asked the question. "How long?"

The corners of Silas's eyes twitched. Otherwise he was carved from stone. "One hundred eighty-seven years. Five months. Twenty-seven days." Silas turned his head and focused on Rhys. "And seven hours. Give or take."

Oh fuck. Rhys stumbled off the bed and ran for the bathroom. Without grace, he heaved the contents of his stomach into the toilet, legs and knees hitting cold tile as he clutched porcelain. That long in the hands of a vampire? The pain, the madness? Another of Silas's memories surfaced for a moment—a flash of immeasurable agony as flesh peeled from bone—and he vomited again.

Bare feet slapped against the bathroom floor. Then Silas sat down on the edge of the tub next to Rhys, a glass of water in his hand.

Rhys brushed moisture from his eyes. "Anaxandros. He's here, isn't he?"

Silas held the glass out to him. "Yes."

Rhys gripped the tumbler and took a swig to clean out his mouth. He spit and then flushed. "How did you survive? I mean—" Rhys stumbled over his words. "Last night. I wanted to die when they had me."

Silas nodded. "It's always like that. They eat life. Consume it." He stretched out his legs. "I survived because I didn't have a choice. Anaxandros set his pack up deep in the woods, in a cave where it was nearly always night. They feasted. I healed. Too much element around me not to."

Day in, day out. Bile rose again. Rhys took a sip of water

and pressed the cool glass to his forehead. "How'd you escape?"

The smile that touched Silas's lips was full of malice and blood. "I broke a clay cup—they had to keep me drinking and eating—dropped it against a rock. Kept a sliver of it with me. When Anaxandros came to exact his punishment, I shoved it into his throat. Then I ran. For a very long time."

Rhys took another sip of water. "He didn't die?"

Something of the man Rhys first met emerged from under that cold, detached expression. Incredulity gave Silas's face warmth, a touch of color. "You can't kill something that's already dead."

"Then how—" Silas held a sword last night, bright silver in the moonlight.

As if reading his mind, Silas reached into the air, and a shimmering sword slid into existence. He appraised the blade, then offered it to Rhys. "Don't touch the edge. It'll cut through you."

Rhys hesitated, but a raised eyebrow from Silas—as if to call him a coward—set his will. He took the sword. He knew metal well enough to know the blade was far lighter than it should've been. The edge glittered like a million gems. "A magic sword?"

Silas shrugged. "It's made from silver and diamond. Forged in the fire of a phoenix. Other than destroying soulless, it's not particularly magical." He paused. "It can cut the Fallen. Not deeply, though."

"Fallen." Rhys turned the sword in his hand, felt the balance, the texture of the grip in his palm. "Daemons?"

Silas nodded.

"You hunt daemons?"

"No. Just soulless."

Well, good. He didn't want to meet a daemon. Rhys

shook his head. *What the hell?* He offered the blade back to Silas. "My life just became really fucking strange, didn't it?"

A chuckle from Silas. He took the sword. "Welcome to Fairyland."

"Why do I have the feeling I'm in this for more than seven years?"

"That's really up to you."

Was it? He mused on that while Silas sheathed the sword, slid it into nothing until it vanished.

"How do you do that—pull it from air?"

"Aether," Silas said. "The sword was made for me—given to me by the Messengers. I know how it fits in my hand. I simply recall that feeling when I need it."

When he needed it. A flash of memory surfaced—Silas turning that same sword on himself last night. Rhys drank the rest of the water and set the glass down on the floor. "Promise me something."

Silas raised an eyebrow.

"Don't ever think of killing yourself again."

Silas's expression remained cool and relaxed. The tension in his arms, his clawlike grip on the tub edge told another story. "I'd not thought you awake for that."

"I guess I was." Rhys struggled to his feet, then perched himself on the counter by the sink. "Why? I mean, why over me?"

A faint smile full of darkness touched Silas's lips. "When the Messengers found me, when they asked if I would hunt the soulless for them, do you know why I said yes?"

"Revenge?"

The laugh that came from Silas raised the hair on the back of Rhys's neck. "I thought if I destroyed them all, then perhaps I'd stop hearing Isatis screaming." He shook his head. "It hasn't worked."

Rhys slid off the counter. "It wasn't your fault."

The hard edge to Silas's jaw softened. "You're not the first to tell me that."

Silas didn't move, not when Rhys sat next to him, not when he covered Silas's rigid hand with his own.

"Figures." Silas might not be human, and Rhys sure as hell didn't understand him—he wasn't sure he understood himself half the time—but he knew pain. Loss. Comfort. He stroked his fingers across Silas's knuckles. "I've noticed you have this thing for not listening."

This time Silas's huff of laughter was light. His arms unknotted. "You're so damn young. Beautiful. Like a spring morning."

"What, cold, foggy, and damp?"

Silas shifted on the tub's edge, turned his hand to capture Rhys's fingers. "Warm and occasionally dense. But full of promise."

Rhys took a breath. "You didn't answer my question."

Through the silence that spread out in the bathroom, the click and whirl of the minifridge in the other room seemed all the louder.

Finally Silas spoke. "There are times when I get tired, Rhys. Soul tired. Seeing what had happened to you because I hadn't been *thinking*…" He looked up. "Perhaps it might be better if you were free of me."

Rhys crushed Silas's hand in his own. "I don't want to be free of you." If he lost Silas, what would he have? A pile of sycophants in New York, hounding tabloid reporters, and a pack of vampires wanting to eat him. "I'm glad you didn't."

"As am I," Silas said, his voice low. "I may be a wretched excuse for a protector, monstrous in my own way, but I'm better than leaving you with nothing at all."

"You're not a monster. You're not…draining me of life. It's nothing like that at all."

ANNA ZABO

Silas attempted to pull his hand away, but Rhys held on tighter.

"I don't want to use you, even if the results are pleasurable for both of us, it's still"—Silas paused, as if searching for a word—"unconscionable."

Large word. Rhys had a few as well. "I think you've misconstrued the nature of our relationship. You didn't use me back there." He nodded toward the bedroom. "Other way around, I think."

That produced a faint smile. "Well, there is that."

Rhys relaxed his grip, and they sat for a moment, shoulder to shoulder, hand in hand. If only they could stay like this, together. Quiet. Just enjoying each other. "They're going to come back for me, aren't they? The vampires?"

"Undoubtedly," Silas said. "Anaxandros knows I'm here, and I'm sure he knows you are here as well." He rose and pulled Rhys up. "We should shower, then have dinner. We both need food."

"Then what?" Rhys strode to the shower, turned on the water, and set the temperature. He heard cloth fall behind him—Silas's robe.

"I do what I was sent here to do. Destroy the soulless." Silas placed his hands on Rhys's hips and pushed him into the shower.

That brief touch, the press of Silas from behind when he closed the shower door, coupled with the warm water sliding down his skin, sent heat to his stomach and thickened his dick. He tried to steady his breath, rein in the desire. He was half-surprised he could even get it up after fucking Silas earlier. But then again, Silas was a walking wet dream—his wet dream. Rhys turned.

Water slid down Silas's body and dampened his dark hair into curls that framed his long face. Lips quirked into a half

112

smile beneath a well-healed nose. Silas spoke. "Whatever am I going to do with you?"

"Wrong question," Rhys said. He pushed Silas against the back of the shower, kissed him until he moaned, then slid— very much like the water—down Silas's body. "You should ask what I'm going to do to you." He took Silas's cock into his mouth.

Hands tightened in Rhys's hair. He let Silas control the rhythm, the depth, opening his throat as much as he could. It was enough to hear Silas's groan, those rough bits of Latin that sounded gloriously perverse, even though he didn't understand any of it. It still tightened his balls. Water cascaded down Rhys's back and tickled his ass and his dick bobbed in time with Silas's fucking.

Too soon, Silas pulled him away. "This is exactly why I can't concentrate. Your damn mouth. Your hands. Your body." He cupped Rhys's chin and stared down at him. "I should've fucked you on the dinner table last night, just to get it out of my system."

Rhys stroked Silas's thighs. "Wouldn't have worked."

"No?" Silas pulled him up and spun him around. In seconds, Rhys found himself against the shower wall, his hands the only things keeping his forehead from bumping against the tile. Silas spoke hot words into his ear. "Shall we see if it works tonight?"

Rhys heard Silas spit. About damn time.

Silas slid his fingers down Rhys's crack and teased his hole, working a finger inside. God, how he wanted to feel Silas's cock inside him. Rhys couldn't help but push back. "I hope you fuck as good as you talk."

Silas ground out a curse Rhys didn't catch. Fingers spread Rhys's ass cheeks. More spit made makeshift lube. Then the thick head of Silas's cock pressed against his hole. Silas grabbed his hips and thrust forward, entering him and filling him deep in one stroke. Silas stretched him wide and hit exactly the right spot inside. Heat raced through Rhys, his hands slipped on the shower wall, and his cry of pleasure echoed off the tiles.

Each time Silas moved forward, he drove deeper into Rhys, hitting places inside no other lover had. Hot light filled Rhys's veins and set his bones tingling. The hard slap of Silas's body against the cheeks of his ass sent heat into his balls. He arched and pushed back, demanding more.

And Silas gave it to him. Somehow Silas understood what Rhys wanted. Unrelenting, masterful, possessive fucking. To be open to Silas and one with him. A sweet curl of tension filled Rhys and wound tighter and tighter until he could barely breathe.

He so needed this. Rhys placed one hand against the shower wall and circled the other around his cock. Every thrust from Silas made him want desperately to come. His balls ached with need.

Silas pulled him away from the wall and slowed his movements. "No."

Payback, no doubt. Rhys's cock throbbed. He squirmed against Silas. "Please. I need—"

Teeth nipped at his ear. "I know what you need." Silas thrust deeper.

Lightning flashed in his veins. He couldn't speak. Couldn't think enough to put words together.

Silas spoke into his ear again. "Both hands on the wall."

His arms trembled, but he complied. A kiss from Silas to his spine raised goose bumps on his arms and nearly caused his legs to buckle.

"Good," Silas said. "Now leave them there." With that, he flattened one hand across Rhys's chest, took hold of Rhys's cock with the other, then started fucking him again. Deep. Hard. Only this time, Silas jacked him off as well, using a completely different set of rhythms—sometimes slow, sometimes fast.

The deep strokes set Rhys throbbing inside, but the erratic rhythm of Silas's hand on Rhys's cock made the want in his balls curl all the tighter. Sweet pain with no relief.

Rhys lowered his head, crying out between breaths, grinding his hips against Silas's thrusts in some effort to gain even a hint of control.

Each time Rhys got close to coming, Silas backed off and changed the tempo. The throbbing light filling Rhys had nowhere to go, but more poured in. His arms shook as every nerve turned to glass. If only Silas would let him break. After the third time, Rhys's legs did buckle. Silas's strong arm about his waist kept him on his feet.

"Silas! Just—" He caught his breath. "Please!"

"Soon." Silas's reply was guttural, almost a moan. "Very." His fucking changed pace again, this time less controlled. There was no backing away, no more games.

The aching in Rhys's balls tightened once more, but this time it broke. Light spread out from the pit of his stomach to each limb and shattered every one of his nerves. He cried out, coming hard and long.

Silas drove into him, harder and faster, until he came as well, his own cry ragged and loud.

Rhys wasn't sure how they were both standing—the greater part of his weight was supported by Silas's arms wrapped around his chest. Silas trembled against him, his rough breathing blending in with the fall of water.

The stream had yet to turn cold. Damn good shower.

After several moments, Silas kissed his shoulder. "Did I hurt you?"

"No." Rhys took in a deep breath of warm, humid air and found his footing. Every muscle in his body radiated with pleasure. His skin tingled where water hit him. "So did you fuck me out of your system?"

A bark of laughter. "No. Not at all." He loosened his arms.

Rhys twisted to face Silas. "Told you."

That earned him a hard but short kiss. "You're too brash for your own good." Silas backed fully under the spray of water. "Had we the time, I'd show you just how quickly I can recover."

Wouldn't that be a night? "What do we do now?"

Silas handed him a bar of soap. "That should be rather obvious."

He took the soap, then poked Silas in the ribs. "Not what I meant. After dinner."

Silas turned and rinsed lather off his shoulders.

Tight-lipped, imperious bastard. "Silas." He jabbed him in the side. Twice. This time Silas flinched, gasped, and that haughty facade broke with a croak of laughter. Silas caught his hands.

"Stop!"

"Not until you tell me what I want to know."

Silas brushed his thumb across Rhys's cheek. "We're quite a pair, aren't we?"

Rhys took a breath, but Silas kissed him before he could speak. A light kiss, but enough to stop his questions. *Damn it.*

"We," Silas said, "or rather, I will destroy Anaxandros and the rest of the soulless, as I was sent here to do."

"By angels." Rhys muttered the words. "You work for fucking angels."

"Angels don't procreate."

Rhys moved to tickle Silas, but he'd already twisted away, a grin lighting his face.

Oh, that was good to see. A true smile, not one that hid other emotions. "What will I do?"

The smile dimmed. Silas wrapped strong arms around Rhys. "You kept me alive. You healed me. You've given me more of my element than I could've gotten, even standing on land. It's enough."

Rhys settled against Silas and let the warmth and strangeness of the man surround him. He didn't reply.

No way in hell Silas would approve of the idea forming in his head.

CHAPTER NINE

*S*ilas studied the impeccable fall of tails over Rhys's ass. "And yet you can't wear a suit to save your life."

They stood in Rhys's cabin. While not as ostentatious as Silas's own, the room still had the feel of luxury, no doubt paid for by some of the millions Rhys had inherited.

Rhys snorted and continued to tie his bow tie in the mirror. "I practically grew up in a tux. All those concerts." He finished and faced Silas. "I take it this meets with your approval?"

More than met. Silas kept his hands in the pockets of his pants to hide just how much he approved. "It'll do."

"Really?" Rhys stepped close and ran the knuckle of his forefinger up Silas's crotch, right over his cock. "You seem rather pleased."

"You are incorrigible." Silas didn't back away, didn't take his hands from his pockets either, lest he start undressing Rhys, and bend him over the nearest piece of furniture.

The dresser was far too high. The coffee table would work nicely, though. He jammed his hands farther into his pants.

Rhys grinned and slipped around him. "Cuff links," he said.

The evening was one of two formal nights on board the ocean liner. They could've dispensed with the tuxedos, had dinner at one of the buffets, and spent the last of the time available in wanton abandon.

Rhys rooted around a suitcase haphazardly tossed onto the bed. Unlike that ill-fitting suit from the first day, the tux fit him to a T. Dressing like this had been worth the extra time, perhaps even worth not fucking Rhys into oblivion.

Silas wouldn't forget the feel of his dick sliding into that tight ass. But there should be other memories too, especially for Rhys.

Even with all of the element Rhys had given him and even with his phoenix-forged sword, the possibility that he would see tomorrow's dawn was no more than a slim fraction of hope.

Five soulless remained. Well, four and Anaxandros. Silas blotted out the memories that came with *that* name and drew a breath. "Would you like for others to see us?"

Rhys paused in his search. His expression changed from one of confusion to understanding. "You mean together? No glamour?"

"Some glamour. My appearance, at least. But no hiding *us*."

"You don't mind being seen with another man?" Rhys pushed aside a pile of clothes in his suitcase. "I mean, at the bar the other night..."

Last night. It had only been last night. "If I minded, I wouldn't sleep with men." He closed the distance to the bed. "But humans can be very strange about their yearnings, and often react poorly to the desires of others." He peered into the ramshackle suitcase.

A glint of silver peaked out from underneath a brochure

for the Hofburg Palace. Silas pushed the glossy flyer out of the way and uncovered a cuff link. The other he found nearby, jammed in the corner of the case.

"Good eyes." Rhys held out his hand.

The links were abstract shapes, almost sensual in their roundness, their dips and curves. Silas rolled a finger over one. Then he handed them both to Rhys. "You made these."

Rhys returned to the mirror and slipped the links into the holes in his shirt. "How'd you know?"

"They feel like you do when you're manipulating element."

Rhys paused in his motions. "Sometimes I still don't believe you. This fae stuff." He studied his reflection. "And then I look in the mirror."

Indeed. Rhys's fae nature had settled down somewhat, but he did look different than he had twenty-four hours before. Sharper. Brighter.

"I suspect that's the new normal for you." Only time would tell how humans reacted to Rhys. Hopefully Rhys's human nature dimmed the sliver of fae enough. Or Rhys would find life much more interesting.

Rhys mock scowled at his reflection. "I suppose it could be worse." He turned from the mirror and inspected Silas. "What do you really look like?"

"This," Silas said. "To you, to me, to anyone with fae blood, I am how you see me, regardless of glamour."

"And to anyone without?"

How to explain? "Fae embody everything humans desire. Unglamoured, we're a bit overwhelming to the senses."

Rhys came close and brushed both lapels of Silas's tux. "You are the hottest man I've ever seen."

"But not so hot that you can't control yourself. There's a reason Thomas the Rhymer followed the Queen for seven years. He would have followed a King, had one ridden forth that day."

"You mean everyone wants you?"

Ah, Rhys and his randy mind. "Not all attraction is sexual." He strode toward the door. "Would you like to see?"

"Love to." Sarcasm gave Rhys's words a sharp edge.

Silas didn't let Rhys see him frown.

Rhys stalked behind Silas the entire length of the hallway to the elevators. Once they stood waiting, Silas put his arm around Rhys's shoulder and brushed his thumb over the soft skin between Rhys's collar and hair. "I've upset you."

"No, it's not..." Rhys pressed against Silas. "Would Thomas have followed you?"

"No. I wouldn't have let my glamour fall. My life is of the road and the sword. It's not one I'd wish on another." The hum of the elevators greeted the end of his sentence.

A long moment later, Rhys spoke. His words cut through the empty lobby like a dagger through flesh. "You're not going to stay, are you?"

Silas swallowed against the sudden tightness in his throat. "You are not Thomas in this affair."

Rhys shifted. His eyes were bright.

"If I see the dawn, I promise you seven years. Seven times seven. However many you wish."

"If," Rhys said. "I don't like the sound of 'if.'"

"Neither do I, particularly."

"And will you always speak true, Thomas?" Rhys's voice was soft.

Silas couldn't have stopped his chuckle had he tried. "I'm not sure I have much choice. I am, after all, a horrible liar."

A soft chime announced the arrival of an elevator. The doors opened to reveal two women on one side of the car and a man on the other. Silas slid his hand to the small of Rhys's back. "Only I am glamoured at the moment." Though unnecessary, he lowered his voice.

A blush crept up from under Rhys's collar, but he strode forward into the car. Silas followed, letting his hand drop—but not before the others saw.

Both women smiled, not unpleasantly, and eyed the two of them. Their gazes lingered longer on Rhys than on him. Curiosity in their inspection, but not longing.

Good. Rhys's human blood hadn't faded too much.

The doors closed.

One of the women—long dark hair and inky eyes that complemented her burgundy velvet dress—turned her attention to Silas and gave him a knowing grin. "Nice."

He said nothing, just smiled back and placed his hand on the small of Rhys's back again. Rhys's breathing hitched, and his lovely blush crept farther up his neck. His smile, however, held.

The gentleman on the other side of them made a noise somewhere between a cough and a growl. He'd moved as close as he could to the button panel.

Silas stepped backward, using Rhys to partially block the women's view of him. He tapped a finger against Rhys's back and nodded toward the man. "Watch."

Silas dropped his glamour completely. "Excuse me, is the promenade button pressed?"

The man glanced back and froze.

His lips parted slightly, and his pupils widened, darkening his brown eyes. An expression close to worship crossed his face. "Oh my God."

Silas rewove the glamour around his body. "The promenade?"

The gentleman blinked rapidly. "What?" He looked back at the button panel. "Oh. Yeah, it's pressed." He gave Silas another look, then inspected his own shoes for the rest of the ride.

Some fae enjoyed holding humans in their thrall. Silas never had. Take away the will, the mind of another, and what did that make you?

But that little moment? Oh, that he'd enjoyed.

Silas drew circles around the small of Rhys's back. He'd only seen that godlike adoration on Rhys when he'd rammed his cock into him, never just in passing.

He dropped his hand to stroke Rhys's ass, not caring that both women could see the act.

The elevator stopped and the doors opened on the promenade deck. The man scooted out of the car.

The other of the two women chuckled. She wore a blue-and-black tea-length gown, and her short hair had been bleached white. She entwined her fingers with those of the first woman and raised them for Silas to see. "Whatever you did, thank you," she said. "He looked mortified."

In answer, Silas offered them a small shrug and a wide smile. The women exited the car.

Silas nudged Rhys forward. "This is our deck as well." He steered Rhys toward the Sea View restaurant.

"Okay," Rhys said. "You made your point. He certainly didn't want to screw you. It was like he'd just seen an angel."

Silas chuffed. "Angels cause quite a different reaction than fae."

Rhys shook his head but said nothing more. Silas let the silence continue, let Rhys digest what he'd seen, what he'd learned.

On large tables near the window, sunlight turned the china to gold as the maître d' showed them to their table for two in the center of the dining room. Only when their server had taken their orders, poured water, and brought Rhys a steak knife did Rhys speak again. "They don't mind you being gay, the angels?"

Rhys might not be entirely human, but he'd certainly been shaped by them—and by Americans at that. "I don't have a particular compunction about sex with women. Men merely provide different challenges and different expectations." Silas ran a finger around the top of his water glass. "If the Messengers have an issue with that aspect of my nature, they've never mentioned it."

Rhys stared at him. "You're bi?" A hint of uncertainty touched his voice.

It was always this way with humans. What type? How many? Who? All the questions another fae never asked because they understood. "Fae love and take pleasure with whomever the spirit moves us to."

Rhys looked down at his silverware. "It must be nice." Anger there, bitterness.

Silas had seen that too, many times, but not the deep fear that Rhys held underneath. Rhys was waiting for Silas to discard him.

That wouldn't happen. Not now. "Seventy times seventy years, Rhys. If you'll have me."

It took a bit of time for Rhys to look up. "You're serious?" Hope flushed his cheeks and honeyed his voice.

"Very." Silas reached across the table and took Rhys's hand.

"Why?"

Love, Silas wanted to answer, because in many ways he *had* become True Thomas, unable to lie to Rhys.

The word never made it past his lips. It caught when his throat closed, when his breath failed to come, when his blood turned to ice, and then burned.

Anaxandros walked into the restaurant. The sun hung in the sky, golden in its descent. These two disparate images clashed in Silas's head, stilled his motions for less than a heartbeat.

That moment of inaction let Anaxandros reach Rhys a fraction before the tip of Silas's sword would have met the soulless's flesh.

He pulled the blow when the soulless's hand closed around Rhys's neck. Silas stood frozen, sword in hand.

Rhys's eyes were wide, his hands nearly as white as the tablecloth they pressed against. He tried to rise, but Anaxandros pushed him back into his chair.

There was no blood. Not yet.

Sunlight filtered through the windows, though they were in shade.

Impossible.

"Quintus Silvanus."

Terror ripped through Silas. It *was* Anaxandros who stood before him, holding Rhys's life in his hands. Time hadn't changed one iota the soulless he'd once called master. Taller than his own six feet and far broader, he looked like frozen gold. Blond. Pale. More angular than any fae. Coldly beautiful. His eyes were black, his teeth very sharp.

His deep voice still made Silas's arms shake and his insides liquefy. He said nothing, could say nothing. The tip of his sword wavered six inches from Anaxandros's chest.

Anaxandros smiled. "Sit down."

Silas almost did, nearly bent to that will. Blazing fury overrode fear and kept him on his feet. "Let him go."

The words came out in Latin. He refused to speak in the soulless's tongue.

"Such a pretty boy." Anaxandros drew a talon up Rhys's cheek, leaving behind a line of blood. "Do you enjoy raping him, Quintus? Sucking down his energy when he screams under your cock?"

Rhys shook beneath the soulless's touch, a deep anger

burning in his forward stare. Only then did Silas realize Anaxandros had switched to English.

He switched languages as well. "Let him go." The tremor of his hand didn't extend to his voice. "If you harm him, I'll cut you down right here."

Anaxandros laughed and the sound sliced though Silas like screeching metal.

No one else in the dining room noticed.

Once more, the soulless changed tongues, this time to Latin. "Sit down."

Those words wrapped around Silas and tightened like a noose. His sword slipped from his hand and clattered against the dishes on the table. His knees bent. Only his iron grip on the table kept him upright.

It had been more than two thousand years. Why did he still need to obey this monster?

As if reading his mind, Anaxandros answered him. "Little fae, your kind never forget, and I worked so very hard to train you."

Truth. Silas's whole body quaked with the shame of it.

"You'll never be free of me."

A thin tendril of energy wound its way up Silas's leg, full of life and vigor. He lifted his head and looked into Rhys's brilliant green eyes.

Cut the fucker down. Those words were in his head, along with Rhys's anger. His love.

Silas gripped the hilt of his sword and lifted it. "I'll be free of you when I slice your head off."

Anaxandros laughed again. "I'm going to take your toy, Quintus. I'm going to break him as I broke you." His talons pierced Rhys's neck.

With Rhys between him and Anaxandros, Silas could only catch the soulless in the leg. If he moved correctly, if Anaxandros didn't block with Rhys's body.

It was Rhys's voice, heavy with hate, that broke the silence. "I'm not his toy." Rhys moved like lightning, grabbed the steak knife from the table, and rammed it backward into Anaxandros's chest.

Silas lunged, his sword catching the cloth of Anaxandros's pants, a bit of flesh too, for the smell of charred meat met his nostrils. Anaxandros retreated before Silas could land another blow. He pulled the knife from his chest and threw it at Rhys.

Or rather, at Rhys's empty chair. Gods only knew where he'd gone or how he could've moved so fast.

Anaxandros snarled at Silas. "I'll have him, Quintus. I'll suck the marrow from his bones while I drown you in his blood."

Rhys stepped out of the shadows and into the sun. "If you want me, fuckhead, come and get me." His hair glowed like a mass of molten copper strands, his skin gold in the afternoon light. He stood as proud and as beautiful as any fae warrior ever had. The element that whipped about him was richer and deeper than any Silas could call. All that was missing from the image was a sword in Rhys's hand.

How many wars had Quarters fought for themselves?

Element struck Silas, filling him, expanding his senses.

Anaxandros surged forward, drawn to Rhys's brightness and Rhys stepped back, stepping farther into the sunlight. Flames licked up from Anaxandros's skin when he crossed out of shadow.

Silas rushed toward Anaxandros's. He'd never have a better chance than this.

Flesh sizzled and popped before Anaxandros's taloned hands reached Rhys.

Rhys bared his teeth, malice in his smile.

Anaxandros fell back into shade, his face and arms blackened, but *only* blackened. No more flame came, no killing curls of fire from within. Silas aimed his blow at Anaxandros's head. The energy Rhys poured into Silas quickened his motions. Time slowed; his aim was perfect.

Claws closed about the gladius's blade. Pieces of blackened flesh fell from Anaxandros's face, revealed pale skin, and turned to ash. "Too slow, sprite." He pushed Silas backward. Turned. In the time it took Silas to regain his balance, Anaxandros had left the restaurant.

A snarl rose in Silas's throat. *So close!* A fraction of a second sooner and Anaxandros would have been dust. He crossed most of the floor before Rhys's voice caught him.

"Silas, don't."

He halted. "I can catch him. Kill him. I'll never have another chance like this." His vision bled red at the edges and his chest heaved against the burning need to follow.

"Silas Quint." Rhys's voice caressed Silas's thoughts. "Kill?"

Cold rushed through Silas. He fell back away from the door, the very words he'd spoken to Rhys echoing in his mind. *"You can't kill something that's already dead."* A moment later, he sheathed his sword. Arms trembling, he'd barely held it properly.

Anaxandros could still affect his mind. More than two thousand years later, the he still possessed a piece of Silas. He ground his mouth closed to keep the wail inside.

A warm arm slid around his waist and fingers stroked the side of his face, gently turning his head back toward the dining room.

Rhys, all copper and green-gold. No blood on Rhys's neck. Who had healed the wound?

"Come eat dinner," Rhys said.

Dinner? Silas looked around the room. They stood in the middle of the restaurant. Not a soul looked at them. His glamour was still intact.

It shouldn't have been. It was Rhys who held the better part of it, his energy propping Silas's weave up.

Silas didn't know a damn thing about Quarters. How in Hades's name was he supposed to protect Rhys?

Rhys pulled him toward their table.

"I'm perfectly fine." Silas shook off Rhys's grasp.

"Liar." Affection and concern softened the reply.

Silas grasped the edge of his chair, pulled it out, and sank down. He would've reached for his wine had his hands not been shaking.

Rhys sat, plucked his glass from the table, and sipped, expression unreadable.

Silas looked away. Anaxandros still played him like a puppet. Had he followed, no doubt the trail would have led him back to a lair with four other soulless. "If you hadn't stopped me, I'd be dead."

"Yeah, I know," Rhys said. "But I'd be dead without you, so it works out."

Silas hazarded a chance at drinking the wine and his hand held steady. "I didn't think—" He stopped and set down the wineglass. "I can't think around him. I'm sorry."

Rhys swirled his wine. "I want to rip that thing apart for what it did to you."

"You have no idea."

"Actually," Rhys said, "I do."

Oh great mother Gaia. Rhys had felt Silas's whole life, that part included. He cast around for words to put together and found nothing.

Thankfully their dinner came, providing Silas with a respite from his thoughts and from Rhys's watchful inspection.

Though how he'd stomach his food, Silas had no idea.

Rhys smiled up at the waiter. "I seem to have dropped my steak knife."

They brought Rhys another.

An image of Rhys's blood welling beneath Anaxandros's claws flashed through Silas's mind. He flattened his hands against the tablecloth, because the tremors had returned. "Jupiter's hairy balls, what the hell is wrong with me?"

Rhys handed him the bread basket. "I don't know. Maybe you just saw the monster that spent a hundred-and-eighty-some years abusing you for the first time since you escaped?"

Silas took the basket and forced himself to pull out a piece of bread. "I should be better than this."

Exasperation was written on Rhys's face. "You're too hard on yourself. What you went through..." He frowned down at his steak and commenced cutting it. "Hell, I kind of lost it around that thing."

The bread was soft and warm. Silas took another sip of wine to wash it down. "You were magnificent. Like wind. I couldn't touch him, and you pierced his flesh." He paused, watched Rhys's hands. "With a steak knife."

Rhys laid the knife on the edge of his plate. "Is that something else I shouldn't be able to do?" Rhys's lips twitched upward.

Cheeky little fox. "Yes." Silas picked up his silverware—and it was real silver—and set about consuming the honey-braised chicken in front of him. At first he nibbled, but the food was surprisingly good. Tender meat and sweet spices. Before long, most of the chicken was gone, and he forced himself to slow down before he stole Rhys's steak.

"I think we make each other better," Rhys said. "I feel you when you"—he waved his fork about in a circle—"do whatever it is you do, and I just know."

"Know when I manipulate the element?" Silas rotated his wineglass, watched the merlot coat the sides. Someone who complemented him in every way. Gods above. "We do seem to share a connection."

Rhys finally looked away, his gaze drifting toward the sinking sun. "Maybe that's why."

RHYS KNEW what Silas's next words would be. He wasn't disappointed.

"Why what?"

He studied Silas. Color had returned to his tan face, stability to his arms and hands. Good. That had been a close call. "Why I followed you."

Silas leaned back in his chair, elbow propped up on the arm, chin resting on his fingers.

A familiar motion. They had been together a day, and yet he knew that gesture nearly as well as he knew his own. "I have horrible boyfriends. Everyone tells me I'm always picking the worst men." He scooped up his wineglass and drained it. "They're wrong."

"You don't pick up the worst men?"

God, he loved that accent, the little dip in Silas's tone that dried his words out. Might as well be a finger trailing up his spine. "I don't pick up men. They pick me up, I fall in love, they use me, then toss me aside."

Silas furrowed his brow as if remembering and dropped his arm. His mouth flattened into a thin line. "I see."

He would. Rhys had Silas's memories, a massive tangle of images and emotions. It only made sense Silas would have his. "I'm not exactly a carpe-diem kind of person when it comes to relationships. I'm...somewhat passive."

"That," Silas said, "is the last word I'd use to describe you."

"Now," Rhys said. "Two days ago?"

"I didn't know you two days ago." Silas stroked the condensation on the outside of his water glass.

Rhys doubted he'd ever get tired of how Silas's fingers caressed everything they touched. "Yeah, exactly." Rhys tossed his napkin on the table and stood. He held out his hand.

A moment later Silas rose, and twined those long fingers with Rhys's. "What do you have in mind?"

He couldn't heal Silas, not from the wounds the vampire had carved into his soul, but he could create ties of his own. Stronger ones. "Wait and see."

A gentle tug was all it took for Rhys to lead Silas from the room. "I would've liked a coffee." Silas's protest was a halfhearted murmur.

Rhys drew Silas outside into the warm glow of the sun. They strolled up the promenade, forward to the bow, then up a set of stairs to an observation deck. Several empty lounge chairs sat on the teak planks. The wind took some of the heat out of the sunlight. No sunbathers. No readers either.

Good. Rhys pushed Silas against the hull and kissed him, forced his tongue past Silas's lips and invaded that mouth. Silas moaned deep in his throat.

How would that moan feel with his cock in Silas's throat? Rhys pressed his erection against Silas's and framed Silas's face with his hands.

Sex would be fantastic, but that wasn't what Rhys needed right now. He broke the kiss. "I want you to listen to me."

"You have the entirety of my attention." A husky response.

"I'm going with you tonight."

Silas gripped his shoulders, tried to open space between them. "Rhys."

He leaned into Silas's body, stroked Silas's smooth cheeks with his thumbs. No stubble. Never any stubble. "I'm not asking. I'm telling you."

The furrow in Silas's brow deepened. "Rhys, you'll be safer—"

"Like last night?" Safer, his ass.

Silas sucked in a breath, but the stubborn, arrogant line of his mouth remained. "You'll be safer in the cabin."

In the cabin? The hell with that. He'd be a sitting duck.

A good fuck was easy to get from Silas. Thoughtful consideration was not, and he of all people should know the vampires.

Rhys shoved himself away from Silas, the pain in his chest sharp and sudden. "Forget it. I guess I'll just give myself to them." He headed for the steps down to the next deck. "Since you don't give a damn." He might have put up with other men treating him like a vapid twit, but he damn well wouldn't from this one.

Silas must have seen what that creature in the dining room tried to do. Didn't he trust Rhys after all that?

Silas caught him by the arm before he reached the railing. "Rhys, don't. Please!"

Rhys didn't shake free of Silas, just pulled taut against his bruising grip. His heart pulsed in his throat. "Either listen to me or let go, Silas. Two choices."

Emotional turmoil flowed over and around Rhys, more turbulent than the ocean surface, far greater than Rhys's anger.

Silas.

Letting go wasn't really an option for either of them. "You're not used to being told what to do, are you?" Rhys said.

Silas's grip on his arm loosened, though Silas didn't let go. "No, I'm not." Rhys barely heard those words over the wind, the slap of waves against the hull.

"I'm not used to ordering anyone." Rhys pried Silas's fingers from his arm but kept ahold of his hand. "But you're being a fucking bastard right now. And I'm not going to let you get yourself killed."

"I could say the same thing to you." Silas's accent thickened his words and made them sharp. Sunlight turned Silas's eyes golden. "He'll kill you, Rhys. Or worse. I can't— won't—let that happen."

The wind lifted those dark curls and fluttered the ends of Silas's bow tie.

Rhys had been wrong. Silas was completely blind when it came to the ancient vampire.

"He?" Rhys placed a hand against Silas's chest, over his heart. It beat faster than his own. "All the other vampires you talk about as things. Creatures. Not that one."

Shock smoothed the lines of anger from Silas's face. His lips parted. Beneath Rhys's hand, his heart fluttered like a bird's.

"You've never noticed, have you?" Rhys said.

Wild despair shone in that beautiful face. No mistaking Silas for human now. Everything about him was untamed. "No, I haven't."

Rhys tightened his grip on Silas's hand. "Listen to me."

Silas trailed a too-warm finger down Rhys's face in the same the way Rhys touched alabaster or marble. "I... Yes. I'll listen."

Rhys swallowed the lump in his throat. Too close, *again*. Any other man Rhys would've left, but Silas was *his*, as surely as he belonged to Silas. "Do you think this vampire, Anex...Anox—"

"Anaxandros."

"—Anaxandros, knows about quarter-fae?"

Beneath Rhys's fingers, the rhythm of Silas's heart slowed. "It's possible." He frowned. "He—it—existed for several millennia before it caught me."

Rhys took his hand away from Silas's chest. His grip on

Rhys's other hand tightened. Silas's gaze never strayed from Rhys's face.

Anaxandros's taunts had been for one purpose. "It tried to take you from me," Rhys said.

Silas got that faraway look, the one that meant he was turning over events in his mind. After a moment his gaze snapped back into focus. "It did try to drive us apart. He—" Silas stopped and spit an angry string of words out Rhys didn't understand. "It knows me better than any creature, save perhaps the Messengers."

"And me."

"You." Silas exhaled. His expression softened into shame. "Gods, Rhys—"

Rhys closed the distance between them and swallowed Silas's next words with a quick kiss. "I swear to God, if you apologize one more time, I'm going to hit you."

"I'm sorry," Silas muttered.

Rhys stepped back and slapped him across the face.

The sting in his palm was well worth Silas's dumbfounded expression. That quickly dissolved into choking laughter. Silas leaned against the overlook's railing, tears dotting the corners of his eyes.

"I did warn you," Rhys said, before laughter overtook him as well.

"Whatever did I do to deserve you, I wonder?" Silas said. Gone were all traces of his earlier despair.

Excellent. The muscles in Rhys's back unknotted. "Probably something really good. Or very wicked," Rhys said. "I'm guessing wicked."

Silas's deep chuckle thickened Rhys's balls. "I was hoping you'd want to do something wicked when you dragged me away from coffee." Silas pushed off the railing. "Rather than argue with me."

"I didn't argue with you." Rhys stepped in. He touched

the ends of Silas's tie, and pulled them apart. "You argued with me, and I won."

"Yes, you did." Silas dipped his fingers between Rhys's pants and chest and stroked his waist. "Have I thanked you for bringing me to my senses?"

"No." Rhys unbuttoned the first three buttons of Silas's shirt and trailed his fingers down his throat. Rhys was hard, painfully so. "How many hours until sunset?"

"Several." He spoke low, his accent caressing syllables. "At least three."

A part of Rhys—the one Silas had awakened—wanted to take Silas right there, bend him over the railing and pound into him as hard as he could.

Instead, Rhys leaned down and pressed his lips against the skin his fingers had so recently touched. He worked his mouth up to Silas's jaw and kissed him. There were other options too, different ways to claim Silas. "Sounds like plenty of time."

"For what?" Silas's hot breath touched Rhys's lips; his hands cupped Rhys's ass.

"For you to put that mouth of yours to better use." Rhys took hold of both ends of Silas's tie, pulled him in for a bruising kiss. When he broke it, Silas hissed.

Served Silas right for worrying him so. For not listening.

Rhys sucked Silas's earlobe, then whispered into his ear. "Now get on your knees and fuck me with your mouth until I come in the back of your throat."

Silas's grip on Rhys's ass tightened, grinding their cocks together. "Deck chair." Silas pulled Rhys across to the closest lounge chair. "I don't want you collapsing on me."

Rhys sat on the end, and Silas knelt between his legs. The sun gilded the edges of his black hair and brightened his eyes to gold. A vision of a pagan god.

Silas tilted his head up. "No man has ever ordered me to my knees."

"Their loss." Rhys ran his hands through Silas's curls. "How do you say 'cocksucker' in Latin?"

Silas grunted and undid Rhys's belt and pants. "*Fellator.*" His lithe fingers freed Rhys's cock and balls.

"You mean like fellatio?"

Silas bared his teeth in a feral grin. "Am I going to have to teach you your own language? Yes, like fellatio." He stroked Rhys's shaft. "Though back then, it was considered a passive act."

Anything Rhys had to say in reply vanished from his mind when Silas tongued the head of his cock, then dipped into the slit, licking at the precome collecting there.

Oh fuck. Velvet lips caressed his glans as Silas lowered his hot mouth and sucked Rhys in. Molten heat shot through Rhys's limbs, and he gripped the side of the deck chair. Silas slid his mouth up and down Rhys's shaft.

A passive act? Hell no. Rhys bit his lips and leaned back on his elbows to watch. Silas's eyes were half-closed. A trace of teeth scraped Rhys's glans as Silas pulled his mouth back, sending a shower of sparks through Rhys. Tongue and lips swirled around the head, and Silas moved his mouth down Rhys's shaft. Lips ringed Rhys tighter than a fist while Silas's tongue skimmed over his crown, teasing and stroking the length. He quickened his pace.

Rhys wouldn't last long at this rate. "Slower."

The arrogant bastard chuckled and then licked the very tip of Rhys's cock before kissing it. Slowly silken lips parted, and Rhys sank into an inferno filled with the slick heat of Silas's tongue. Feather touches pushed into his slit and around his glans. Light flared in Rhys's veins, and his arms shook.

Silas sucked Rhys in, a fraction at a time, massaging every

inch of Rhys's shaft as Rhys slid deeper and deeper into Silas's mouth.

Warmth curled into his balls.

Silas reversed direction. The pull of silk and the caresses around his shaft made every nerve in his body swell and ache. Rhys threw back his head and moaned. Shit, he was going to—

The grip Silas had on his cock tightened painfully at the base. That was the only thing that kept Rhys from shooting right then and there. Rhys twisted his hands in Silas's hair. "Oh, God."

Silas's other hand massaged Rhys's balls.

His lovers hadn't blown him that often and never this well. "For someone who doesn't suck dick, you're damn good at it."

Silas's reply was to take Rhys back into his throat, even more slowly than before, sucking hard.

He needed to come. Now. He pushed on Silas's head. "Faster."

The amused grunt that vibrated the length of Rhys's shaft tightened his balls more than before. But Silas didn't speed up. He took Rhys in farther and then pulled off again.

The wind against his wet cock wrapped cool feathers around the shaft and sent a shudder through Rhys. Then the inferno of Silas's mouth descended and burned his skin with wet, velvet touches. With each stroke, the air cooled his blood before Silas's mouth set him on fire again. Light filled Rhys, pooling around his core, aching for release. It had nowhere to go. Rhys's arms trembled, and he fell back against the lounge chair.

Yes, he'd ordered Silas to his knees, told him to suck cock, but Silas had complete control over when Rhys would shoot down that lovely, tight throat.

Silas took him in completely surrounding him with a wet

fire that burned more than just Rhys's flesh. His chest ached. Did Silas understand? Did he realize? Fucking was like everything else between them—a partnership.

"I know." Foreign thoughts caressed Rhys's mind; then a lighthearted laugh vibrated him from the tip of his dick to his balls. *"I understand."*

Silas released the base of Rhys's cock and quickened the pace, his lips a tight circle, his throat open.

Rhys thrust his hips upward, hard and deep. He knew what it was like to be on the other end of a face fucking, the surrender it took, how hard it was to breathe. Even painful sometimes. He pounded into Silas's mouth.

Silas met each of his relentless strokes and never let him slip out. He fondled Rhys's balls with the utmost care while taking him to the root.

The light pooling in Rhys's core blazed and arced down every limb in a storm of energy. This time there was nothing to hold Rhys back. "Oh fuck, Silas!" He thrust upward, pulled Silas's head down, and came with his balls against Silas's chin. He moaned deep and long until he couldn't catch his breath. An eternity passed before the lightning in his veins lessened and he stopped coming.

His hands slipped from Silas's hair, his cock from Silas's mouth. Silas laid his forehead against Rhys's leg and gulped air, his breathing as harsh as the ocean waves crashing against the hull of the ship.

A breeze blew across them, the scent of salt water mixing with the musk of sex and the smell of sun-warmed grass and pine. Goose bumps rose on Rhys's arms under his jacket. Even far away from the garden, the energy of the forest and the field swirled around them.

This was him—his element. Fae. The part that had been missing all this time. He shivered and watched Silas's perfect face. And there was his home.

Silas stirred and licked his reddened lips. He tucked Rhys's cock back into his underwear and pants, then zipped and buttoned him closed. Finally he buckled Rhys's belt.

Neither Silas's hair nor his eyes were golden, but he still had the look of a god—a smiling being of beauty and desire.

"I think I understand Roman mythology better," Rhys said.

"That would be a trick." Silas crawled up into the lounge chair and settled himself onto Rhys. "Romans didn't understand Roman mythology. It's rather convoluted."

Rhys wrapped his arms around Silas, soaking in his warmth. His hair smelled like sunlight on leaves. "How do you fit into it?"

"I don't." Silas slipped his hand beneath Rhys's jacket and stroked his side. This time the shudder that ran through Rhys wasn't from the chill of the wind. "Though Silvanus is the name of a Roman forest god."

"And Quintus?"

Silas raised an eyebrow. "Fifth."

Heat spread up Rhys's face. "I should know that. Quintet. Quintuplets."

"Yes." Silas kissed him on the cheek. "Mine was the fifth family of our court. Or so they said."

"Quintus Silvanus," Rhys said, tasting the name on his lips. It didn't sound right. "I prefer Silas Quint."

"So do I." Silas laid his head down on Rhys's shoulder. "So do I."

They lay for several minutes, wrapped in each other's arms, bathed in the light of the western sun, the ocean the only voice on the wind until Silas spoke again.

"Tell me how it is that you developed such wisdom in only twenty-eight years?" He nuzzled Rhys's neck.

Wisdom? "About the vampire?"

"Yes."

Rhys rolled a lock of Silas's hair between his fingers. He wasn't wise at all. "It's not me. It's you. All the stuff you know. That Anax-bastard just rattles you too much for you to see it."

Silas pressed against Rhys. "It's a problem." His tight voice barely rose above the sound of the waves.

"Yeah. But we'll work it out." Rhys found Silas's lips and kissed him deeply. Silas shifted, and his hard shaft pushed against Rhys's thigh. "Want me to do something about that?" Rhys spoke against Silas's lips.

Silas hummed. "Everything I want to do to you at the moment requires far less clothing, higher furniture, and a shower afterwards."

Pinpricks traveled outward from Rhys's stomach, raising the hairs on his arms. Amazingly his dick stirred too. "We could go back to your cabin."

"That had occurred to me." Silas kissed Rhys's neck, and hands found the ticklish spot on Rhys's side under his arm. "And I'm sore tempted. But I think we should remain in the sun."

The vampire. The flame of desire dwindled. "It's never come out before dark before?"

"I've never known any soulless to walk in daylight. I don't know how Anaxandros could."

The vampire had burned in the sunlight and felt pain from those burns. That had been plain in the snarl the creature had given when it tried to reach Rhys. "There're stories about really old vampires being able to walk in the day."

"The old ones are hard to destroy. That very well might be the case." Silas's desire had deflated too.

Pity. But Silas was right. Better to stay in the light and plan rather than fuck in the shadows and get eaten. "Will your sword work against it?"

"Yes. The Messengers wouldn't have sent me here unarmed."

Of course not. They were angels. Rhys shifted, caught Silas's head in his hands, and made Silas look at him. "They also wouldn't have sent you here if there wasn't hope of success, Silas."

Silas squirmed against the truth. "A fool's hope."

"More than that." Silas tried to look away, but Rhys held him fast. He stroked a thumb over Silas's cheek. "Listen to me."

"I *am* listening. I'm no match for Anaxandros. There's only one fae who might have been."

"Might have been?"

"He died hunting daemons."

Oh. The thought of Silas hunting daemons froze Rhys's veins and he shuddered. "I'm here." Rhys let Silas go. "You're stronger now."

Silas laid his head on Rhys's shoulder. "Not enough. Even if I could touch Anaxandros, there are four others." He paused, then added, "And please don't tell me the Messengers sent me to save you."

Stubborn, foolish man. Rhys tasted the truth. Why couldn't Silas? "Maybe they sent *me* here to save *you*."

Silas raised his head and peered into Rhys's face, his expression a mixture of worry and wonder.

"That never occurred to you, did it?"

"No." Silas's fingers were warm against Rhys's cheek. "But that makes far more sense than the other way around."

Rhys couldn't help the snort. "For someone who's lived a goddamn long time, you really don't know yourself very well."

Silas stiffened. "For someone who has known me less than two days, you seem very sure of your knowledge of me."

"But I do know you." He kissed Silas, smoothing out

some of the angry lines on his brow. "Please stop fighting me."

Those lines folded into worry. "If I fail, it's not just my life. I'm not afraid to die. I've never been afraid. But if you—" His voice cracked, and he fell silent.

Rhys stroked Silas's hair. "Then use that clever mind of yours to figure out how to beat them." He kissed Silas again. "Because I don't want to die on this boat. And I want that thing's head."

CHAPTER TEN

*S*ilas lurked under a set of stairs and against the bulkhead, his glamour wrapped close about him. He loosened the grip on his sword for the fourth time. An odd thing, to have apprehension nipping at his heels. He'd never been so anxious on a hunt, not even during his first. But the longer he and Rhys waited for the soulless, the more worry pooled in his mind and the harder he clenched his sword.

That wouldn't do at all in a fight.

Ten or so feet away, Rhys leaned against the deck railing outside the Piano Bar, his back to Silas. Long strands of elemental energy flowed about him, dancing in a wind of their own making. The smooth curve of Rhys's ass peeked out from behind the tails of his tuxedo.

Rhys was, as he himself would've said, the perfect image of vampire bait. A living being full of energy and beauty.

Silas loosened his grip again. This wasn't the most clever plan he'd ever devised, but given all the factors, including Rhys's insistence that he hunt with Silas, it was the best he had.

There were some merits to using Rhys as bait, though. Proximity to Rhys hid Silas's elemental signature under that brilliance and chaos. Rhys was also far safer here under Silas's watch than alone in one of their cabins.

Not that he would ever admit that to Rhys—the imp was smugger than a cat on a fishing boat. No need to encourage him further.

One hitch marred their little trap. Three hours after sunset, not a single soulless had appeared. Frustrating didn't even begin to describe the night.

As if sensing Silas's thoughts, Rhys sighed loud enough to be heard over the ocean and kicked at the metal band on the bottom of the railing. "Maybe," he said, "I should go back in and dance some more."

Oh, Silas knew with whom Rhys wanted to dance. Heat settled in his stomach and made his face warm. "If you'd like." Even though his glamour swallowed the words to human ears, he kept his voice low.

Rhys peered over his shoulder. "Jealous?"

He didn't deign to reply. Rhys snorted and went back to watching the sea.

And to think the night had started out so promising, even if a bit windy. Silas ran his tongue over his upper lip, but the salt he tasted there was from the sea air, not Rhys.

Close to sunset, they'd left the lounge chair and returned to Silas's cabin. Rhys needed very little cleaning up—a side benefit to Silas sucking him off—and no change of clothing at all. He, however, changed into something more appropriate for destroying soulless on the windswept decks of a ship. For the rest of the night, he'd followed Rhys, a silent and deadly shadow, while Rhys enjoyed all the nightlife the ship had to offer.

Enjoy Rhys did. With abandon. While no soulless had taken the bait during his romp through the ship's clubs, plenty of humans had noticed him. Most of his admirers had been women, but a few had been men.

Now *that* had pleased Rhys. For the gentlemen, his grin was true, his laughter infectious. He'd even danced with a particularly handsome blond, close enough that their hips had touched. Rhys hadn't cared one whit what anyone thought.

Silas's little experiment in the elevator had certainly unlocked the exhibitionist in Rhys. Or perhaps it was his fae blood finally showing.

Rhys's change in attitude should've delighted Silas. Glamouring the both of them could be tiring, even with an abundance of element. Rhys being comfortable in his own skin was a blessing. It boded well for the future.

Silas repeated that thought during the very long five minutes he'd watched Rhys on the dance floor. It was a wonder he hadn't ground his teeth to nubs.

Jealous? Life was too long to worry about what any given romantic partner was up to. Silas's life being what it was, his affairs had always been blessedly brief. He preferred it that way.

No, he wasn't jealous in the least. Never mind that he and Rhys were inexorably bound together, that looking at Rhys drove breath from his lungs and blood to his cock.

Silas shifted his weight from one foot to the other. Oh, he was quite the wretched liar.

"Do you dance, Silas?" There was too much amusement in Rhys's quiet voice.

"Of course I do." When this was over, he was going to thoroughly enjoy showing Rhys just how well he *danced*.

At the railing, Rhys straightened and spoke louder. "Once more into the breach, dear friends."

"Come now, it can't be that bad." A woman's melodious and fluid voice floated down from the next deck. Footsteps on the metal stairs over his head followed, descending from above.

Silas felt nothing living above him. He loosened his grip on the gladius.

Rhys stepped away from the railing. Shadows sharpened his features, exposing the deep worry written on his face.

"You seemed to be enjoying yourself." The creature that stepped onto their deck had once been a woman. Long black hair, pulled into a braid, swung against its back. More details than that, Silas couldn't see.

The soulless clicked its tongue. "Why are you all alone, little Quarter? Where's your friend from the dance floor?"

The accent was Hindi. A surprise. The lust for physical immortality wasn't as strong in cultures that believed in reincarnation. Silas took two silent steps away from the stairs and the bulkhead.

"He's probably still on the dance floor. I'll go check." The reply was cavalier, but a tightness in his voice betrayed Rhys's fear. He angled toward the door.

The soulless shifted, cutting off Rhys's retreat. "Why don't you dance with me, Rhys?"

A shudder ran through Rhys at the sound of his name. "Dead's not exactly my type."

Laughter, strangely close to the sound of glass bells, echoed across the deck. "Did he tell you that, your fae? That we're dead?"

Silas took three more steps. The last one took him within sword's length.

"And just where is Quintus Silvanus? Has he abandoned you already?"

"What do you think?" Annoyance and dejection flashed across Rhys's face. "I guess he had his own plans."

The soulless stepped forward and touched Rhys's arm.

"He's more of a fool than I thought, to leave you alone for us to take."

Rhys froze under the soulless's touch, even as he fought against its thrall.

Silas raised his sword, cocked his hips, and waited. So that dance with the blond hadn't been entirely out of lust, but part of a ruse for the soulless. Clever Rhys.

"Now," the soulless said, "where is Quintus Silvanus?"

Rhys spoke the truth because he had no choice. "He's behind you."

It turned. Silas swung and cleaved its head from its shoulders. The trunk fell, smoldered, and burst into flames. The head rolled to a stop, before collapsing to ash. A length of braided hair fell to the deck, limp as an old rope.

Rhys rubbed his arm. "That's a bit disturbing."

"The hair?"

"Yeah. I kind of like it when there's nothing left. Like before."

So did Silas. Others who hunted the soulless sometimes took trophies and kept track of the numbers. He didn't. The Messengers knew the count. That was enough. He knelt and tossed the braid onto the pile of smoking ash that had been the soulless's body. The hair ignited, flamed, and was gone.

"Better." Rhys toed the edge of the ash pile. "What about this?"

"The wind will scatter it into the sea." Silas rose and listened for other movement. "We won't be able to do that again, I believe."

"Pity. Even you believed my performance." Rhys shoved his hands into the pockets of his pants. "Now what?"

"Up." He nodded to the stairs. "Let's see where this thing came from."

"From me, Quintus. She came from me." Anaxandros stood at the top of the stairs to the next deck. His jagged teeth gleamed in the moonlight for a moment. "Just as you did."

Breath refused to enter Silas's lungs. Years fell away in a rush of memories, and he stood on the blood-soaked grass of Campania, the corpses of his family and the rest of the fae court lying at his feet. Anaxandros's hand wrapped his throat, and that voice slipped into his ear, into his soul. *"You belong to me now."*

Rhys gripped his wrist, snapping the image and pulling him sideways. "Come on!" He headed toward the port deck.

An uncontrollable burning rose up from Silas's chest, setting his heart and soul in motion. Twisting away from Rhys, he rounded on Anaxandros, his sword flashing forward.

Anaxandros caught the blade with one hand, skin hissing under its edge, then stepped in and drove the other into Silas's side.

Pain, so intense white spots flickered before Silas's eyes, replaced rage.

"Do you need this, Silvanus?" Cool, whispered words licked against his ear. Anaxandros's tone was conversational. Friendly. Then the soulless squeezed what he held.

Agony shunted every other sense out. A whine, like the high-pitched sound only electricity produced, filled Silas's mind. His vision turned completely white.

A voice overrode the whine. "Perhaps not. What is it you Romans say about the liver? The seat of passions? You always had too many."

Oh great and powerful gods, preserve him. Silas tasted blood in his mouth. Not again. He couldn't bear this again.

Under the roar in his ears, metal clattered to wood. His sword falling to the deck. His muscles spasmed, and every nerve shrieked in time to the squeezing of Anaxandros's hand. He shouldn't be standing, yet he was, held upright by Anaxandros's arm about his waist.

"Are you in such a hurry to join your court? Have you truly lived long enough?" Words murmured against his throat.

No. Not nearly long enough. Wait—horror snaked through his thoughts—what was he thinking?

Another sound cut through the cacophony in his mind— Rhys yelling. "You leave him alone, you fucking bastard." Rhythmic banging followed. "Let him go!"

Anaxandros did, with a cry that was half a snarl and half pain.

Silas crumpled, but falling to the deck hurt less than having his liver palpitated through a hole punched into the side of his body. His vision cleared enough for him to stare at the painted steel underside of the deck above.

"Have you lived long enough?"

"No."

He wasn't ready to lose— Oh Great Father Jupiter. Anaxandros would tear Rhys apart.

"Rhys!" Silas tried to push himself up. A searing like hot iron on flesh burned down his spine, and his limbs spasmed. "Rhys, run!"

"It's okay." Rhys loomed over him. Knelt. "It's gone." Blood—and something else—coated his hands. "Don't move."

Easy enough. Silas closed his eyes, took a painful breath, and then opened them. Element whipped around Rhys like tongues of flame, but his faint color and the rising panic in his face betrayed his youth and humanity. "God, what do I do? How do I stop the bleeding?" He stripped off his coat.

"Not like that." He had no idea what his side looked like, but from the blazing stabs stripping his veins, he had a good guess. Cloth against that would likely hurt more than Anaxandros's claws. "Give me your hand."

"I have to stop the bleeding."

Silas grabbed Rhys's arm and pulled as much element as he could into his body. Contact made it so much easier.

Rhys hissed, and his face twisted. After a moment, he relaxed, and the flow of element increased.

"Sorry," Silas said. "First aid's a bit different for fae."

"It's okay. I wasn't thinking."

"That makes two of us." He let go of Rhys. He needed more element, but there wasn't time. He struggled upright. "We need to move. Anaxandros won't be gone for long."

Rhys sat back on his heels. "Actually he might."

Silas took a closer look at Rhys's hands. Then surveyed the ship deck. A metal box—an ashtray from the railing—lay on its side, one end mangled and covered in blood, flesh, and hair. "What did you do?"

"I beat it in the head until it let you go." Rhys looked at his hands. "I think I broke its skull."

"You think..." There were little flecks of brain matter on the deck. Words fled Silas. Once more, Rhys had injured Anaxandros when he couldn't even lay a finger on the soulless.

"I didn't kill it...destroy it. Whatever. It went back the way it came, up the steps." Rhys stood, wiped his hands on his pants, and held one out to Silas. "I thought about following, but I couldn't leave you bleeding like that."

He hated the tremble in his limbs and the malaise in his body, but losing that much blood was one of the few injuries he couldn't heal quickly. He grasped Rhys's hand and climbed to his feet. It was far harder than he wanted to admit. Every inch of him felt battered. The ship lights seemed to dim and brighten, and the world felt more tenuous

ANNA ZABO

than he liked. If Rhys *had* followed Anaxandros, he wouldn't be standing now.

On the teak planks of the deck, his sword lay in a large puddle of blood.

"We should find Vasil. Ash will blow away. But this?" Rain at sea wasn't something he relished, but just this once, it would've been nice. Stars studded the achingly clear sky.

"I should find Vasil," Rhys said. "You should stay here and hide the blood. Glamour up some caution tape or something."

If only it were that easy. He ignored Rhys and walked over to retrieve his gladius. Or rather, he tried. After a few steps, he collapsed into Rhys's arms. Agony traced lightning in his veins.

"When will you fucking listen to me?" Rhys dragged him over to a wooden chest set against the bulkhead. LIFE JACKETS, the sign read. "God, Silas. That thing had its hand in your side. That's not something you just walk away from."

"Says the human."

Rhys gripped his chin and forced Silas to look up into his face. His bloody and sticky fingers smelled like iron. "Says the quarter-fae who has more than a little bit of your memories."

Rhys's grip was like iron too. Silas couldn't turn away.

"I don't want to die," Rhys said. "I don't want you to die either."

Unease stirred in Silas, like a forgotten memory triggered by a smell or a song. "I have no plans to die."

"You could've fooled me."

Silas grabbed Rhys's arm and struggled to push him away. It was rather like fighting against a mountain. "This isn't the time or the place to have this argument."

"Yeah, well. Here we are." Rhys let go and straightened. "What do you want, Silas?"

Not the question he'd expected. "I... What do you mean?"

Rhys looked down the ship deck, toward the stern of the ship, his profile strong, proud. "My life was chaos when I got on this boat. No idea what I wanted, what I was going to do when I got home. God, there are a thousand people clamoring to take my money and run. Funny how being hunted by vampires changes your worldview." Rhys licked his lips. "I want to walk off this boat in New York with you. Then spend a week in bed, preferably fucking you. Then I'm going to tell those thousand people to go screw themselves."

"After that?" The rapid rate of Silas's heart had nothing at all to do with his injuries.

Rhys turned to face Silas. "I don't know. It gets kind of fuzzy after that. Something about spending the rest of my life with you."

Silas leaned his head against the bulkhead. "You hardly—"

"I know you better than anyone else in this world." He paused and added, "And you know me."

There was no defense against the truth. Oh, he cast about to find some lie to throw in front of Rhys, but there was nothing. Fate had thrown them together, Quarter and fae. He *knew* Rhys.

"What do you want?" Rhys asked again.

Silas spoke the truth to the wind and sea and to Rhys. "Hope. A future. Not to care when the sun sets and rises. To be free of this pain. To stop seeing Isatis's lemur. Stop hearing his screams."

Rhys said nothing. Young, beautiful Rhys.

"You deserve so much better than I can give you." Silas gestured at the blood-strewn deck. "Look at this. Look at my life. I'm...a shell. Nothing but pain and hatred and blood."

"You're lying again." Rhys sat down next to him on the

wooden trunk. "Or you really don't know yourself. One of the two."

Silas stared out at the dark ocean. A bit of both, most likely. He'd been running for so very long. "I want to give you the world. There's so much you haven't seen, that you don't know." He exhaled. "A week in bed sounds like a fine place to begin."

"Yeah. Well, there's still the whole walking-off-the-boat bit before we can get to that."

"Quite." He didn't like saying the next words. "You're right. I need to stay here."

Rhys didn't smile. He simply turned his head and kissed Silas. His lips and mouth were warm and tasted of rosemary and red wine. Tender and sweet.

It had been a very long time since anyone had kissed Silas so.

When Rhys drew back, more truth slipped free from Silas. "I love you."

This time Rhys did smile. "I know."

He didn't ask how and refused to ask if the feeling was mutual. Later. Later he would, if Anaxandros didn't kill him first. He clutched his side, though it wasn't his liver that hurt.

Rhys caught his chin again, brushed a thumb over his jaw. "Silas."

"You should find Vasil." His voice was as raspy as the ocean against the ship's hull. He pulled away. The burning in his throat wasn't from any wound.

"*Te amo.*"

It took a moment for the words to register. Gods, his pronunciation. They'd have to work on that. Then the meaning hit, and for the third time that night, he had trouble catching his breath.

"I mean it," Rhys said.

"You don't know 'quintus,' but you know *that*?"

Rhys shrugged and looked out at the ocean. "There was a guy once who made me memorize 'I love you' in fifty different languages. Had me recite them when he fucked me."

Cretins. Self-absorbed plebeians, every single man who ever let Rhys go, who ever treated him with such disrespect. "Does he have a name?" Silas dug through the memories he had from Rhys.

"No." Rhys's eyes were dark in the fluorescence of the ship deck. "You're not allowed to kill him." The corner of his mouth, though, was fighting against a smile.

"I won't kill him." Silas shifted. When he made it to New York, he'd start a different kind of hunt. "I'll only break a few of his fingers."

"No." The smile won. "Save the violence for the vampires." Rhys stood. "I'll go find Vasil."

"Take your coat," Silas said. Blood stained the side of Rhys's white shirt. "I can't glamour you when you're gone."

Rhys scooped up his jacket and donned it. It hid all but a trace of the blood on his shirt. Hopefully that would be enough.

Rhys stooped again, this time to pick up Silas's gladius. "You might need this." He handed it to Silas. "I'll be as fast as I can."

Element flared when their fingers met.

Silas nodded. He didn't trust himself to speak. Only when Rhys had vanished down the deck did he allow himself to voice the moan he'd been holding.

Rhys knew. He had to have felt how much damage Anaxandros had done. Casting a glamour over the floor— even the simple caution tape Rhys suggested—sapped more of his strength than he'd hoped. He laid his sword across his thighs and leaned his head against the bulkhead.

It wasn't the loss of blood or the breeze that set him shivering, but the memory of Anaxandros's lips against his throat, the question he—*it*—had posed, and the fact that the soulless hadn't killed him.

Silas had never been afraid to die, especially during that long century of torture in Anaxandros's cave. No, death had held no terror.

That had changed. Utterly and completely.

Silas shivered again. Anaxandros had felt that change and knew its source.

"Oh, Fortuna," Silas prayed into the night, "be with Rhys. Smile on him. Bring him back to me."

RHYS BREATHED DEEPLY upon entering the tropical garden and slowed his steps a fraction. If he was a battery, this was where he could recharge, and certainly Silas needed all the energy Rhys could give him.

The damn fool kept going after Ajax—or whatever that thing's fucking name was—and nearly getting himself killed. Rhys balled his hands into fists in his pants pockets. They were still stained with Silas's blood and whatever the vampire leaked.

Silas.

Rhys stopped walking and drew in the energy of the trees. Or at least he hoped he did.

Silas wanted to stay with him. Silas loved him. They could be together in New York. It would've been a dream come true, but for the nightmare of the vampires and all that blood…

Long strides took him across the distance between the far end of the garden and the bar in moments.

Vasil—and no one else—was cleaning the empty bar. He

didn't look up from his task. "I'm sorry. We're closed. We open again at six for breakfast."

"Vasil."

At the sound of Rhys's voice, the waiter snapped his head up, and his hand froze in midwipe. "Mr. Matherton." He let go of the rag. "You're bleeding."

"It's not mine. It's Silas's. He's been injured."

A bit of color drained from the waiter's face. His lips pressed thin before he spoke. "I'm not a doctor."

"It's not that. It's the deck. We need to clean it. He can't hide the blood forever."

"Blood?" Vasil let go of the rag. "On the deck?"

"Yeah. The vampire—"

Vasil cut him off with a gesture and something that sounded like a hiss. "Don't speak of them." He sighed and glanced around the bar.

"I can help you clean up here afterward."

Vasil furrowed his brow. Then the skin smoothed. "Perhaps," he said. "Take me to Mr. Quint, and let's see how bad the deck is."

Silas was where Rhys had left him, his eyes closed, one hand wrapped around the handle of the sword resting across his thighs.

No one else was on deck—at least not in this section.

Vasil slowed to a stop and peered around the deck. "I don't see the issue."

The deck was covered in coagulating blood, smeared in some places, and the smell—how could he not notice the smell?

Because Vasil couldn't see what he did. "Silas."

Silas opened his eyes and exhaled. "You found him."

"I thought you said—" Vasil then spoke in a language Rhys didn't know. He made three quick gestures over his chest—the sign of the cross, but not in the way Rhys was used to.

Silas's chuckle was wrapped in pain. "Quite."

Rhys ignored everything but the pale, sickly cast to Silas's skin. He crossed the deck and placed a hand against Silas's forehead. Either his own skin was cold or Silas was burning with fever. "What happened?"

"Nothing." Silas brushed Rhys's hand away and then wiped his mouth with the sleeve of his coat. "Poison claws. It's a bit hard to rejuvenate a liver and fight that at the same time."

"Holy Mother of God," Vasil said.

Rhys lowered his voice and gripped Silas's shoulder. "Let me help you."

"Later." Silas didn't push his arm aside this time. "We can't afford to have both of us weakened. And you need to help Vasil."

The waiter looked about ready to heave the contents of his stomach over the railing. "How is it that you live?"

"I'm stronger than I look," Silas said. "Even now." He glanced up at Rhys during that last comment.

Vasil inspected the planks of the deck for a moment. "Do you truly work for angels?"

Rhys's face felt hot. He probably should've mentioned his conversation with Vasil to Silas at some point.

Rather than responding with anger, Silas smiled. "I do, yes." He held up his sword. The edge glinted in a manner no blade should, like a blaze of tiny stars. "A gift from them."

Vasil followed the path the blade cut through the air. "I'll help you." His gaze fell on Rhys. "I'll need your assistance."

Silas gripped Rhys's arm. "Be kind to him. He's seeing more than any mortal should."

Rhys swallowed past the lump in his throat and nodded,

and followed Vasil toward a door marked with a STAFF ONLY sign.

Vasil was mortal. But what was Rhys? Not quite human, not nearly fae. Dark tendrils of doubt crept into Rhys's mind. If he hadn't met Silas, would he be oblivious to the vampires? Would they even have noticed *him*?

Had he never spilled drinks on Silas, would he still be a normal human, as mortal as Vasil?

He couldn't pin a label on the emotions rolling inside him. What he most wanted was for Silas to be safe.

The rest he'd deal with later.

The door led to a closet with cleaning supplies inside. Vasil handed him a large squeegee on a broom handle, then hefted a coil of hose. "Your Mr. Quint isn't well, is he?"

"No." Had he not met Silas, would he even be alive? "Look, I'm sorry about all this." He gestured to the deck, to Silas. "It's a lot to take in."

"It is." Vasil dragged the hose out to a spigot and connected it. "I come from the intersection of practicality and faith. We do what we must, even when the world"—Vasil glanced at Silas—"is not what we might think."

"I wish I had your fortitude."

The look Vasil gave him was almost the same as when he'd tried to bribe the man. "You do." He aimed the hose at the bloody deck and cranked on the water. "Push the puddles toward the channel along the edge."

Rhys did as instructed, and in a short amount of time, they had the deck cleaned. Rhys washed his hands in the cold stream of the hose and dried them on his jacket. This tux he'd never wear again. With the amount of blood on it, it was fit only for an incinerator.

He and Vasil stowed the gear back in the closet. "I have no proper way to thank you," Rhys said. "Hell, I don't even know what way would be proper."

Vasil smiled. It was a tiny thing, just a slight upturn of his lips, but it lit up the man's face like a firebrand. "If you happen to see an angel, please ask him to pray for me."

Rhys caught himself against the hull. *"If you happen to see an angel."* Nothing would ever be normal in his life again. The flutter of light-headedness might have been fear or elation. "I'll remember."

They returned to Silas. He gripped the hilt of his sword so tightly that his hands appeared skeletal. Paler and thinner, he looked even more wilted than before they had cleaned the deck and far worse than the night he'd nearly died.

"My God." Vasil's voice cracked. "Mr. Quint!"

Silas wasn't glamoured. Rhys caught the waiter's arm before he touched Silas.

Vasil shook him off but didn't reach for Silas again. "He needs to see a doctor!"

"If I were to see a doctor," Silas said, his voice as thin as paper, "they'd cut me apart to see how I work." His eyes were close to black and full of pain. "Thank you, though, for your concern."

Vasil stilled. "What can I do to help?"

"Forget this night ever happened," Silas said.

"Oh, I can help with that." A man's voice—not one Rhys recognized—snaked out of the night, soft and delicate. Delectable. The air about Rhys felt like shattered ice. He stepped closer to Silas, even as he turned to find the speaker.

A man dressed in a suit as dark as the ocean at night walked toward them from the stern of the ship, hands in his pocket. With his black hair and golden, sun-drenched skin, Rhys would've mistaken him for a normal passenger had he not been smiling. Bright, jagged teeth shone in the deck lights. Inhuman and sharp.

Vasil, too, took a step back and clutched at something beneath his uniform.

Behind him, Silas cursed in a string of guttural Latin syllables.

The vampire clicked its tongue. "And here you called our people barbarians." The creature took its hand from its pockets and curled a clawed finger at Vasil. "Although you did bring me a snack. How kind."

Vasil took a step forward. *Shit.* Rhys grabbed Vasil's arm and yanked him back. The waiter stumbled onto the box of life jackets, his chest heaving.

"Little Quarter."

The need to move forward, to surrender to that voice shot through Rhys. He twisted his hands into fists, and his nails bit into his palms. The pain cleared his head. He turned to Silas—and saw terror in those eyes.

Silas couldn't stand. While upright, he leaned over the life jacket chest, his arms and legs trembling with exertion. No way he would remain on his feet if he pushed off the chest. He still gripped his sword, though.

"Oh shit."

The vampire chuckled. "You needn't worry, Quarter. Neither you nor your master will die—not tonight." It stepped closer, held out his hand to Vasil. "This one, however…"

Vasil rose and took the vampire's hand.

"Sword." Rhys touched Silas's right hand. "Give it to me."

"You don't know—"

Of course he knew nothing about swords, but this wasn't the time to argue. He wrenched the hilt from Silas's grip and ignored the hiss of pain that followed.

"Let him go." Rhys took a swing at the vampire.

It laughed, avoided the blade, and pulled Vasil against its body. Vasil, held in the vampire's embrace, faced Rhys—a living shield.

"Careful. The angels don't like it when you harm one of their precious humans."

"Rhys!" Silas hissed his name. There was pain there and fear too. The vampire must not have been kidding about the angels.

But what else could he do? He adjusted his grip and tried to find some memory of Silas's that might help.

Nothing.

Vasil's eyes tracked the blade of the sword. So he wasn't entirely in the thrall of the vampire. Whatever Vasil wore beneath his shirt, he still clutched at it.

Silas must have noticed as well. "Vasil," he said, and spoke words Rhys didn't know, but they held the same clip as the waiter's speech.

The vampire bared its teeth and answered in the same language, talking over Silas.

Vasil closed his eyes. When he spoke, it was in English. "I'd rather die by an angel's blade than from the bite of an upyr." Then he began to sing in his own tongue.

It was, Rhys realized, a prayer.

The vampire snarled. "You're a fool if you think that will save you." It bit into Vasil's neck.

The chant broke off into silence. Though Vasil mouthed words, no sound came from his lips. Tremors raced through his body.

Rhys gripped the hilt of the sword with both hands. He might not know how to swing the blade, but he damn well could run it through something. He lunged forward while the vampire gnawed at Vasil's neck and pierced its side. Smoke and the smell of searing flesh rose into the night air, as did the wail of the vampire. It let go of Vasil.

And took hold of Rhys. Claws pierced his arms. Ice and fire traced up his veins as the burning vampire held him close. "At least I'll take one of—" Flame licked out of the vampire's mouth, before its face fell inward.

"Rhys!" Arms wrapped around his waist and pulled him backward. Metal clanged against wood—he had dropped the sword. He felt nothing in his arms below where the vampire had held him. There was no way to break his backward fall.

Rhys toppled over onto Silas; then a different kind of fire burned in his arms—pain, yes. But the itch and fire was of healing flesh.

"No!" He threw himself away from Silas. He scrambled a bit farther and lay still on the deck. Cold, uneven grain ribbed his cheek and smelled faintly of damp wood and blood.

Once more, Silas called his name. This time it was a mere whisper.

"Sorry," Rhys said. "I'm not letting you die for me."

Silas didn't answer, but the metallic *clang* of his sword scraping across wood caused Rhys to sit up. What remained of the fabric of his tux was crisp and blackened. His arms were a red patchwork that looked like freshly scrubbed flesh peeking out from under flakes of burned and curling skin.

He should've been screaming in agony. Was it the poison that blocked the pain or something Silas did?

Even as he watched his arms, old skin flaked off to reveal new underneath. Healed.

"Goddamn it, Silas."

Silas sat on the wet deck, hunched over his sword. For once, Rhys was glad he couldn't see Silas's face. Something about the way he sat, the way his hands shook as they curled around the hilt of his sword, filled Rhys with fear. Maybe Silas was angry, but Rhys wouldn't let Silas hurt himself even more. If only the man would *listen*.

Near the bulkhead, Vasil groaned.

Shit. Vasil. Rhys crawled over to the waiter. Vasil clutched his shoulder, blood weeping from between his fingers.

"Let me see." He pried the waiter's fingers up and then pushed them back down. "Oh God." A chunk of skin had been torn away—bitten off.

Vasil's pupils were huge. "I can't feel my legs."

Poison claws. Poison fangs as well?

"Bring him here," Silas said, his voice harsher than the crashing waves.

"I don't think we should—"

"Now." That one word shot through Rhys like lightning and left a bitter taste in his mouth.

Vasil pressed his lips thin but nodded.

Rhys helped the waiter crawl—pulled him, really—to where Silas sat.

Gone from Silas was any sign of kindness. He said nothing, just gripped Rhys's thigh and drew a painful amount of element out of him.

His bones—his skin—ached, and he gasped for air. His heart twisted.

Silas didn't even flinch. "Vasil, move your fingers."

The waiter did as told. Silas cupped his hand over Vasil's shoulder. Silas's lips curved into a deep frown.

Lightning seared Rhys's veins as another pull of element flowed from him, and a hot coal of fury formed in his gut.

Vasil exhaled and twitched his foot. Silas folded his hands into his lap. "You may feel weak for a bit. I can't heal the loss of blood. Only time can."

"I'll manage. Thank you, Mr. Quint." Vasil shifted his gaze to Rhys. "And thank you. For my life."

"I couldn't let you die." Truth. He would've been happy to help heal Vasil, if only Silas had *asked*. Rhys's arm shook, and his fingers felt numb. *Damn it.* "But all that effort to clean the deck…"

"Not a waste." Vasil climbed to his feet. He swayed a bit but managed to walk back to the storage closet and pulled out the dented ashtray. "If we leave this, the crew in the morning will assume a drunken passenger caused some trouble." He placed the box near the pile of ash that used to be the vampire.

"Good," Silas said. "Might we use your garden?"

We. Rhys finally looked at Silas who had turned an even more unhealthy shade of yellow. His forehead glistened with beads of sweat. Fury at being used mixed with concern for Silas and turned Rhys's stomach.

Vasil brushed his hands off on his pants. "Of course."

"I promised Vasil I'd help him finish cleaning up the bar."

The sword in Silas's hand flashed as he shifted his arm. He didn't reply.

"It's not necessary." A gust of wind swirled the ash at Vasil's feet. "And I believe Mr. Quint needs your assistance more than I do." He nodded to both of them and walked toward the stern of the ship.

Silence fell over the deck. Then Silas spoke. "I owe him quite a recompense for what I have done to him."

"What you have done to him?" Rhys didn't bother to keep the anger from his voice. Emotions tumbled like rocks in his gut. Fear that Silas would die, bitterness that Silas had stolen element without thought, and terror that they'd never see morning.

Silas laid his sword down on the deck. He placed both hands on his thighs and looked at Rhys. "He can't be glamoured. He's seen too much of the truth. Bitten by a vampire. Healed by a fae." He shook his head. "He won't be able to ignore us anymore. His mind has learned how to see."

"So he's like me?"

Lines formed on Silas's forehead for a moment before smoothing out. When he spoke, his words were gentler than before. "In a way, yes."

"Then maybe he should be the one giving you assistance."

Rhys rose, turned toward the sea. The view held no comfort. He watched Silas from the corner of his eye. A cold nausea rose in his throat. All that talk about Silas not wanting to use Rhys. The arm Silas had gripped while healing Vasil still felt like lead.

Silas grunted. "Fine." He gripped the sword and used it to help him to his feet. Twice he swayed, and Rhys almost—almost—reached out to catch him.

When Silas straightened, he ran a hand through his matted and bloodstained hair. "We should discuss what just happened."

Understatement of the year. "Yes."

"I do need to sit in the garden for a bit. As I said to Vasil, there's nothing I can do about the blood loss, but the poison... Well, let's just say that Anaxandros knows quite well how to cripple me."

Rhys stared at the waves, caught between the desire to scream at Silas and the need to take the man in his arms and soothe his pain.

Silas grunted again. "Take my key card, then. I'll meet you back in my room when I've healed a bit more."

Heat touched Rhys's face. He turned away from the sea. "I didn't say I wouldn't come with you."

The key card in Silas's too-pale hand shook. "Nor did you say you would."

"I'll come," Rhys said. "I could use some time in the garden too." Despite his healed arms, his joints ached, and the tips of his fingers prickled.

Silas slid the card back into his pocket and walked toward the garden. With each step, he paused to correct his balance. At this rate, it would be dawn before they saw the inside of the greenhouse.

Rhys's throat tightened. He caught up in three short steps. "May I help you?"

There was no change in Silas's expression or tone of voice. Both remained flat. "I'd greatly appreciate that, yes."

Rhys supported Silas's trembling frame the entire walk to the garden, but the pulling of element Rhys expected wasn't there. Worry warred with his anger. Was Silas holding back out of pride? Or was he too ill to draw from Rhys? Then again, he wasn't sure how he'd feel if Silas took energy unasked from him.

When they reached the garden, Rhys helped Silas to a bench—the same one they had used before. But he didn't sit. "Try not to kill any plants this time."

"Why not?" One hand gripped the edge of the bench; the other was still wrapped around his sword. "You can heal them."

True. And he would, if needed. He could heal Silas too, if he put his mind to it. He glanced at Silas's sword. "Why don't you put that thing away?"

Silas's bark of laughter bared his teeth. "Because if I do, I won't be able to draw it again for some time. It's not an effortless task, you know."

Rhys didn't know. How could he? Silas's memories were there, yes, but they were visions and emotions. Nothing practical. He wanted to reach for Silas but couldn't decide if that was to comfort or to shake him.

If Silas had only listened, if he hadn't returned to face Anax-bastard, he'd be well. Around Rhys, life shifted and groaned as it made its way to Silas. "The sword is important. You should take better care of it."

Silas leaned back onto the bench. "Ultimately it's just a sword. Important to me, yes." He laid the blade down next to him. "But there are worse things to lose."

Rhys chewed on his tongue. Pressure built in his heart, in his head.

"I meant what I said, Rhys." Quiet words.

Everything burst. "Then why do you keep trying to get yourself killed?" Rhys spun about, looking for something, anything to grab and throw. Nothing. He slapped his hands against his thighs. "Why don't you listen to me? Why don't you ask for help?" His words echoed up to the glass roof of the garden. Palms swayed out of sync with the rhythm of the ship.

Then silence descended around them, but for the hum of the ship.

Silas shifted on the bench and rubbed his side. "I could ask you the very same set of questions."

Rhys turned on his heel and walked away, through the garden and toward the doors that led outside. White-hot fury haloed his vision. The joints of his finger ached nearly as much as his head. It wasn't until he stepped outside and reached the railing of the ship's deck on the other side of the garden that he realized why—he'd balled his hands so tight for so long that his fingers had locked in place.

He massaged his fingers and stared out at the night sky.

Damn it all to hell. He grasped for anger but found it flaming out, leaving cold despair in its wake.

"There are worse things to lose." Silas's words seemed to linger on the sea breeze, as if it were those soft words that ruffled Rhys's hair, stung his eyes.

He didn't want to lose Silas. But he was—either to the vampires or Silas's own death wish. He leaned over the railing as exhaustion seeped up his legs. What the hell was he going to do?

"Mr. Matherton?" Vasil's voice was soft, almost reverent.

Rhys lifted his head and pushed off from the rail. The waiter stood by the door to the garden. "Are you all right?"

Rhys nodded. It was a lie, but one not spoken.

Vasil glanced at the sea, then back. "I..." He rubbed his shoulder. "I've finished up. Cleaning."

Rhys nodded again.

Wind whipped the collar of Vasil's uniform. He inhaled. "I can't imagine what has happened to you and Mr. Quint. But I do know that he'd move the world for you. You should know that."

"I don't want the world moved for me." His voice sounded alien in his ears. Too broken. The sea spray must have kicked up. He tasted salt water on his lips.

"Of course not," Vasil said. "You want to move it for him."

Rhys froze.

"Good night, Mr. Matherton." Vasil slipped away, up the deck and into the night.

How long it took him to walk back into the garden, Rhys didn't know. His face was wet, his eyes stung, his breathing harsh in his ears. Thoughts flicked about his mind. Silas's laugh, the sharp hatred of Anax-bastard's snarl, his father's dismissal of him at the reading of his mother's will. The flash of a silver blade.

Rhys found Silas where he'd left him, on the bench in the garden. Silas had lain down on the length of wood. His eyes were closed.

The sword lay under the bench.

Rhys knelt down by Silas's head. "I don't want you to die."

"Nor I, you." Silas didn't open his eyes.

"I don't want you to sacrifice yourself for me."

Silas flicked open his eyes. They had returned to their warm-honey coloring. "Nor I, you."

"You didn't ask when you took energy to heal Vasil."

Silas turned onto his side and brushed two warm fingers over Rhys's cheek. "You didn't ask when you took my sword."

"There wasn't time."

Silas said nothing. Loudly.

"Damn it, Silas."

"You very nearly burned to death."

Silas's fingers against his lips stilled his next words.

"You nearly burned to death," Silas said, "because I couldn't act. Because I let myself get caught by Anaxandros. Because I let my emotions get the better of me. Again." Fire in those words. "Vasil nearly died and now has the burden of Sight, and you nearly burned to death because of my weakness."

Rhys wrapped his fingers around Silas's wrist and pulled Silas's hand away. "You're blaming yourself again."

"Who else is there to blame?"

No one. Guilt twisted in Rhys's stomach. Not too long ago, he was heaping similar words on top of Silas. He let go of Silas's wrist. "You could let me help you. I mean, really help you."

Color touched Silas's cheeks. "I don't want to."

Yes. Obviously. "Why?"

Silas stroked Rhys's cheek again. "I chose this path for me. I took the Messengers' sword. My life..." He withdrew his fingers. "Blood and ash and nights and death. That's the heart of my life, Rhys. It's far from the normal life of a fae. Why would I want to drag someone I love into that?"

Rhys fingered the burned edges of his tux's sleeves. Pieces of fabric broke off and fell to the tile floor. "But I'm already here."

Silas swallowed hard. "I know." Voice tight, he looked down at Rhys's arms. "And I'm so very sorry I've done this to you. If I'd known—" He croaked a bitter laugh. "Ah, gods."

Rhys leaned forward and kissed him, pushing his tongue against the other man's lips until Silas relented and opened his mouth. Rhys plunged in, shifting to find a less awkward angle. He cupped Silas's face and kissed him until Silas uttered a deep groan. Then he pulled back. "If I'd known, I still would've chased you down that hall."

Breathing hard, Silas lay his head back onto the bench. "Impetuous, rash—"

Rhys took his mouth again, just to shut him up. Energy swirled around them with the sweet smell of summer apple blossoms. But small lifeless spots hovered around them—and thin lines of pain. Not his own.

Silas. He broke the kiss. "Let me help you heal."

"I'm fine."

"Liar." He touched Silas's side, his arm. "I can feel—see—where you're hurt. Where you're dying."

Silas stilled for a moment. Then sighed. "That's far from fair. How am I supposed to stoically lie to you about my injuries now?"

"You're not." Rhys brushed a curl of hair out of Silas's face and sat back on his heels. "Besides, Stoics aren't supposed to lie."

"How would you know that?" A hint of amusement entered into Silas's rough voice.

"I read Marcus Aurelius in college."

"You don't know Latin, but you've read Aurelius?" Silas rubbed his face. "Americans."

He poked Silas in the side—hard. That elicited a painful hiss from his fae. "You are such an arrogant jackass sometimes," Rhys said.

"I'm an arrogant jackass all the time." He coughed a laugh and massaged the spot Rhys's fingers had hit. "It's just that some of the times you enjoy it."

True. Some of the time, that arrogance made him furious with rage—and sometimes it made him rock hard with desire. But most of the time? Most of the time, Silas's whole being made his heart squeeze tight and his mind tangle itself into knots. Right now, it was a bit of all four. He placed a hand on Silas's chest. "Will you let me help you heal?"

Silas caught Rhys's hand and kissed it before replying. "Yes."

The last of Rhys's anger melted away. He touched his lips to Silas's. This time he didn't need to badger Silas to respond —he did, deeply and passionately. But beneath that...

God.

Silas's veins burned with poison. Muted pain rippled through Rhys. He reached for the energy of the garden and pushed what he gathered into Silas.

Silas moaned and broke off the kiss.

Shit. He let go of Silas. "Sorry, I thought—"

Silas caught his arm and gently pulled him back. "Just too much, too fast." His face had lost color—or rather had become jaundiced again. "I'm not as strong as you." He paused, and spoke lower. "I'll never be as strong as you."

The inside of Rhys's skull itched. Quarter-fae. What would happen if he forced too much energy into a fae? Best not dwell on that. He reached for his element again but this time pushed a tiny stream toward Silas.

"Better," he said.

The damaging fire of the poison in Silas lessened, like a riverbed drying up. The festering death eating at Silas's side stopped and reversed. So slowly, though. So much pain in Silas. Rhys laid his head on Silas's stomach. "You shouldn't be conscious, let alone walking."

Silas stroked his hair. "Well, one good thing Anaxandros gave me was a very high tolerance for pain."

Rhys couldn't stop the shudder. "I hate that thing."

"As do I."

In his ear, Silas's heart beat a steady but quick rhythm, but his breaths came in shallow gulps. Memories—not his own—stirred in Rhys. "It's stuck its hand inside you before."

Silas stilled his hand. "Yes."

"Did it—did they—" Rhys didn't know if he wanted to ask this question. But now that he'd thought of it, he couldn't stop. "Were you raped?"

Silas's breathing slowed. "I suppose it depends on what you mean." He took another handful of breaths before continuing. "The soulless have no sexual capacity or ability. They can stir our desires, make us want them, but they themselves?" Rhys felt Silas shrug. "On the other hand, everything Anaxandros ever did to me was about taking power and will from me. About degradation."

Silas's voice was so calm, but underneath Rhys heard an unbridled wail of fear and pain. He sucked air in through his teeth.

Silas resumed stroking his hair. "There's nothing you can do to change my past."

"I know." The streams of poison in Silas were nearly dry. Another question nudged at Rhys. "What about Vasil?"

"He should feel better in a few days, as I said."

"That's not what I mean." Rhys lifted his head and sat back. He kept the trickle of energy seeping into Silas, though. "It bit him."

Silas's confused look gave way to one of clarity. "You can't become soulless from a bite."

"But the legends…" Then again, if someone could, Silas would probably be a vampire, given the flashes of memory Rhys glimpsed. Heck, he'd be one too.

"You can't lose your soul or have it taken from you. To become soulless is a choice."

"No accidental angsty vampires?"

"No. They—every last one of them—chose to be what they are." Silas sat up.

The sickly color had fled, leaving a somewhat paler but much healthier-looking Silas behind. The muscles in Rhys's

173

back unknotted, and he broke off the stream of energy. Exhaustion slammed into him. He leaned against the bench. "Is it morning yet?"

Silas caressed the back of his neck. "Look." He pointed up.

Rhys tilted his head back. Through the glass of the roof, streaks of blue and golden clouds painted a pale sky with luminescent color.

Dawn.

"Your place or mine?" Rhys said.

"Mine." Silas reached under the bench and pulled his sword out. "The bed is bigger."

"I'm not really up for anything other than sleeping." Rhys climbed to his feet, using the bench for support.

"Likewise." Silas rose, and caught himself on the back of the bench. "Mercury's balls."

The poison in Silas's blood was gone, as was most of the damage to his liver. Rhys steadied him. "I don't understand."

Silas twisted his mouth into a bitter expression. "Lost too much blood. Not a damn thing I can do about that."

Silas had told Vasil the same. Rhys wrapped one arm around Silas's waist. "Together, then?"

"For as long as you wish."

Rhys pondered that answer while they worked their way through the ship to Silas's cabin. He turned it over in his mind when they undressed, heaped their bloody clothes into a corner of the bathroom, and washed blood and ash off themselves in the shower.

When they crawled into bed, Rhys finally spoke. "For as long as I wish?"

"True Thomas never lies."

"You're not Thomas." Rhys snuggled into the length of Silas's warm body. "And you do lie."

"Yes, but not well. And not now." Silas spoke the words

into Rhys's ear. "I promise not to leave you if you wish me to stay."

"And if I wanted you to be with me forever?" He breathed in the scent of shampoo on Silas's wet hair and kissed the curls stuck against Silas's forehead.

Breath tickled Rhys's neck. "Then I best not get myself killed, eh?"

"You'd better not. *Te amo.*" He paused and then added, *"Je t'aime. Seni seviyorum. Ich liebe dich…"* By the fifth phrase, Silas trembled. By fifteen, Rhys's eyes stung. Only this time he couldn't pretend that the salt water on his cheeks and on his lips was sea spray.

He kept speaking, up to the fiftieth language. With daylight streaking across the walls of the cabin, he whispered that phrase one last time into Silas's ear. "I love you."

CHAPTER ELEVEN

For the first time in decades, Silas didn't wake from a nightmare. Isatis's lemur wasn't standing in the shadows of the room. Strange. Strange, too, was the delightful sensation of another person burrowed against his side and the smell of pine and sea grass that permeated the room.

Rhys.

The previous day's events rolled over Silas, waves of memories crashing over the moment of serenity, breaking it down and washing away his peace. *Anaxandros.*

Silas slid his hand down and rubbed where the soulless had ripped into his side. Smooth skin and an intact liver, thanks to Rhys.

He should be dead. They both should be dead.

Rhys snuggled closer in his sleep. Silas resisted the urge to run his fingers through that tangled mess of hair.

Very few people had handled his gladius and only with his permission. No one—not a single soul—had ever used it before. The Messengers had been rather explicit that this task was his and no other's. But Rhys had been correct; Vasil would've died.

Still, watching Rhys burn because of his own inability to fight—that had been worse than Anaxandros's claws crushing his liver. Worse than the humiliation of Rhys snatching the sword from his hand.

Silas rolled sideways to look at the man tucked under the covers with him. Glorious and blissful in sleep. Rhys's fae nature—the copper strands of his hair, his narrow face—peeked out from behind very human stubble and a whorled mass of hair.

No, he'd not ever get tired of waking up to Rhys in his bed.

Silas's dick, already semierect, hardened when Rhys's lips parted and a content snore issued from him. Unable to resist any longer, Silas brushed a finger over Rhys's rough stubble, savoring the glint of red among the brown hairs.

Rhys opened his eyes.

"Good morning," Silas said.

Rhys stretched, his leg sliding against the hard length of Silas's erection. "Is it still morning?" Vestiges of sleep slurred his words.

"No idea." Silas cupped the back of Rhys's head and drew him forward for a kiss. No resistance, just a murmur of pleasure that vibrated Silas's lips. He plunged his tongue into Rhys's mouth and sucked on each of his lips until Rhys squirmed against him. "Good morning," he whispered again against Rhys's swollen lips.

Rhys exhaled. "Very." He rolled, pulling Silas on top of him. "God, you're still here. This isn't a dream." Joy in his voice.

Silas didn't reply. He set about devouring those lips and that tongue.

Rhys's fingers scraped against his scalp and tugged at his hair. His hips thrust a rock-hard cock against Silas's dick.

Want and need pooled in Silas. He ground himself into Rhys and bit at his bottom lip.

Rhys's gasp and the deep groan that followed sent a spike of desire that tightened Silas's balls. He shifted and rose up over Rhys, breaking the contact between them.

Slow. He had to pace himself. His wounds and the poison were gone, but he couldn't say he was entirely over the attacks from last night. He felt better than he should've, but the tremble in his arms wasn't from lust, nor was the rapid thrum of his heart entirely the product of desire.

The angle of the sun was high. They had time. And by the gods, he wanted to hear Rhys moaning beneath him, wanted to see him thrashing with pleasure. That much, at least, Silas could give to the beautiful man in his arms who'd said, "I love you," over and over in all the languages Silas knew. And more.

Certainly that was a goal worth exhausting himself over. He leaned down and sucked Rhys's kiss-bruised bottom lip again.

"Please." Rhys's voice was a mix of sleep and desire. "I want..." He slid his hands over Silas's shoulders and down his back, warm fingers tracing pleasure over Silas's skin.

"Everything." Stubble scratched Silas's lips as he drew his mouth over Rhys's chin and kissed the cleft in the middle. He tongued those tiny hairs, nibbled at them, then wandered lower, kissing his way over Rhys's throat. He tasted of sea salt and smelled of spice. Rhys swallowed, his Adam's apple prominent for a moment. Silas licked at it.

Rhys hissed. The tug on Silas's hair grew sharper, tighter. Rhys had probably balled his hands into fists, just as he had while fucking Silas's mouth yesterday.

Silas slid his fingers over the sensitive skin on the sides of Rhys's stomach.

Thrusting upward, Rhys growled when his cock met nothing but air. "Damn it, Silas! Let me—"

When Silas rolled Rhys's nipple between his fingers, those words turned into an unintelligible string of syllables.

He'd pay for that later, undoubtedly, but it was worth the frozen wide-eyed expression of surprise. Rhys bucked and squirmed to get away from his ministrations. Silas flattened himself on top of Rhys and replaced his fingers with his mouth. Though hard, the nub of flesh yielded nicely to the play of his tongue as he licked and sucked it. Rhys's wordless cry turned into gasps and whimpers. His hands tightened in Silas's hair, and sparks danced over Silas's skin.

At some point, he'd let Rhys know just how much having his hair pulled turned him on. Right now? There were better things to contemplate. Silas scraped his teeth over the nipple. Beneath him, Rhys's whole body shook. He pulled back and loomed over Rhys.

Rhys worked hard to catch his breath. His eyes were wide with expectation—and just a hint of fear.

"I'm going to teach you a word in Latin," Silas said. After all, he'd only worked over one of Rhys's nipples.

"What word?" Rhys croaked the question.

"*Symmetria.*" He descended on the other nipple with lips, teeth, and tongue and pressed his full weight down onto Rhys to keep him still.

That didn't entirely work.

"Oh fuck." Rhys trembled and dragged his fingers along Silas's side. The heat and sting jolted like electricity to Silas's balls. He thrust his cock into Rhys's thigh. The sweet friction sent tingles of warmth through his arms and legs. He needed to feel more of that heat, but it could wait. It *would* wait.

Rhys's nipple, however… He sucked the nub between his teeth and tugged.

"God." Rhys clawed at his back. "I can't—"

Silas relented. "But you can. You will."

"Please." Rhys's voice was breathless.

He sat up and traced fingers across Rhys's chest, following the fine line of hair down to just before Rhys's cock. "Do you want more?"

Rhys sucked in a deep breath of air. "From you? Always."

Silas laughed. There was no doubt that fae blood lingered in Rhys. Wanton, lovely Rhys. "You're utterly delightful."

"And you're sexy as hell." Rhys wrapped a warm hand around Silas's cock and stroked. "Let me suck you."

There were very few things more enjoyable than Rhys's mouth around his dick. But that wasn't his aim at the moment. He brushed a finger over Rhys's lips. "Later."

Brash man that he was, Rhys took that digit into his mouth and tongued it in rhythm as the hand he stroked up and down Silas's dick. *Gods.* Lightning traced down Silas's veins, and he very nearly abandoned his plans so he could sink his cock into the wet heat milking his finger.

Silas pulled his hand free, then caught both of Rhys's arms and pinned them down to the mattress. "Later."

Rhys smiled up at him. "I thought you liked coming in my throat."

"Immensely. But I have other ideas for that lovely mouth of yours."

"Such as?"

"Moaning, screaming in abandon. Gasping. Random pleading to deities." He leaned down so that his lips hovered over Rhys's. "And that'll be before I actually fuck you."

Rhys's warm breath tickled Silas's wet lips. "Promise?"

He chuckled and then stole a quick kiss from Rhys. "Yes." He planted another kiss on his chin, his neck, his shoulder, sucking and nibbling down the length of Rhys's body. He kept his hands locked around Rhys's wrists.

When he dragged his teeth across the left side of Rhys's taught stomach, Rhys twisted and moaned.

He loved that sound. Nothing got his cock tighter than Rhys's exquisite babble. He worked his way to the dip of Rhys's belly button and plunged his tongue in.

Rhys bucked his hips. The tip of his dick slid across Silas's chest, leaving behind a trail of wetness that cooled against his skin.

"So demanding," Silas murmured. He regretted having to let go of Rhys's wrists—being caught seemed to excite Rhys even more than sex in public—but if he truly wanted to hear Rhys in ecstasy, he'd need his mouth and his hands.

He slid his fingers over Rhys's thighs, then pulled them apart. He lowered his mouth to the sensitive skin under the curly hair near Rhys's sac. Rhys tasted of salt and smelled of soap, pine, and grass.

Silas couldn't help but utter his own moan. He pushed his cock against the soft, cool sheets of the bed. *Amores above.* The urge to jack himself off was almost overpowering. Even more so when Rhys's fingers tangled in his hair and ground Silas's head into his balls.

Randy bastard. Silas wrapped his hand around Rhys's cock and ran his thumb over the slick head, while sucking one of Rhys's balls into his mouth. Thick hairs tickled his tongue as he rolled it around the hard nut and swallowed the musky taste of Rhys.

Rhys gasped and loosened his grip in Silas's hair.

He switched to Rhys's other ball.

"Oh, God." Rhys said.

Silas slid his cock along the sheets, his body aching with the need for release. Soon. But first he wanted Rhys's inarticulate cry. He nibbled up Rhys's hard length and drew his tongue over the scar left from where Rhys had been cut and kissed the head.

The velvet skin tasted of salt and the sharp tang of Rhys's seed. Silas licked deep into his slit. Silas's cock throbbed, the sweet pain mixing with the savory taste of Rhys.

Rhys had grown still and quiet but for delightful gasps and a constant shaking in his legs. Silas opened his mouth and drew Rhys in.

"Oh shit!"

Not exactly the cry Silas wanted. He'd have to do better.

He pulled Rhys into his mouth, loving the contrast from the silky head to the hard-veined length of Rhys's shaft.

Ragged breaths from Rhys heated Silas's blood. Wanting to hear more, he milked Rhys's dick with his mouth, then sucked hard. He withdrew so slowly that he could map each bump and vein as they passed beneath his lips. Rhys quivered against Silas.

Slowly he took Rhys back in. And there was Rhys's cry he so desired, a sound of abandonment and wonder. Silas answered back with a low moan he couldn't have stopped had he tried.

Now, at last, Silas could give in to his own body. He fisted his cock and then spread precome over the head and down his shaft. Need twined in Silas's belly, and his arms trembled with exertion, even as he pulled his mouth up on Rhys's cock again.

Would that they could stay like this forever, caught between pleasure and release. But even he didn't have that kind of control.

When the tenor of Rhys's moans changed, he stopped sucking on Rhys's cock.

Nails bit into his skull. "Damn it, Silas!" Rhys's voice was rough and angry.

He sat up and stroked himself faster. He wasn't about to

search out his bottle of lube, but his cock was slick enough. With one hand under Rhys's ass, Silas pushed the head of his dick against Rhys's hole.

Rhys threw back his head, his anger replaced by a throaty cry.

Silas slid the head into Rhys, then stopped. Blazing heat surrounded him and gripped Silas tight, milking him, and a flash of euphoria hazed his vision. He held himself there, savoring the moment. Gods, did he love entering Rhys. Being one with him.

Rhys closed a hand around his arm. "Don't you dare stop." There was more growl than speech in his words. Sweat had beaded on Rhys's forehead and dripped down his face. Wet lips, open mouth, he stared up. "You damn well better finish what you started."

Silas pushed himself farther in. Rhys moaned and let go of Silas's arm.

He placed his other hand under Rhys's ass as he thrust in and out. Perspiration rolled down Silas's face, into his mouth. His grunts mixed with Rhys's moans and the slap of flesh as he drove himself forward. Pinpricks danced along Silas's veins as light curled into his stomach. He fought the growing tension. *Not yet.*

Rhys bucked beneath Silas. All well and good, but anyone could do that to Rhys. Silas wanted—needed—to give Rhys more. Inscribe himself onto Rhys's memories. Brand Rhys into his being. Silas shifted angles, looking for the one that would slide him against the correct spot, the one that would shatter Rhys to pieces.

He'd better find it soon. The pool of fire in Silas threatened to blaze out of control. He couldn't hold it back much longer, though he wanted to. Wanted to hang in that sweet pain and give Rhys all he could, forever. Silas pounded in and up.

Rhys gripped the sheets with both hands and arched his back. He opened his mouth in what would've been a scream had any sound come out.

There. He slowed his strokes but hammered in harder.

Rhys squirmed and tried to reach for his cock, but Silas thrust into him before he touched himself, eliciting another shattering tremor in his body.

A different fire flared in Silas. Why hadn't any other lover given Rhys this? He'd seen enough of Rhys's past to know no one had. Anger gave way to satisfaction. Now no one else ever would. Rhys was his to love. To cherish. Entirely. Silas pistoned Rhys's ass as fast and deeply as he could.

"Oh fuck!" Rhys's eyes were wide, his hands balled into fists against the bed. He threw back his head and groaned as ribbons of spunk landed on his chest.

That cry, the sight, and Rhys's ass tightening around him cracked what little control Silas had. Lightning clouded his vision as his balls tightened. He slammed into Rhys and every inch of Silas's body seemed to cry out as he emptied himself. His yell was just as guttural and long as Rhys's.

Silas fell next to Rhys, unable to hold himself up any longer. Not any of his lovers had ever made time stop or poured such fire into his veins. His soul ached.

He'd find a way to keep Rhys alive.

Silas couldn't tell which of them was trembling more. His vision turned white about the edges and faded, his lips suddenly dry.

Oh.

Well, that had certainly been worth it. Rhys was going to be furious, though.

"God, Silas." Rhys's voice was breathless. "That was awesome!"

He felt Rhys's lips brush his cheek. "I'm glad you enjoyed

it," he whispered. Then his vision turned dark, and he fell into oblivion.

———

SILAS WENT LIMP AGAINST RHYS. *What the fuck?*

"Silas?" Rhys kissed his cheek again. No response. And none when he slid out of Silas's slack embrace.

Rhys rubbed a shaking hand through his hair. Jizz slid down his chest. *Shit.* He was still pretty high from the best orgasm of his life.

He was going to kill Silas when he woke up. If he woke up.

Hell.

Other than the sweat and mess of sex, Silas was pristine, if a little pale. He was breathing. All his wounds had been healed and the poison gone. Surely he'd have noticed—

"Damn it, Silas!" Rhys flopped down on the bed, his heart thumping.

Blood loss. Silas had said he'd probably be weak for a while, and yet the fool had gone and fucked Rhys with abandon. He should've stopped Silas, but he hadn't been awake enough to think.

Sunlight slanted in the windows. Rhys glanced over at the clock: 1:27. Not too late. He rubbed his eyes and cursed. How the hell had *he* become the smart one in a relationship with a guy more than two thousand years old? What if that asshole vampire came out in the day again? Rhys hauled himself out of the bed. He knelt down and found the hilt of Silas's sword.

Good. So if Anax-bastard showed up, he'd have a weapon. Silas would be furious he'd taken the blade. *Tough shit.* He pulled it from under the bed and made his way to the bathroom.

He left the blade on the sink counter and the door open, just in case.

Ten minutes later, he placed the sword on the coffee table and then stood in front of Silas's closet. Sadly all that remained on the hangers were slacks, collared shirts, and sedate sweaters. Everything was a bit too corporate. It was like the crap his father—

Not his father. Derrick Matherton wasn't his father.

Pinpricks ran up his arms. What was the man—that half-fae who had fathered Rhys—like? He'd never find out now. He'd taken the millions rather than the opportunity to search for him.

Perhaps that had been a mistake. On the other hand, he didn't want to be beholden to anyone, not even Silas. His inheritance granted him freedom, provided he could keep the vultures away.

He grabbed a pair of black pants and a dark blue shirt and dressed.

On the bed, Silas lay sprawled among pillows and sheets, alive but otherwise unmoving.

"Silas."

Nothing.

At least there was coffee. And room service, if it came to that. He popped a pod into the coffeemaker and brewed a cup. Wrapping his hands around the warm mug, he settled into a chair at the coffee table and waited.

Maybe it was the aroma, but as Rhys sipped his coffee, Silas stirred, rolled over, and burrowed under the sheets. A groan issued from beneath a mound of white cloth.

Rhys snorted. He might have found it endearing in any other circumstance.

A few moments later, Silas emerged from beneath the covers and sat up. He looked around the room before settling his gaze on Rhys. If he noted the sword—and Rhys was sure he did—he had no reaction to it. "How long have I been unconscious?"

Rhys glanced at the clock. "About a half hour."

Silas grunted, then scrubbed his face with his hands. "My apologies."

"What the hell were you thinking?"

"I was thinking," Silas said, his words all honey and heat, "that I wanted to see you writhing in ecstasy."

Rhys pressed his lips together and fought to hang on to anger, even as his cock threatened to harden.

Silas climbed out of bed, stumbled, then sat back down. "I don't suppose you'd be willing to get me a cup of coffee?"

Rhys rose, slapped a pod of French roast in the machine, stuck a mug underneath, and turned it on. "You shouldn't have." He watched the coffeemaker cycle through its brewing. "Don't get me wrong, it was the best damn fuck I've ever had, but there *are* more important things than sex." The machine finished.

He took the cup to Silas and sat back down at the table. He ran a finger over the leather-wrapped handle of Silas's sword.

Something in Silas's expression flickered—anger, embarrassment, Rhys couldn't tell. That changed completely when he sipped his coffee. Silas frowned into the cup. "I knew you'd be angry, but not this angry." He sighed but sipped again.

"Think of it as penance for being a complete fool." Irritation faded as he studied the blade of the sword. Faint knot work twisted up the middle channel of the blade. He'd missed that before. "It really was the best sex I've ever had."

"Good. Now I have a bar to rise above."

Good God. Rhys shifted in his chair, his balls tightening at the thought. "Doesn't mean you're not an ass for exhausting yourself."

Silas placed the mug on the side table next to the bed, and stood. This time he remained standing. "An extra half hour unconscious won't make a difference. By sunset, I'll have recovered as much as I would've otherwise."

"And had Anax-bastard shown up?"

"Anax—" Silas cuffed a laugh, but sobered. "Yes, fucking you was a risk. But then so was sleeping. Had Anaxandros come during either, we'd both be dead."

He had a point there. "I just don't want to see you the worse for wear because of me." There were no scars on Silas that he could see, no sign of injury. But his sun-kissed skin was a shade too ashen.

"I'm alive because of you."

Rhys sipped his coffee as cover for the sudden ache in his chest and throat. It didn't help. "So, what now?"

Silas wore his patented thoughtful look.

Rhys shook his head. "We're so not having sex again. Not now."

Silas waved the words away. "There are other things I can show you. But first I need to shower." With that, he strode across the cabin and disappeared into the bathroom.

Other things. Rhys chewed on those words and finished his coffee while he waited. *What other things?*

In short order, Silas emerged smelling of almond soap. He dressed—tweed pants with a black belt and a green button-down shirt, which he tucked in. Silas looked like some hot-as-sin accountant. The clothes might be corporate, but Silas would never look like a pencil pusher.

"Now come here. And bring my sword."

A voice like bourbon, velvet and rich with a bite at the end. He still must have been miffed at the whole sword thing. Rhys rose, picked up the sword, and joined Silas.

"What do you think of it?" Silas gestured at the blade.

"It's lighter than I expected." Rhys twisted his wrist, moving the blade a few inches. "It feels like I'm cutting air."

"You are." Amusement touched Silas's voice. "Your grip's wrong. Here." He grasped Rhys's arm and shifted the position of his hand and fingers on the hilt. "Better."

And it was. Rhys took an experimental swing.

Silas clicked his tongue. "Use your hips, not your arms."

That made no sense. "How the hell do you use your hips to swing a sword?"

"Have you ever played baseball?"

"Of course I have. I—" Hips. Swinging a bat. "Oh."

"Exactly."

"But that's with two hands."

"Same idea and a similar form. In a pinch, swing with both hands. Just aim for the soulless's neck, if it comes to that again."

Vampires. Though the sword didn't weigh any more, it suddenly seemed more substantial in Rhys's hand.

"Or stab, as you did last night. But pull back or let go."

The sharp memory of the flesh curling as it burned caused him to ball his free hand into a fist. "Do they usually go up that fast?"

"Sometimes. It depends on the age and the wound." Silas stepped back and seemed to study him. "I want you to try something."

"I don't think I can learn sword fighting in a day."

"You can't." Silas rubbed his chin. "But if you're willing, it wouldn't be a bad skill to learn." Rhys opened his mouth, but his reply was forestalled by Silas raising his hand. "It's not something you need consider now."

Rhys nodded. If—when they reached New York, the possibilities were endless. "What do you want me to do?"

"Feel the sword in your hand, the weight, how the grip feels against your skin. The texture of the hilt when you shift your fingers. Imprint that into your mind. Remember it as if your existence depended on recalling this moment."

Closing his eyes, Rhys focused on his hands. He'd done this type of thing before, memorizing the shape and texture of items. It helped when sculpting. He flexed his fingers, felt the slide of the leather wrap against his palm, the cool kiss of the guard along his forefinger and thumb. "Okay."

"Keep your eyes closed." Footsteps on carpeting, then the gentle heat of Silas standing behind him. Almonds and pine. "And focus. On the hilt, please."

Warmth suffused Rhys's face. "I am focusing." He turned his attention back to the sword.

"Now imagine that the air to your right is solid, that you can pierce it with the tip of the sword. See the blade slip through this space, as if reality were a sheath."

Silas had done that, pushed the sword into somewhere else. His heart fluttered. What happened if he got this wrong? "All right."

"Now sheathe the sword."

Rhys kept his eyes closed, painting a picture of his movements. As he cut into the air, a pressure that he hadn't felt when swinging the blade ran down the length of his arm. He pushed against that, shoving the sword deeper into the slit he'd painted in reality.

Ice bit into his hands, and cold tendrils wrapped his wrist.

"Let go, Rhys."

He did, opening his eyes in time to see his hand missing from the length of his arm before he snatched it back from a swirling mass of...something. Light? Dark? The hole in the air snapped shut.

Rhys flexed his fingers. The sword was gone.

"Well done." Silas kissed the back of his neck and pulled him tight against his warm body.

Holy hell. Rhys stared at the spot where the sword had

been. The tingling in his spine had nothing to do with Silas for a change. He looked at his hand. "Why'd you want me to memorize how the sword felt?"

Silas's chuckle vibrated against his back. Hot breath caressed his ear. "Because now you're going to pull it out."

Put his hand back in there? "You've got to be kidding."

"Frightened?" Amusement in that honey voice, and a hint of mockery.

"You're an ass. You know that?"

Another kiss to the nape sent a shudder through Rhys. "Yes, actually, I do," Silas said.

Bastard.

Terrified was a more apt description. The freezing slickness that had wrapped around his hand while it wasn't here chilled him to the marrow. But knowing how to draw a sword out of thin air... Well, that could come in handy.

He clenched his hand, shook it out, then closed his eyes and plunged it back into that awful place.

God, it was cold. Something that felt like feathers tickled across the back of his hand. Where the hell was the sword?

Silas's voice rang in his ear. "The hilt, Rhys. Remember."

He did. And then it was there in his hand. He tightened his grip and pulled the sword free. When he opened his eyes, the blade was there, diamond edge sparkling in the sunlight pouring in from the windows.

"Well, shit," Rhys said.

Silas laughed, rolling peals of pure amusement and love.

This time the tingling in Rhys's limbs had everything to do with Silas. "You're going to tell me I shouldn't be able to do this, aren't you?"

"It's a fae trick, to store things in the Aether. You've enough fae blood."

"But it's your sword."

"Ah, yes." Silas sobered. He took the sword from Rhys's

hand and stepped away to twirl it in the sunlight. He frowned. "The Messengers gave the blade and the burden to me. But you've used it once. You may need it again." In a flash of light, he slid the sword into nothingness.

"How do you do that so quickly?"

"Practice," Silas said. Then he smiled.

Shit. "Again?"

"Until you can draw it without thought."

"Really, really an ass."

Silas stepped forward, cupped Rhys's chin, and pulled him into one of those devouring kisses that set every nerve in his body on fire. When Silas broke it, he spoke. "Yes."

God, this man. "Fine."

He was able to draw the sword five more times before his hand turned numb. It had gotten easier and quicker. Not as fast as Silas, but his final draw before he dropped the sword onto the cabin floor and cupped his frozen hand against his chest had been deemed acceptable by the rat-bastard-fae he loved.

Silas took Rhys's hand and held it between his. "That's why speed is important."

"Yeah, I get that now." Rhys snorted. "You could've warned me."

Silas shrugged and let go. "It wouldn't have helped. The first time is pretty much the same for everyone." He bent to retrieve the sword but swayed when he stood.

Rhys caught Silas when he stumbled and righted him.

"I'm fine," Silas said, but he didn't struggle against Rhys's support.

"You don't look fine." Too pale. Silas's skin had a sudden clammy feel to it. Rhys walked him over to the edge of the bed. "Sit."

Silas rubbed his forehead, sat, and slid his sword back into nothing.

Aether. It was a freaking scary place, whatever it was.

"You need to rest," Rhys said.

A gesture from Silas dismissed that idea. "I need to eat."

And at those words, Rhys's stomach rumbled.

Silas chuckled.

"We could order room service."

"No." Silas looked up. "I want to feel the sun on my skin. Hear the laughter of others. Smell the salt air." There was a wistful but melancholy tone to his voice.

Silas still thought he was going to die. *Damn it*. Rhys brushed his fingers against Silas's cheek. "We're going to be okay."

A ghost of a smile might have flickered across Silas's lips. "Quam minimum credula postero. I have no trust in the future." He stood and framed Rhys's face with his too-pale hands. "But you give me hope." This time the smile, though slight, stayed.

Rhys swallowed, his throat once more too tight to speak.

Silas released him. "Come. Let's try the buffet on the lido deck. I suspect they'll have what I want."

It seemed like Rhys's stomach was better at communicating, since it growled a hearty response.

Silas's smile grew. He held out his hand.

Rhys took it.

CHAPTER TWELVE

*A*las, the buffet had no liver, so Silas settled for steak, cooked rare, a haunch of lamb, and a salad of spinach and chickpeas. It was a start, iron-rich foods. Not that they would help that much before nightfall.

But after? It took effort not to dwell on the possibilities that lay along that road, not to give in to the warmth of delight and hope that lurked in the shadows of his heart.

He and Rhys had made their way outside to the sunny side of the deck. Windy, but it was warm enough for June, even on the open sea. Rhys eyed the contents of Silas's plate but said nothing. He'd chosen lighter fare, despite the rumblings of his loud gut—fruit, salad, and a small hunk of seared salmon. A wise plan if they had to run tonight.

They would. Two soulless, likely older ones, plus Anaxandros.

Silas put down his fork. Why hadn't Anaxandros killed him? The opportunity had been there. After two thousand years, did the soulless simply wish to recapture him? That made little sense. Surely there had been other fae. The occasional stories that surfaced told him that. Why taunt? Why not kill and take Rhys?

He should've hunted Anaxandros years ago. Yet another failure to crown the heaping pile of inadequacy. *The great Silvanus. Hah.*

"Silas?"

He retrieved the fork from his plate. "Just thinking."

"About?" Rhys sat back in his chair and toyed with his water glass. A charming furrow formed between his brows.

Silas took another bite of lamb, stalling for a bit before speaking. "Anaxandros. He's..." *Jupiter's balls!* He fisted his hand into a ball and tried again. "It's toying with me, but I don't know why."

"Because it gets off on your pain?"

There was truth there, yes. This was an old, familiar game, to some extent. Still... "I'm sure it does. But Anaxandros wants something more from me, more than agony, more than despair." Silas certainly had given more than enough of that during his captivity. "It vexes me."

Rhys fell quiet for a moment. "I think you're the only person I know who would seriously use the word 'vex.'"

Silas ever so gently kicked Rhys in the shin. "'Vex' is a fine word."

"It's an old word." Rhys stabbed a piece of pineapple.

"It's a Latin word."

He pointed the fruit-laden fork at Silas. "I rest my case." He popped the pineapple into his mouth, looking far too smug.

Americans. "Half the words you dribble from that pretty tongue of yours are Latin." He cut into his steak. "And you do realize that I'm as old as 'vex.'" Silas saw the trap Rhys had laid as the words left his mouth.

"Well, you certainly are vexing."

Silas kicked him again, harder this time. Rhys laughed.

That was contagious enough. He found himself joining in until the joy overwhelmed him.

Gods. Silas set down both his utensils and ran a hand over his suddenly damp eyes. When was the last time he'd sat so with anyone, let alone a lover?

He didn't remember. Even with his very few friends, he'd never opened himself up this much.

"Silas?" Humor had fled from Rhys's voice.

He waved the concern away and looked up. "You're absolutely marvelous. Even if you are a complete git. And that"—he pointed his fork at Rhys—"is from German."

Rhys snorted.

"Now let me eat in peace." He failed horribly to keep the laughter from those words.

This, the arguments and the humor, and the companionship. Desires of his heart. Everything he'd lost when Anaxandros killed his court. Everything he could build with Rhys.

If they survived.

If.

Hope squeezed his heart. *When.* They would survive. They had to. The alternative was too horrible to contemplate.

They ate in silence, Rhys's leg pressed against his under the table, until a waiter came and took their plates.

Rhys shifted his chair to stare out into the sea. "Why doesn't he want to know me?"

Silas's shifting mood had become infectious, it seemed. "Pardon?"

"My father." Rhys wrapped his fingers around the arm of his chair. "My biological father."

The half-fae. Silas sat back. "That may not be his motive at all."

Rhys turned back from the sea. "Why else would he have given me hush money?"

Oh, this would be an interesting conversation. "As I said before, most of what I know about quarter-fae is myth. But here's something to consider. All that you—" He stopped and corrected himself. "All that we've done together here, we've done while floating in an ocean with only a greenhouse garden to draw on."

Rhys furrowed his brows. This was obviously not the answer he'd been expecting. A moment later, however, understanding dawned across his face. "What we'll be able to do on shore..." Rhys rubbed a hand over his gaping mouth. "Oh shit."

Indeed. "A new set of issues, for sure. Quarters are mythic for a reason."

"What will happen to us?"

"I'm not sure. You'll be noticed by the courts. I don't think there's a way to avoid that."

Rhys shifted in his chair but kept silent.

"Do you want me, Rhys? Want me by your side?" He knew the answer.

"Yes."

"Then there's not a being in this world that will keep us apart."

Rhys glanced out to sea, his jaw working. "Even Anaxandros?"

So Rhys did know the soulless's full name. Silas held out his hand. "Not even Anaxandros."

Rhys nodded and twined his fingers with Silas's. "About time you came around."

That forced an honest chuckle from Silas. Three days. Why did it seem longer?

He brushed a thumb over the back of Rhys's hand. "What do you think a court might do if they knew a half-fae was fertile?"

Rhys reacted as if someone had slapped him. He jerked

197

back, his hand slipping from Silas's. After a moment, he stood. "You can't tell me that they would—" Rhys made a croaking sound, and sank back into his seat. "That they would force him to have more..." He fell silent, trembling.

Most likely in rage. It was an abhorrent idea, one he'd never abide. "Not all courts. Not even most. But some, yes. I said fae are passionate. Some let the passion for control and power consume them."

A deep frown and clenched fists were Rhys's only answer.

"If I were a half-fae who fathered a quarter, I'd hide," Silas said. "For both that child's sake and for my own."

A change in the wind whipped Rhys's hair, setting the copper highlights ablaze in the afternoon sun. Element seeped around them, twisted up Silas's legs like a caress. He doubted Rhys even knew what he was doing, so focused was he on the thoughts in his head.

Finally he spoke. "If we could find him, would you protect him? From the courts?"

The question sent a prickling up the back of Silas's neck. He'd had plenty of offers to join various fae courts. Refused them all. "I don't know if I could."

Rhys's lips formed a very thin and pale line.

"It's not a lack of desire, Rhys. I have power, yes. I'm old, yes. But the courts leave me alone because I'm of little concern to them."

The muscles near Rhys's right eye twitched. "That'll change, won't it? When we reach New York?"

"Yes." Silas folded his hands in his lap. It kept him from gripping the edge of the table. "I'm not without resources, and I do have a few favors I can call on."

"But if we find my father?"

"There are not enough strings in this world to pull to keep the courts from hounding us."

The deep thrum of the ship's motor changed pitch for a

moment. Rhys exhaled. "That doesn't exactly sound like a fun life to live."

"No." Silas reached across the table, palm up. Rhys covered Silas's hand with his own. Warm, a slight tingle of element. "But if you wish it, I'll do all within my power to keep you and yours safe."

"But you said—"

"I said I didn't know if I could. I never said I wouldn't try."

Astonishment filled Rhys's expression in the same manner that a sharp clap of thunder might shock someone. His mouth worked, but no words came forth.

Silas couldn't help but smile. That earned him a bruised shin of his own.

"Bastard." The word was wrapped in affection.

If only they could stay like this for the rest of the cruise. If only.

Damn the Messengers. Or bless them. Looking at Rhys, Silas couldn't decide which.

His sudden change in mood must have been noticeable. Rhys squeezed his hand. "Do you have a plan? For tonight?"

No. He had nothing. "We've lost the element of surprise. Our trick from last night won't work again." It would've never worked on Anaxandros, anyway. He must have been— He. "Juno's tits."

Another squeeze. "We'll work something out."

Silas stifled the urge to sigh. "I suppose the only thing to do is to hunt. We wait until dark, find them, and kill them."

Rhys snorted. "Easy as ice cream."

So very young. But not at all naive, despite his flippancy. Silas studied the man who held his hand. His fae blood had sharpened his features, coppered his hair, but there was something still so very human about him, most likely that sense of cocky assurance.

It might save them both. "Your thoughts?"

Rhys tapped his water glass and chuckled. "You won't like it."

"Probably not."

"We hunt now. During the day." He picked up his water glass and sipped. "And if we don't find them, then we wait in hiding and pick them off as they hunt us."

He pulled his hand from Rhys's. "We have no idea where their—"

Rhys had enough manners not to smirk, not to gloat. He sat there, as calm as any Stoic.

Silas stood. Of course they knew where the soulless's lair was. It was on the boat. Probably internal, likely deep in the bowels. Hunting alone, it had always been too dangerous to confront the soulless in their stronghold. He walked to the rail and stared down at the twirling white ripples along the side of the hull.

Behind him, a chair scraped across the deck. Rhys wrapped his arms around Silas, kissed the back of his neck. Pine and sea grass. "Stop berating yourself."

There was no point in asking how Rhys knew his thoughts. Predictable. Constant. Like the little cyclones of white that spun out from the boat to be lost in the churn of the ocean waves. He didn't bend into Rhys's embrace. "I'm better than this."

"I know." Rhys didn't let go. "I remember."

Hades. Those memories. "For that I'm sorry. I should've never—" Rhys's fingers pressed against his lips, blocking the words. He knew the taste of that skin.

"Let's find the fucker and put a stake through his heart. Or a sword. Or whatever."

Silas had to blink back the salt spray when he opened his eyes. "It's a good plan. I'm not sure I would've thought of it."

He felt Rhys's laugh. "Good. Then the bastard won't expect it, will he?"

No. While Anaxandros knew him, the soulless didn't know Rhys. Deep within, the shuttered spark of hope flared to life. Minerva bless them both with wisdom and strength.

They were going to need it.

———

COFFEE. Rhys needed coffee to get his mind in gear. Not just the drip-brewed stuff at the buffet, but a nice, hot double shot of espresso. Thankfully, the boat had a coffee bar by the library.

He glanced back and grabbed Silas's hand. Damn everyone else on the ship if they had an issue. Last thing he needed was to lose Silas to the crowd around them. Midafternoon seemed to be a very popular time to roam the decks.

Silas wasn't well. Worse, he didn't seem to notice his ill health. Pale and shaky, he wasn't putting much into his glamour, given the looks he was garnering. Rhys attempted to push element toward Silas, but he couldn't concentrate on that while walking.

Silas's mind certainly wasn't in the game. Not that Rhys blamed him. Flashes of memories not his own had been intruding into his thoughts over the past day. Scarred didn't even begin to express Silas's mental state.

But there was a will so strong there—strength Rhys doubted he could match, not in the face of that much pain for that long.

He understood now how someone could rip apart a vampire. He certainly had that desire.

"Two double-shot cappuccinos to go, please."

The woman behind the bar nodded and set to work.

"Cappuccinos," Silas murmured, then shook his head. "What?"

"Somehow I don't think we'll find what we're looking for at the bottom of a cup." The dry tone, as whip sharp as it was, warmed Rhys's heart.

Good. This was the Silas he needed now, the arrogant one. He handed one of the paper cups over. "Fuel for the road." He took the other.

"If only we had a map."

Rhys glanced over at the entrance to the library. "Librarian."

"What?"

Oh, he'd regret this. "You know, book person. From the Latin?"

Silas choked on his coffee. His expression moved from shock to annoyance, then straight into that smile he got whenever he thought about sex.

Yup. That would cost. But in a good way. "Come on."

"If we didn't have other plans..." Silas trailed his warm fingers down the back of Rhys's neck.

"I'll hold you to that." But later. Last thing he needed was Silas passed out again. Rhys stepped around two ladies filling out a giant crossword puzzle printed on a table and headed toward the back of the library.

The librarian was a woman with short black hair and three piercings in her left ear. She smiled as they approached. "How can I help you gentlemen?"

Rhys matched her smile. "Well, this is kind of odd, but do you have a map of the ship?"

"There's a digital map on every level by the elevators. Touch screens." Her cheerful tone didn't waver, though creases formed in the corners of her eyes.

"We're actually looking for the ship plans," Silas said.

"My friend was curious to know what all those other decks are used for."

"Oh!" The tightness around her eyes vanished. "There's an old copy of the plans hanging in the aft stairwell between decks eleven and twelve. It's not quite accurate, but it's very close."

"Excellent." Silas sipped his coffee. "Thank you."

"Anything else I can help you with?"

Rhys stifled the urge to ask for a Latin-to-English dictionary. "Nope. Thanks."

He let Silas lead the way to the map. Once off of the main entertainment decks, the crowds thinned down. Only cleaning staff roamed the halls, wiping down banisters, refilling hand sanitizers, and vacuuming. The crew must have been working their way down the ship. Once Rhys and Silas climbed past deck ten, they saw no one.

The map—ship's plan—spanned the entire wall of the landing between decks eleven and twelve and included a cross section of the ship and detailed deck plans for every deck—even the ones without any cabins.

"It's huge," Rhys said. "I hadn't thought…"

Silas rubbed his chin. "Well, we can discount all the cabins with windows, I should think. I doubt any of Anaxandros's followers can stand the light."

That made sense. "If only we knew the names they used to board."

"It's highly unlikely they bought tickets." Silas swirled his coffee cup. "That would require the whole check-in procedure. Photographs. Passports. Documentation. It's rather a bother."

That never occurred to him. He inspected Silas's profile. "You have all that?" And what did he look like in a photograph anyway? Did his glamour appear on camera?

Silas shrugged. "I do. To live in the world, you need such things now."

Vampires didn't live. They preyed. Rhys suppressed a shudder. "How? I mean, I guess they're faked, but you'd have to keep getting..."

Silas turned. "I have an exceptionally good lawyer." The amusement in his expression shifted to worry. "If I don't survive..."

"Don't."

"Please. This is important."

"You're not going to die." Rhys stepped closer to the map. "So there's nothing to discuss."

Stillness behind him, then a sigh. "Do you know who Justin Peters is?"

That lawyer? Good God. A million bucks an hour, or something like that. Rhys placed a finger on the engine area. The decks below that held fuel, water, and ballast. "Of Peters, Sebastian, and August?"

"Yes." Silas paused. "If something ever happens to me, go to him. He'll know what to do."

"Nothing's going to happen to you." Rhys studied the map as best he could, considering his damn eyes kept blurring. "I don't want to talk about this."

Silas kept his mouth shut. All he did was brush the back of his hand over Rhys's cheek.

Rhys jerked away. "Are you going to help me here or not?" If Silas kept talking like this, he'd lose it. Life without Silas was incomprehensible. There was no other path. He tapped the map. "Shall we start here?"

Silas studied the layout. "Near the engines would be too hot," he said. "The smells would carry too much." Flat tone, clipped accent. No emotion.

Smells. This time Rhys couldn't suppress the chill that ran down his body. His heart ticked up a beat as a memory of cold darkness, the sharp stab of heat, and the ever-present scent of earth and blood invaded his senses. Silas's memory. Someone rooting around in his side.

Rhys ripped off the lid of his cup and downed the rest of his coffee—as warm as it was—in one gulp. His eyes stung. "The storage areas, then." His voice sounded rough and high to his ears.

"It's a good place to start." Silas moved closer and wrapped his free arm around Rhys's waist.

They stood like that for some time, staring at the ship plans. It was only once he stopped that Rhys realized he'd been trembling.

Finally Silas spoke. "It happened long ago."

"But it did happen." The torture. The pain.

"Yes."

The bitter but comforting smell of coffee drifted between them, a much better scent than the iron tang of blood. "I'm going to make sure nothing like that ever happens to you again." The words poured from Rhys, from his soul. "If I have to beg the angels to make me a sword."

"Are you to be my protector, then?"

"Aren't I already?"

Silas pulled him closer. "The world is certainly strange and full of surprises. Even after all these years."

Rhys took Silas's cup, shoved it into his own, and then planted a kiss onto Silas's lips. "We should get started."

Silas caught Rhys's face in his hands before he could pull away. "I love you."

Those words. That look. Rhys's vision blurred again. "I'm not losing you."

"But if—"

"Silas." He said the name like a command. It seemed to work, because whatever protest had been on Silas's lips died. "Promise me. Promise me you won't leave me."

"I'll try not to."

"Not good enough." Rhys caught one of Silas's wrists and held it as tightly as he could. "Promise me."

Time seemed to slow as a struggle played out over Silas's expression. At last he shrank in defeat. "I promise I will do everything within my power to stay with you."

It wasn't exactly what he wanted, but it would have to do. Rhys kissed him. Not a peck, either, but a kiss that would've dragged them both into bed, had there been one.

Had they the time. If Silas weren't so hurt.

Rhys broke the kiss. "I love you too." He moved away, tossed the cups into the trash, and looked back at Silas, who stood exactly where Rhys had left him.

He recognized that dumbstruck expression, pretty sure he'd worn it himself at some point in the past three days. "We should start. While it's still light."

Silas nodded. "Let's go, then."

They headed to the nearest elevator.

———

TWO HOURS LATER, they had searched through the cramped storage areas and even the hot engine area. No signs of any vampires.

"Fuck." Rhys scrubbed a hand over his face. Silas's color hadn't improved. If anything, he seemed more drained. Maybe from the heat, maybe from the glamour he had to cast to hide them. He'd tried to push energy into Silas, but nothing seemed to improve. As far as he could tell, there was no flow to Silas. Which either meant he couldn't accept any element or he refused to.

Silas wiped a pale hand across his brow. "So we scout through the unused interior cabins."

"We should rest for a bit." Maybe if he concentrated more.

Silas peered upward, as if looking through the decks. "Perhaps. There's still some time before sunset. But if Anaxandros is about..." He pushed through a doorway into a service stairwell.

They started to climb. If that vampire found them first, they were in a heap of trouble. "How the hell are we going to know which cabins are free?"

Silas didn't answer. Probably because he was gulping down air as they ascended the stairs.

Rhys watched the play of fabric stretch across Silas's ass. *Nice.* Too bad he could also see the slight tremble in his legs. "Are you okay?"

Silas paused on the landing, his breathing shallow and fast. "I'd say yes, but you'd know it for a lie. But I'm as well as to be expected." He turned the corner and continued up. "I'll manage."

Crap, crap, crap. But what else was there to do? Rhys ran after him. "We could rest until sundown. Maybe if you slept?" He knew the likely answer but asked anyway. "Or the garden?"

At the next landing, Silas leaned against the door but didn't open it. "I need time, Rhys, to heal. We have none." He pushed through the door on to the lowest of the common levels. "As to your earlier question, I'm going to check the ship's hotel computer system, find the records we need, then borrow a master key card."

Rhys followed through the door. "You're going to do *what*?" This was the same man who chided him for trying to bribe Vasil?

"I'll need you to sit out by the front desk and provide a distraction." At the elevator, Silas punched the Up button and leaned against the wall.

"Do you even know how to use a computer?"

Silas drew himself up to his full height. "Likely better than you do." A healthier color washed over him as Rhys felt the unmistakable pull of element.

Ah, so he'd been holding back, the arrogant asshole. "Well, you *are* stuck in a different era."

The elevator dinged. Rhys entered, Silas close behind. The pull of element increased. Silas punched the main deck.

"What, pray tell, is that supposed to mean?"

"Pray tell?" Rhys mimicked Silas's accent. "You're about as modern as ice skates with keys."

Silas opened his mouth, and snapped it shut. A moment later, he burst into laughter.

"What?"

The elevator slowed to a stop; then the doors opened.

"You," Silas said. "It's roller skates that had keys." He sauntered out of the elevator.

Rhys had to hurry to follow Silas's spectacular ass before the elevator doors snapped shut. "Ice skates, roller skates."

Silas stopped by the grand staircase, near a cluster of chairs that faced the front desk. "I know what you're trying to do." He leaned near Rhys's ear. "And I thank you for the thought. But I want you to keep as much energy as possible for later."

Heat rushed to Rhys's face. "You're not well."

Silas shrugged in his infuriating manner. "I'm not so horrible that I can't function. And if Anaxandros is about, it's better he think me worse than I am."

Oh. Rhys dropped his voice and gripped Silas's shirt. "You could've *told* me, you know."

"You think better when you're worried or angry."

Warmth washed over him, followed hotly by fury. "You little—"

Silas stopped his words with a kiss that tingled every

nerve in his body, from the tips of his ears down to his little toes. Desire coiled in his belly.

When Silas broke away, he whispered in Rhys's ear. "No glamour, my love."

This time it was heat that chased through his body. He probably had a blush so bright it would light a dark room. What conversation there had been in the area had gone silent.

"Wait here." Silas spoke loudly enough to be overheard. "I'll be back in a bit."

"Right," Rhys croaked, and sank down into a chair as Silas walked away. A quick glance around confirmed his fears. Everyone looked at him. Or at Silas. Or between the two of them. One woman tucked away her cell phone.

Rhys cleared his throat and leaned back. Well, that'd probably put a stop to his womanizing rumors. At least for a while.

Really, he couldn't do any better than Silas. Rhys brushed the back of his hand over his mouth and tried not to laugh.

A few moments later, Silas returned, but this time no one noticed. Rhys picked up a newspaper from the table to his right and flipped through it while trying not to watch Silas slip behind the front desk counter.

Now he wore a glamour. One so good, no one saw him as he sat at an unused terminal. A minute or so after that, he scooped up a piece of paper from a printer, slipped past the man behind the desk, and lifted a key card.

Holy hell. Fae were born thieves. Rhys struggled not to stare as Silas worked.

Silas slid back out into the lobby and vanished around a corner. Rhys continued to not read the newspaper until he felt the press of Silas's fingers on his shoulder. "Back so soon?" He leaned back and looked up at Silas, who stood behind him.

Not nearly as pale as before, Silas smiled and kneaded Rhys's shoulders. "Shall we go somewhere more private?" The rich, deep tone of that question fired Rhys's blood and dried his mouth. *God.* What Silas did to him.

"Sure." He folded the newspaper, set it down, and then rose.

A number of folks in the lobby still watched them, some with admiration, others with curiosity. A few with fear. He ignored them all and followed Silas to the elevators.

Rhys dropped his voice to a near whisper. "I'm going to fuck you so damn hard the next time I get a chance."

When the elevator opened, Silas pushed him inside. "I'll hold you to that." He hit the button for deck four before he leaned against the wall. "Thanks for providing such an enticing distraction."

"I think that was your kiss." He still felt that warmth of Silas's lips, the plunging of his tongue.

"I've never kissed anyone in public like that before."

Rhys would've laughed, but the seriousness in Silas's tone and in his expression spoke truth.

"Not even Isatis?"

"No, not even Isatis."

The elevator opened. Once more Rhys had to rush to follow Silas before the doors closed on him. In two thousand years? Never a passionate kiss in public?

There was no lie in those words, though. "I've changed you." How could that be possible?

Silas drew a piece of paper from his back pocket and unfolded it. "You have, yes." He paused, as if choosing his next words. "Mind you, that is not such a bad thing." He handed the paper to Rhys.

Room numbers. All the unoccupied rooms on the ship, the ones the staff didn't need to clean until they arrived in

New York. One hundred five in all. "This is a crap-load of rooms."

"Ah, however, all but twenty-five are external." Silas pointed to a second column.

So they were.

They searched, very carefully, starting with the cabins on deck four. Nothing.

Nor on five or six. Seven had no cabins, and eight only had balcony rooms. As they exited the elevator on nine, Rhys's skin itched. His room was on this deck.

"I think I'm going to be very wigged out if they're my neighbors."

Silas scanned the room list. "There's only one unoccupied interior room on this level."

Much to Rhys's relief, it was like all the others. Empty of anything other than furniture, fixtures, and towels.

Two unoccupied rooms stood next to each other on deck ten. As they approached, Silas clasped Rhys's wrist. Pulled him to a stop.

"What?" And then he felt it. A tug of element, but not toward Silas. Every hair on his neck rose.

Here. They were here. Sandwiched between Silas's deck and his. *Holy shit.* "They must have felt everything."

Silas's face was unreadable. He reached into the tumult of the Aether and drew his sword. "Stay back. Behind me."

The pull came from the door to their left. Cabin 1013.

Figures.

Silas unlocked the door and pushed it open. Stillness from inside. And something else—the sticky smell of decay. Silas's sword was already in motion when he ran into the room.

Rhys remained outside, waiting. The stillness shattered into an unnatural howl, followed by an angry guttural cry.

"Rhys!" Silas shouted. A vampire burst through the door and hit the opposing wall. It recovered quickly. No beautiful seduction here, this one came at Rhys with fangs and claws, its face twisted into a snarl. He threw himself down the hall away from the thing but tripped as the boat bobbed, and he fell onto the carpeting.

No way Silas could save him. No time. Rhys plunged his hand into the Aether in hopes that something—anything— would be there. A familiar touch of leather against his skin, then the sword was in his hand. A moment later, the vampire impaled itself on it. Flame burst out of the vampire's leering mouth and blackened its teeth. Eyes boiled off with a hiss. Hot ash stung Rhys's face as he scrambled backward away from the sudden inferno consuming the vampire.

Rhys choked back the bile rising in his throat. The smell of charred flesh lingered in the hall. Rhys stared at Silas, who stood, sword in hand, just outside the cabin door.

No alarms. No sprinklers went off. Silas let go of the door frame, took two steps forward, then stopped. He stared at the floor.

The sword Rhys had pulled from the Aether lay on the carpet amid a pile of ash. Rhys sat up and touched the hilt.

Yup. Real. Just like the one in Silas's hand. "Oh my God."

"I thought…" Silas took another step forward, and ash fell from his blade. "When you drew before…" He stopped. "Pick it up. We need to get out of here."

"But—"

Silas's tone changed to a command. "Now. Anaxandros will have heard that."

Shit. Rhys staggered to his feet and grabbed the sword. "Which way?"

"Whichever is fastest to the outside."

"That would be behind me, Quintus."

Rhys dodged to one side as Silas skittered down the hall, his whole body pale and tense. His eyes were wide.

Anaxandros stood between them and the closest set of

elevators, as well as the only outside deck on this level. In his hand, he held a black blade twice as long as the ones Rhys and Silas carried. Looking at it made Rhys's stomach churn. Something about the metal—it crawled through his mind.

"Run," Silas said.

He didn't have to say that twice. They tore down the hall toward the other set of elevators, Anaxandros's laughter pounding off the walls behind them.

Rhys hit the door marked STAIRS and pushed it open.

"Down," Silas called. They both half ran, half jumped down to the next landing.

And then Silas screamed.

A knife jutted from his shoulder, and he bounced off the stairwell wall into Rhys, nearly sending him tumbling down to the next level.

"Get it out!" Raw words. Silas flailed wildly but couldn't remove the blade without dropping his sword that he clutched so hard his fingers had turned white.

Rhys wrapped his hand around the hilt of the knife, and it seared into his flesh. He shouted as agony traced up his arm, but he ripped the knife out of Silas anyway. The flesh of his hand didn't blacken—it turned gray, then white, rimmed with red. His whole hand hurt as if he'd stuck it in glowing coals.

Silas shoved him. "Go!"

Too late.

Anaxandros landed on the platform and kicked Silas down the next flight. The cry and the sick thud that followed turned Rhys's vision red. He dodged. The vampire's black sword screamed as it cut nothing but air.

Rhys gripped his sword like a bat and swung. The tip scraped along Anaxandros's chest. Smoke curled into the air. The vampire hissed and stepped back.

That gave Rhys enough time to flee. He jumped down the stairs to where Silas stood near the door to deck nine.

Silas stood. *Thank God.* But his left arm was bent in a way no bones should ever be. Silas kicked open the door. "Aft. There's a deck aft."

Sunlight. They sailed east. There'd be sun behind them. As they ran, Rhys didn't dare look back. From the thudding footsteps, the vampire had to be close. At the same time, they pushed through the double doors to the small observation deck and shot out into the sunlight. Silas crumpled against the rail. Rhys turned to face the vampire.

Aside from a few deck chairs, they were alone. But the murmur of passengers on deck eight filtered up from below.

The vampire was still fucking tall, still had hair the color of the sunlight.

Anaxandros stood just inside the shaded part of the deck, his lips pulled back to expose his jagged teeth. It might have been a smile. "This," he said, sweeping the tip of his black sword through the air, "is your doing. Quintus would never dare hunt during the day, never approach a lair."

"Yup," Rhys said. "My idea." Swollen flesh peeked out from the cut Rhys had made in the vampire's shirt. It pulsed and wiggled like a nest of maggots. "By the way, how's your head?"

Anaxandros's expression darkened. "I'm going to enjoy cracking open your bones and drinking your marrow, Quarter."

"And I'm going to enjoy watching you turn into a pile of ash, you fuck." Rhys stepped back until he stood next to Silas. "Can you stand?"

"Yes." And he did. Once on his feet, he faced the vampire. "It's just you now, Anaxandros."

The vampire shrugged, a movement that was eerily close to Silas's own. Rhys felt ice flow down his spine.

"It was only ever you and I, Quintus."

"Perhaps. But no longer."

Those words drew Rhys's attention away from the vampire for a moment. Silas moved his left arm and winced, and the angle of Silas's wrist made Rhys's innards twist. Silas couldn't fight the vampire, not like this. The moment he stepped into the shade, Anaxandros would be on him. Rhys turned back.

"No, you went and found yourself a Quarter." He twirled the sword. "How's the shoulder?"

Silas said nothing.

Rhys looked at his own hand. The wound had spread. *Shit.* He looked up. "I found him."

Anaxandros frowned.

"I'm not his Quarter. He's *my* fae." He put his arm around Silas's good side. "Come on. Let's get out of here." Retreat seemed the best plan. Heal, regroup. Rhys steered Silas toward a set of stairs that led down to the outside deck below.

"Rhys Alexander Matherton."

His name—his full name—on the vampire's lips caused him to stumble.

"Rhys," Silas said, "don't look back."

He didn't. This time he listened to Silas. But the words from Anaxandros lashed out anyway.

"The sun will set, Quarter. Soon. Then you'll both belong to me."

Rhys helped Silas down two flights of stairs and into the garden, oblivious to the people around them, heedless of the fact that both he and Silas carried swords. Maybe they were glamoured, maybe not. It didn't matter.

All that mattered was healing Silas as best he could in the time they had left. He would *not* lose Silas to that thing.

CHAPTER THIRTEEN

*T*he sunlight that streamed in the greenhouse windows was tinged orange, a color Silas had grown to hate over the long years of his life. It brought death and blood and fire and pain. He closed his eyes and let Rhys walk him through the garden. What he could still feel of his arm burned as if it had been dipped in acid.

Only when Rhys sat him down on a bench did he open his eyes and speak. "You should leave me."

"No. Never. So shut the fuck up."

The words that poured from Rhys's mouth were perhaps the most violently loving and curse-laden statements anyone had ever said to Silas.

"You beautiful shit-head, why would you even say that? After all we've been through?" Rhys balled his hands into fists.

It hurt to laugh. The daemon-forged knife had cut deep, spreading its venom into his blood. What was left of that, anyway.

He'd truly been blessed to find Rhys. "I don't want you to die," Silas said.

"Yeah, well, I don't want you dying either. And I'm not having that *thing* take you." Rhys laid his sword on the ground.

Element pushed into Silas, almost painfully. He didn't bother to ask Rhys to be gentle.

Rhys has a sword.

Silas lifted his own blade and stared at it for a moment before handing it to Rhys. "Put both of them back into the Aether. If we lose them here, we can't get them back."

Rhys's rage ticked down a notch. "Why are there two swords?"

"I don't know." Truth, but Rhys looked dubious. "I truly don't. The Messengers must have known." They always knew.

"But you got your sword years ago."

"Two thousand years ago. Yes."

Rhys exhaled. Inhaled. Croaked.

Silas knew that expression well. He'd worn it several times because of the Messengers. "It's not important right now. You needed it. You have it."

Rhys swallowed and nodded, then shoved the blade back in the Aether. Silas's sword followed. "Now, what can I do to help you?"

The amount of element Rhys poured into Silas's body was extraordinary. Had he not taken so much of a beating in the past thirty-six or so hours, he'd have had no trouble healing himself. But now? "Give me your hand. The one that touched the daemon knife."

Rhys extended his right hand, palm up. "It burned. But not like fire."

"Onyx, edged in black diamond, forged in daemon-fire." Silas examined his palm. No nicks. Good. "I'm going to heal you. See if you can sense what I'm doing with the element."

It was a long shot, but Rhys had become more sensitive to

the energy around them. And everything else he knew about Quarters had proved wrong—perhaps Rhys could consciously manipulate the element after all.

He'd done enough of that without thought.

Though a simple healing, it took more of him than he'd expected to lay the element out and bind it to Rhys's flesh, coax skin to grow and heal. By the time he'd finished, his unbroken arm trembled.

Rhys laid his now-healed hand on Silas's forehead. "You're going into shock."

"Probably. Did you feel what I did?"

For a moment Rhys looked as if he might slap Silas. Then he nodded. "Yeah. I think so."

"Good. Do it to me, where the knife entered." He leaned back against the bench and closed his eyes. "It'll be harder. There's poison. Blood is tricky because it moves."

"I have no idea what the hell I'm supposed to do." Panic tinged Rhys's voice higher.

"I'll help as best I can." Which wouldn't be much at all. "You've done this before. From across the ship." He opened his eyes and looked at Rhys. "I trust you."

Rhys furrowed his brow and placed his hand over the knife wound. "Fine." A distant, internal gaze followed.

Then the pain came, burning his veins. Not the sting of death or poison, but of every cell cleansing itself all at once. Silas bit his tongue to keep from vocalizing. Like everything else about Rhys, his healing was brash and bold. He probably sculpted in a fury too.

It was a very good thing he'd been unconscious when Rhys had healed him the first time. With his good hand, he gripped Rhys's arm. "Enough."

Rhys lifted his palm and blinked. "Shit. I hurt you." He brushed a hand against Silas's cheek.

Only then did Silas feel the trail of wetness left behind on his own skin. Tears. His own. "What you lack in finesse, you make up in power. It only stung a bit."

"Liar," Rhys murmured.

"No." He shifted on the bench. "*Now*, you're going to hurt me. We need to set my arm."

All color drained from Rhys's face. Still, he studied the bones. "I think I know what to do. All those anatomy classes."

"Good. Give me a moment." Silas braced himself, drew up a glamour to cover sound, then nodded.

Rhys yanked. Twice.

Silas screamed at the glass ceiling. Twice.

The fire of Rhys's subsequent healing left him racked with sobs, and he curled up on the bench.

Not one of his most glorious moments. The worst bit was the horror writ on Rhys's face and the litany of "I'm sorry, I'm sorry" over and over again, like some damn priest of an apology god.

Still quite a bit of young human in Rhys. What power would he possess in ten years? In one hundred?

Silas grabbed him by the hair and kissed him, tasting his own tears—and Rhys's—in the process. "It's your turn to shut the fuck up," he said. "Sometimes pain is good."

Rhys's green eyes were rimmed with red. "Not this kind of pain."

"I'm alive. I wouldn't be without you."

Rhys wiped a hand over his mouth before answering. "Yet you keep asking me to leave."

Silas stilled. Orange and red clouds glowed in the sky. "Anaxandros is coming for me. I'm in no condition to fight him. I can't win."

"I can." Rhys's bravado both warmed and chilled Silas, because Rhys believed what he said.

"No, you can't." He shifted to sitting and held up a hand

to stifle Rhys's retort. "You can wound him, yes. But in a long, drawn-out battle?"

That belief wavered. Rhys set his jaw, but fear lingered in his eyes, in his shuddering breaths. "They wouldn't have sent you if there was no hope."

The Messengers. The truth of Rhys's words dislodged the ghost of an idea. Silas exhaled. Then he pulled in a lungful of air that smelled of earth, leaves, and Rhys and said a single word. "Bait."

The retort he expected didn't come.

From the tight pull of muscles in his face, across his shoulders, Rhys didn't like the idea. He stretched out one long leg. "So, what? I chop off its head when it comes to take you?"

"Something like that."

Rhys let out a strangled laugh. "That's the shittiest idea I've ever heard."

As plans went, it *was* the most pathetic he'd ever concocted. "Have you a better idea?" He said it without sarcasm.

Rhys rubbed his face. "No." He dropped his hands into his lap. "Do we wait here?"

There was a certain advantage to the garden. "This seems as good a place as any. Better, perhaps."

"Anaxandros will know. I mean, he'll see the trap. Every other time I hit him, he hadn't been expecting it."

"Not true."

That caused Rhys to turn.

"You managed to catch him with your sword. He knew you had it, should've expected you'd use it."

"I don't even know how to use the thing. I just swung."

So Rhys had. And with a speed even Silas couldn't manage. "You're fast."

After a derisive snort, Rhys reached into the air and drew out his sword with an ease that sent prickles across Silas's skin. Everything about Rhys was quick, including his ability to learn.

Rhys looked down the length of the blade. "The pattern's different." He offered the blade to Silas.

He took it and examined the fine etching down the center. The impossible thought that there could even be a second sword had blinded him to the differences. It felt nearly like his, but not quite. Rhys was correct. The weave that ran up the center was tighter than the pattern that ornamented his.

"I should've noticed."

"Didn't you? I saw you look at one point."

He handed the blade back to Rhys. "I'd thought there was something odd, but put it down to my light-headedness and your handling of the blade."

Rhys laid the sword flat across his legs. "I'm not fast."

"You move like wind and water. Like a blade of grass in a stiff breeze." Silas paused. Sea grass and pine. "Where were you born?"

Rhys's skin took on a ruddy hue. "Nowhere special. Nowhere like Italy."

"There was no Italy when I was born, and I was rather provincial." He swallowed a laugh. "Still am, in many ways."

"Provincial." Rhys imitated his accent again. "You should see the way you look. The way you dress. Hear how you speak. There's nothing provincial about you."

"Rhys—"

"New Jersey. I was born in New Jersey."

Silas chewed on his tongue for a moment. "Near ocean and pine."

"Close to the Pine Barrens. Why?"

"Curiosity." He took one of Rhys's hands in his own.

"You're of the forest and the field but smell of the sea. And pine. I didn't understand."

"And do you now?"

"Shifting sand."

"Oh." Rhys twined his fingers between Silas's. "You mean I'm unstable."

Silas couldn't help the chuckle. "You're adaptive and quick. Whereas I'm old and set in my ways."

"Grounded."

Opposites. Complementary. Gods below, if only there were land beneath their feet. Silas stood. "Come. Let's get a drink and watch the sun set."

Rhys rose and sheathed his sword back into the Aether. "Love to."

———

THEY HAD SINGLE MALT SCOTCH, the best on the bar list, poured by Vasil. The waiter looked grim. "People are starting to notice odd things," he said, his voice low.

Silas took a sip, and the drink seemed to evaporate on the back of his throat. Peat and smoke. "It'll be over tonight, one way or another."

Vasil paled and looked at Rhys.

"Everything will go back to normal," Rhys said.

Vasil nodded and headed down the bar. Silas strode to a table by the window, Rhys close behind. The fiery ball of the sun hung low and red in the sky, its reflection in the water churned by the passing of their ship.

"What will happen to him if we fail?" Rhys drank, then he peered into his glass. "I always thought scotch took the skin off your throat."

"Cheap scotch does."

Rhys glanced at the receipt in his hand and looked up. "Provincial, my ass."

Silas shrugged. "Wait until you meet other fae before you make that judgment."

"Other fae." Rhys examined his glass again. "What will happen if we fail?"

"If" they failed. *If.*

He wanted to carve that word out of the English language. Slice the concept out of every tongue he knew.

"If we fail, and if the passengers and crew are lucky, Anaxandros will be too busy with us to bother with anyone on the ship."

A shudder ran through Rhys, and he took another longer pull of scotch. "I thought we'd die."

There were worse, far worse things than dying. Hanging in the dark, throat raw from screaming, smelling blood and piss and excrement for endless days of pain. That voice, that deep, haunting voice, laughing.

Needles pricked the insides of Silas's bones. He set down his glass and looked out at the sunset. "If we fail, we won't die. Not for a very long time."

Rhys swirled his glass, his color draining away. "I guess we better not fail."

"No." Silas finished his drink. "We best not."

But hope had stretched so thin, he felt it fray and split as the sun sank into the ocean.

RHYS'S MUSCLES ITCHED. Every time anyone walked down the path through the garden, he tensed, thinking it was Anaxandros. But the number of people in the garden had dwindled to nothing. The last person to walk down that path had been Vasil. The waiter had nodded to Silas and then hurried into the main part of the ship.

Vasil hadn't seen Rhys at all, which was good. Sort of.

He should've been the one sitting as bait.

But Silas had insisted, and so Silas sat. Well, he paced now. An hour after Vasil left, Silas had risen from the wooden bench and started walking up and down the path they'd chosen as their battleground.

Rhys lurked behind a stand of rhododendron, his back against a lemon tree, sword leaning next to him. At first he'd clutched it like a talisman, but after his arm cramped he had set it down.

He didn't even know how to use the damn thing. Swing it like a bat? Right. He resisted the urge to sigh.

All he had was the knowledge that he was quicker and, at the moment, stronger than Silas. And they knew Anaxandros wanted them. Would stop at nothing to have them.

Rhys glanced at his watch and stretched his back. Four in the morning. The vampire should've come by now. Standing here was pointless, and his legs hurt. He sheathed his sword into the Aether and slipped out onto the path.

Silas turned on the ball of his foot, unsheathing his sword from the air. His expression slid from wary to annoyed. "What are you doing?"

"Sitting down." He made his way toward the bench. Or would've, had Silas's look not morphed into fear.

Shit.

Rhys dived for the floor as stinging fire raked across the back of his neck. The blow hurt more than bouncing off the pavers. He rolled away.

From where he'd been came an unnatural screech of metal sliding against metal—swords colliding—then silence. That was broken by Anaxandros's soft, dark laugh. Something warm and wet ran down Rhys's neck. As he scrambled to his feet, he rubbed at the liquid. The stinging bloomed into a throb of stabbing heat. His hand came away sticky and red.

Blood. His. So not good. Neither was the scene before him.

Silas stood, one hand clutching the back of the bench, the other holding his sword in front of his body.

The vampire lingered just out of Silas's reach, his black blade pointing down. Anaxandros bared his teeth. "So you can use that thing after all."

Silas straightened and let go of the bench but said nothing.

"Pity you're spent. I would have liked to test you in your prime."

The laugh Silas gave was nearly as dark as the vampire's. "No, you wouldn't have. But you were never one for fair and equal."

"Fair?" Anaxandros raised his sword. "Equal? From the lips of a fae?" He leaped forward.

Rhys didn't see the series of blows that came crashing down on Silas, or Silas parrying, only the blur of black and silver and that same horrible scrape as before. He reached into the Aether, ran into the fray, and swung his sword at the vampire's head like a batter after a fastball.

His sword whiffed air. He never was very good at hitting the fast ones either. The swing took him too close and set him off balance. But it stopped Anaxandros from attacking Silas.

The vampire's claws ripped through Rhys's shirt and raked bloody lines down his chest. Ice stung his veins and chilled his lungs. A flash of silver slid through Anaxandros's wrist, and the air around Rhys filled with the smell of burned flesh. The clawed hand convulsed before it fell and burst into flame.

Rhys sucked in air through his teeth and tried not to scream as he fell backward, away from the vampire. It felt like bees had replaced his blood. A spasm racked his arm, and his sword slipped from his hand. The clatter of the blade on the stone path was drowned out by a howl of fury so powerful Rhys felt the hate deep in his bones. He scrambled to his feet.

Anaxandros rained blow after blow down on Silas, his dark blade ringing against Silas's sword like a blacksmith's hammer. Silas fell to his knees under the onslaught.

And then the silver sword in Silas's hand shattered into countless pieces.

No! He threw himself at Anaxandros. It was all he could do, all he had left. The next blow would kill Silas.

Finally some use for those years of football. A well-placed shoulder into the vampire's hip kept the thing from cleaving Silas in two. It should've knocked the vampire over.

It didn't.

Anaxandros growled a single word Rhys was sure was a curse. Dark liquid oozed from the stump of the vampire's arm as the vampire straightened and eyed Rhys.

"You will lose this dance, Quarter." The black blade swam in Rhys's vision, the edge wavering and twisting as if it were alive. His own sword lay a good fifteen feet away.

No way out of this.

There had to be a way out.

"Yeah." Rhys took a deep breath and angled himself between Silas and that blade. "Probably. But you never know."

For an instant, Rhys saw a flash of doubt in the vampire's face, but then the black sword moved. And so did Rhys—right into Anaxandros, as close as a lover. Given their height differences, it was easy enough to duck under and grasp the vampire's good arm. Rhys pushed up.

"Silas!"

There was no way for the vampire to claw him off, not with a stump, and no way for the thing to strike him with the blade. Maybe he'd give Silas just enough time to get the other sword.

As Anaxandros snarled and fought against him, an odd sense of euphoria filled Rhys. They were going to survive!

Teeth sank into his neck. Spears of flame tore through his body, ripping apart his bones, shredding his lungs. All hope, all love, all the things that made living worth the time and effort flowed out of him. It was all Rhys could do to grasp on to the moments of his life as they slipped by. One by one, they slipped away, only to be replaced by acid and fire. Above them, the palm trees shook and groaned.

Silas yelled, his words unintelligible but full of malice and wrath. Only when Rhys fell hard onto Anaxandros's shoes did the burning in his body stop.

"Do you wish to see him dead, Quintus?" The point of the vampire's sword clicked against the stone mere inches from Rhys's eyes.

He wouldn't have moved had he been able to. As with Radmila and Jarek, he was paralyzed, blood screaming in his veins, but he was also far too aware. Moisture blurred his vision.

So much for winning.

"Do you understand yet, Quintus?" The question was almost gentle. "You'll never be strong enough to protect him."

Silas gave no answer. Nor was he anywhere in Rhys's view. All Rhys saw was a slice of black metal that twisted and danced before him.

The blade was alive.

It screamed in the same way Rhys wanted to, reached out toward life even as it killed all it touched. Fear crept into

Rhys and mixed with the sparks of icy fire that burned through his organs.

"They'll take him from you. Pull you two apart. Try to force another to him." Anaxandros spoke in that same almost reasonable tone. One that seemed true. Caring.

Don't listen to him. But Rhys couldn't speak. Couldn't help Silas see through the lies the vampire spoke.

The black blade whispered with the voice of a woman, with the voice of summer trapped in ice. *"He's not lying."*

Oh God. In that moment, Rhys understood.

SILAS DIDN'T UNDERSTAND why Anaxandros hadn't attacked him again. Rhys lay at the soulless's feet—alive, thank all the gods for that, but unmoving. He had Rhys's sword, but Anaxandros surely saw the tremble in his stance. There was no way Silas could withstand another series of blows like the ones that had shattered his sword. He could barely stand. His vision wavered, his blood still too thin to support him.

Every nerved tingled. He was on the verge of fainting.

Yet all the soulless wielded were words. It gave him a moment of rest he desperately needed, so he'd play this game.

"What do you know of fae?" Silas said. "Of Quarters?"

There was that smile again, the curl of contempt, those razor teeth coated with Rhys's blood. "Far more than you, Quintus."

Silas slid forward a step. Anaxandros tilted his head and fingered the hilt of the daemon sword he balanced on a spot just in front of Rhys's nose. He twirled the blade on that point.

Silas froze.

"I once underestimated your intelligence," Anaxandros said. "Don't disappoint me by playing the fool now."

"I have no desire to please you," Silas said while his mind spun around the soulless's words. He was missing something. Diana help him, there was meaning in the vampire's talk.

He didn't understand. He felt all the more helpless as he looked down at the crumpled form at Anaxandros's feet.

He'd give anything to save Rhys.

"Anything, Quintus?"

He hadn't realized he'd spoken out loud. Part of him was sure he hadn't, and he didn't want to contemplate what that meant.

"Anything?" the soulless repeated. "Your life?"

This wasn't the game he intended to play, but he found he couldn't keep silent. "Yes." His voice was a whisper.

"Your soul?"

For a moment, breath failed to fill his lungs. Then he managed a mouthful. "Fae can't..." Or so he'd been told. Humans could relinquish their souls. Messengers could fall. But the fae were fae, always.

Anaxandros stood tall, inhuman, and looked like the most glorious day of summer. Silas had never thought—never seen that possibility before. He took a step back and wielded words like a shield. "Fae can't give their souls."

The soulless chuckled. Then it spoke in a tongue none of its kind should know, a tongue older than humans. "Is that what they told you?"

He hadn't heard the fae language in so long. It was for the court, for family, and he had none of those things.

Horrible, horrible understanding blossomed like a bloodstain on cloth. The death of his court, those long years of torment and pain. Why the Messengers had chosen him. They had to have known, because they *always* knew.

Fae. Anaxandros had been fae.

It took all his strength not to drop the sword in his hand. Rhys's sword.

Rhys.

As if the soulless—this fae soulless—could read his thoughts, it lifted the point of its sword and stepped over Rhys. "The Messengers are fond of choices, aren't they?"

Silas backed into the wall of the planting beds behind him. He hadn't meant to move at all. An instant later, Anaxandros pushed the sword away with the stump of his arm and laid the daemon blade on Silas's shoulder. The edge kissed the side of his neck.

"I'll give you a choice." Anaxandros spoke in fae, in the tones a brother might use. "Give your soul to me, and I'll spare his life."

The daemon blade burned against his neck as Anaxandros kissed his cheek. "Or keep your soul and see him dead, and I'll keep you alive to remember him for the rest of eternity."

Those are not choices!

"There are no other options, Quintus."

Become soulless so Rhys could live. Or let Rhys die.

"You can keep him safe. Forever."

Silas couldn't push any words from his lips.

Anaxandros lifted the sword from Silas's neck. "Choose."

The moment hung like the last leaf of November. But in the end, he couldn't let Rhys die. "I—"

"No." Rhys's guttural voice boomed through the garden. Branches shook above, sending showers of debris down on them. From the edge of Silas's vision, Rhys leaped at Anaxandros, his bloody hand holding something jagged and silver. He jammed the sword shard deep into Anaxandros's neck as the soulless turned to block.

Anaxandros mouthed a voiceless scream. Then it clubbed Rhys with the stump of its arm. The blow caught Rhys hard in the head, sending him flying down against the stone path. He hit, rolled, and then lay still.

Rhys!

Smoke poured from Anaxandros's mouth. Silas pushed the soulless away. When Anaxandros swung his black blade at him, he parried, his muscles trembling against the force of the blow. The blades screamed.

Any other soulless would be in flames, but Anaxandros's eyes were clear, his blacking mouth twisted in anger. He parried Silas's every stroke.

Silas had no strength left, only enough to slip through the tiny opening in Anaxandros's defense. He plunged forward just as Anaxandros stepped out of the way.

No! Silas threw himself sideways in an attempt to avoid the next stroke. He crashed to the ground. Anaxandros, his neck now black, followed after him. Silas rolled away but not fast enough.

Anaxandros plunged the daemon blade through Silas's shoulder and into the stone paver. Death flowed into Silas, corroding his blood, eating his flesh and bone. Every good thing inside him withered. Darkness stabbed deep, cut through his heart and pierced his lungs.

Silas screamed and thrashed against the blade, but it didn't move, just cut all the deeper. Grasping the blade only sliced and corrupted his hands.

Over him, Anaxandros loomed. Words ripped through Silas's mind. *"I had you at the end. You were mine."* Then the soulless's head toppled from its body and bounced off Silas's chest.

The trunk fell forward and burst into flames. Ash and fire rained down on Silas. Flames seared his flesh. Hot air burned his throat. The sword remained and sucked his soul like marrow from bone, cracking and splintering what was left of his life.

His vision blurred. Smoke, blood. Rhys above him.

Rhys. Rhys was alive.

Too many words, not enough languages. He couldn't even move his lips.

I'm sorry. There was so much I wanted to show you.

CHAPTER FOURTEEN

*R*hys scrambled over to Silas and grabbed the hilt of Anaxandros's sword with his left hand. Hundreds of knives flayed his skin from his muscles, then muscles from bone. He gritted his teeth, tightened his grip, and yanked the blade out. He tossed the thing as far from Silas as he could.

His hand turned bluish gray. The other was in ribbons.

Vampires might not have souls, but he knew the blade did. It was like him, that soul. Rhys sought for a pulse at Silas's neck, but his fingers had gone numb. He laid his head on Silas's chest.

The only sound, only beating, came from Rhys's own thrumming heart.

No.

Rhys balled Silas's shirt in his hands. Gray and black lines ran up the side of Silas's neck. They spread as Rhys watched, creeping across Silas's cheek.

No!

Life swam around him, his element, Silas's element. Rhys took all that he could and slammed it into Silas. In his mind, he ripped out the damage the blade had done, built new, healthy flesh, and pushed at the blood that grew stale in Silas's veins.

Move, damn you!

Silas's heart did, slowly at first, then faster. A thump, then another, and another. More. A steady rhythm.

Good. Rhys pulled back slowly, but as he did, Silas's heart faltered and slowed.

Oh fuck.

He laid his head on Silas's chest once more and listened to a heart that only beat because Rhys forced it to beat. After a while, he lessened the flow of element and let Silas's heart slow and stop. He closed Silas's empty eyes.

There was nothing else he could do. Rhys sat up and swallowed the lump in his throat and rubbed his neck. No blood. No wound. He didn't have to glance down at his chest to know he'd healed those injuries too. All except the ever-growing crack wrenching his soul apart.

Fan-fucking-tastic. Rhys lurched to his feet. He could heal himself, even fix Silas's body, but that meant nothing. Nothing at all.

Because Silas was dead. Rhys screamed and kicked at the nearest ash pile. He hadn't even had the satisfaction of watching Anaxandros burn. All that was left was a dead Silas, piles of ash, and a living sword.

Three long strides took him to the blade. He picked it up and felt the flesh of his hand wither. A strong pull of element fixed *that.*

So he could wield this thing. And there were plenty of other ways to seek his revenge, a way to right the injustice that had happened here.

He pulled more element. Nearby, ivy withered and died.

Good. The last thing he wanted was life. The blade whispered a thought to him. *Angels.*

Yes. They'd sent Silas here. He'd start with the angels.

"Rhys Alexander Perun Matherton." His name thundered through the garden like the clear tone of a giant bell. A man of average height with short brown hair stood in the center of the garden path. "Put the sword down."

He eyed the stranger. No accent. Clean and oddly elegant features. He wore jeans and a white button-down, shirttails out. Red high-top sneakers. Rhys stared at the shoes for a moment. Then he eyed the man again.

"Strike him down."

Rhys took a step forward.

"Put the sword down." Same booming voice, though the man didn't shout.

"Make me."

The stranger smiled beatifically, but what appeared around him was as monstrous as it was beautiful. Wings tipped with gold and scarlet and swords of light encompassed the height of the garden and beyond. Lidless and large eyes— countless numbers of them scattered throughout the wings— all turned to look at him.

"Rhys," the angel said. "Put down the sword."

He did, and stumbled backward and to his knees under the angel's many-eyed gaze.

Minutes passed. Or maybe millennia. It was hard to tell because Rhys watched as galaxies were born, lived, and died in those eyes.

Beauty. Death. If he could have crawled under a rock and hidden, he would have.

"My name is Nathaniel." The man walked forward, and the image of the angel's true form vanished. "You need not fear me, Rhys."

"But you... I..." He had thought to slay angels. The truth pinned him to the ground. Stole his breath and left nothing behind but shame.

"A thought is not an action." He touched Rhys on the head, as if in benediction, and the weight of his guilt cracked and frayed. "You were not entirely in control of yourself, and were also half-mad with grief. You are forgiven. We are not capricious beings, Rhys."

Good thing. Because he really ought to be dead right now. But breath came once more.

Another smile graced Nathaniel's lips, and movement returned to Rhys.

The angel walked to the black sword. "Do you know what this is?"

"A trapped soul."

Nathaniel picked up the blade. "Most blades like this contain the soul of one of the Fallen. They're meant to destroy my kind."

The guilt Rhys expected with those words didn't come. "But not this one."

"No." He pushed it into—not the Aether, for the glimpse Rhys saw was as blinding a light as the Aether was dark.

"She was—" Rhys choked on the words, cleared his throat, and tried again. "She was Anaxandros's Quarter."

Nathaniel nodded, his expression grim. Or sad. "He chose a path that cut them both off from the living."

"What will happen to her?" The whisper of the sword had been as dark as Anaxandros.

"She is free, and her soul can rest." The angel seemed to read his thoughts. "Her recompense has been paid out over many millennia, Rhys. As I said before, we are not capricious."

"Silas is dead," he blurted out. "He did what you asked, but he's dead."

"No."

Rhys finally found the strength to stand, but that single word sank him to his knees again. "He's alive?"

"No." Nathaniel held up a hand. "He walks between the two even now, pondering which choice, which path to take."

"What will he choose?"

A brief look of consternation passed over Nathaniel's face. He gazed at Silas for a moment before speaking. "I do not know." There was wonder in his voice.

The angel didn't know. Rhys chewed on the inside of his mouth. Silas hung between two choices.

Shit.

Rhys scrambled over to Silas's side. "Silas," he said. He gripped his shirt and gave the body a shake. "You said you'd do everything you could to stay with me. Well, I'm still here, so you damn well better come back!"

Oh God, he hoped Silas could hear him. Bright red sneakers came into view next to him. Rhys felt Nathaniel's hand touch his head once again, this time in encouragement.

"He will hear you."

Rhys shook the limp body and called again. "Silas!"

SILAS STOOD on a hillside in Campania. He hadn't been here in hundreds of years, and yet he knew exactly where he was, knew the touch of the earth, the pull of the grass and shrubs. He could name the trees. Just down that path and over that knoll, past the sentry stone pine lay home. His home.

Only they were all dead, and this...this... Silas took a better look around.

This was very odd. The sky was blue and clear—too clear. No contrails.

He closed his eyes and listened. No sounds of cars. No hum of anything electrical. The air smelled of wood smoke—not diesel or petroleum.

A strange tingle ran down Silas when he looked around again. This was Campania exactly as he remembered from his youth. A land that didn't exist anymore.

He still wore slacks and a button-down shirt.

Very, very strange. Something sounded on the wind, and he turned toward it, but the noise was indistinct and muffled. Silas paused, shook his head, and headed down the path that would take him home. He cleared the knoll, smelled the sweet scent of pine, and stopped.

Pine. There was something familiar about the scent, like the tickle of a memory. Something was missing, though. What was he forgetting?

He brushed his hand against the bark. He'd first kissed Isatis here, all those years ago. Yes, that must be it.

Still, that didn't seem quite right. Silas traced the lines in the bark. Why was he here?

A dream. It must be a dream. He let out a breath and continued down into the valley. There was a break in the hills just past that stream that led to the court. The scent of bread and honey wafted to him, and he quickened his pace. Baking bread. Smoke. They were here.

He'd never dreamed them here before. Never. The court was always empty and cold.

He ran. All he had to do was cross the water—

Water?

Silas stopped and stared at the thin stream that trickled across his path.

There hadn't been a stream. Ever. Not in life, not in his dreams. Yet here was one. More troubling, though it was only a hand span in width and full of clear water, he couldn't see the bottom.

The odd tingling returned. He looked up.

Isatis stood on the other side of the stream. Not his shade —his lemur—but Isatis, clear-eyed and smiling.

"Silvanus."

He bit back the automatic correction, because he wasn't Silas here, had never *been* Silas here.

"Isatis?" The name was rusty on his lips. When had he spoken it last?

Memories bubbled like sea foam on a wave. A tile floor, cool beneath his feet. A man with eyes the color of summer grass and a soft voice. *What was his name?* His own response. *Vel Calavius Isatis.*

Silas took a step back. "You're dead. I saw you die."

"Yes."

The pinpricks that had been chasing up and down his spine dug in. The stream. Dark and thin. When he lifted his gaze again, it wasn't just Isatis who stood on the other side of the tiny, insignificant stream.

The whole court stood there. His mother, her hair as dark and curly as his, and his father with his straight light hair and honey eyes. Their king. Tall and broad with laughter like wind ruffling grass.

Everyone.

Words stuck in Silas's throat. Home. He'd truly come home at last. He could be at peace.

He'd been so tired for so long.

"We've waited for you," Isatis said and held out his hand.

Everyone he'd ever loved was just a step away. Everyone.

"Silas."

His name sounded on the wind, like the distant roll of thunder. Or a crash of a wave. He turned toward it.

Everyone he loved?

His name came again, louder this time. With it flowed a breeze that smelled of pine—not the stone pines that grew here, but shorter tenacious pines from a distant shore, and sea grass.

"Rhys." As he spoke the name, the memories came.

Rhys's smile. Coffee. The touch of skin and a passion that made him feel new and young again. A ship, the soulless. Anaxandros. The daemon sword plunging into his flesh. Seeing Rhys before he died.

He had *died*.

Silas looked back at the court, at Isatis and his family. Long moments passed before he spoke. The words were for Isatis. "You've haunted me since that night."

His smile was sad and loving. "No. You only ever haunted yourself."

Rhys called his name again. This time it came with the words "fucking bastard." Silas couldn't help the snort. *Rhys*.

Isatis raised his head at the sound, and the sadness vanished. "Let me go, Silvanus."

"I think I can now." Before he turned away, he ran a hand through his hair and searched for words. They were all inadequate, but he tried anyway. "I love you all. And miss you. But Rhys—Rhys found me. Saved me. Now there's so much more to do. I can't leave him."

It was his mother who replied. "Then the gods keep you safe until we meet again."

"And all of you." He looked over his court, those who had died before him all those years ago. They were at peace.

Silas let them go.

His rest didn't lie here, not yet. His solace was behind him, back in a world of chance and danger—and love. He turned from the stream and began the climb out of the valley. By the time he passed the stone pine, he was running.

"Rhys! Wait!"

When he cleared the valley, fog rolled in and swallowed him whole. He stumbled and fell, pain bursting in his chest. He gasped for breath, large lungfuls that hurt and felt sweet all the same. When the ringing in his ears subsided, he heard Rhys's voice. "It's okay, Silas. You're going to be okay."

"Rhys." His vision swam but eventually settled down. He had an excellent view of Rhys's torn-open shirt. But the skin beneath was unmarred.

Gods, did he hurt. He cleared his throat and touched Rhys's chest. "You're alive."

"Yeah." Rhys sat back on his heels, and that beautiful grin of his stretched his lips wide. "So are you."

"I am, yes." Silas felt his smile grow, until he realized they were not alone.

He knew the other being. "Nathaniel."

Rhys stilled and glanced up at the Messenger.

"Silvanus," Nathaniel said.

"You—"

"No. It was Rhys who healed your body and Rhys who called you back. I came to collect Anaxandros's sword and to see."

"See? See what?"

It was Rhys who answered. "See what you would choose. He didn't know."

That knocked him speechless for a moment. The Messengers *always* knew. They stood beyond Saturnus's reach, not touched by time. "How is that possible?"

Nathaniel gave him an enigmatic smile. "Call it a gift from the universe."

Silas pulled Rhys into his arms.

Rhys struggled for a moment before leaning his head against Silas's shoulder. "I thought you'd left me."

"I did," he said. "But I came back."

Nathaniel exhaled a breath that sounded exceedingly close to a sigh. Then he set a sword down next to them. "This is yours, Silas, should you want it. And for Rhys." He set a second sword next to it. "And now I'll take my leave."

Rhys called after the Messenger. "One more thing!"

Nathaniel paused. "Yes, but only one, Rhys."

Rhys tensed, and his breathing hitched. Then he relaxed and nodded. "There's a waiter named Vasil. He asked if you would pray for him."

True smiles from angels were rare. Nathaniel graced Rhys with one. "And so I shall." From his pocket, he produced a loop of beads that ended with a tassel and handed them to Rhys. "Give these to him."

"I will," Rhys said and closed his hand around the strand.

The Messenger turned and walked away.

They were alone, but for the plants and two piles of ash.

Silas kissed Rhys's neck. "What else did you want to ask him?"

"When I was—" Rhys shuddered in Silas's arms. "No. I'll tell you that part later." He started again. "He called me by my name."

"They do that."

"He called me Rhys Alexander Perun Matherton."

"Yes?"

"I've never been called Perun before, and yet…"

No doubt the name had felt correct. They might use misdirection, leave pieces out, but the Messengers never lied. "It must be your name, then. Or will be."

"Or was," Rhys said. He voice was very soft.

In that instant, much of the annoyance he'd felt for the Messengers fell away. "That too was a gift, I think. A clue."

Rhys was quiet. Thoughtful. After a time, he spoke. "What about the swords?"

Another choice. Silas looked at the blades. Two. His and Rhys's. "It's not always an easy life to work for the Messengers."

"So I've noticed." Wry humor, even now after all that happened. "I don't want to live every day like the past few."

"This was the worst it's ever been."

Rhys's lips against his neck spread a deliciously distracting warmth down his back. "That's over now."

Over. Anaxandros had been destroyed. He could put down the sword, stop hunting. "Shall we leave them, then?"

"Is that what you want?" Rhys's thoughtful expression returned.

No. Yes. There were other soulless out there, perhaps even others who had once been fae. And he'd miss the feel of the blade in his hand, the thrill of the hunt. But his life wasn't entirely his own, and he'd no desire to pull Rhys into that world unwillingly.

Rhys snorted. "Yeah, I thought as much." He slid from Silas's embrace. "I don't want to spend all my nights hunting vampires."

"Then we—"

Rhys picked up both swords and held out Silas's. "Once in a while would be fine, though. When they really need us."

Silas tamped down the sudden tightening of his throat and took the blade from Rhys. "That will work quite well, I think." He sheathed it into the Aether.

Rhys put his sword away, and stood. "Besides, I want you to teach me to use it. We can't do that if we give up, right?" He held out his hand.

Silas grasped it and let Rhys pull him upright. "True." Beyond the glass walls of the garden, it was still night.

"What are you thinking?" Rhys said.

"I think"—Silas brushed his fingers over the tears in Rhys's shirt—"I'd like to go to bed before dawn."

"There's a novel concept." Rhys stepped in and kissed him. Hard. When he let Silas's mouth go, he spoke again. "I hope you hadn't planned on sleeping."

"At some point, but not right away."

"Good." Rhys pulled him toward the elevators.

CHAPTER FIFTEEN

Once inside the foyer of Silas's cabin, Rhys pushed Silas up against the wall and kissed him with the same passion Silas had used on him just two nights before. It seemed like a lifetime ago. Rhys needed to touch Silas, taste him, and hear his breath. Beneath Rhys's hand, Silas's heart fluttered. *Alive.*

When Rhys broke the kiss, Silas spoke, his voice rough around the edges. "This seems familiar."

Bits of element swam around Silas.

Rhys stroked Silas's throat. "A bit." He unbuttoned the top button of Silas's shirt, then the next, working his way down. Silas tasted of honeysuckle and sunlight. "You're not covered in drinks, though." He planted a kiss on Silas's collarbone and pushed his shirt off. "You've got more energy now."

"I can feel the garden." Silas gripped Rhys's hair, tugging just hard enough to send a bolt of desire straight down his spine to his cock. The only way to stifle the moan in his throat was to suck on Silas's earlobe.

The groan that echoed through the foyer was Silas's. Rhys

couldn't help the chuckle. That died when he ran his fingers over flesh that should've been smooth.

Rhys pulled back and touched the spot where Anaxandros's sword had run Silas through. "There's a scar."

The remnant of the wound was just a shade lighter than Silas's bronze skin, a single rough line. He'd been injured before, by the dark knife, by vampire claws, but none of those seemed to have left a mark on Silas's body.

Only the one wound that had nearly killed, nearly taken Silas away from him. Silas traced his finger over the scar and grunted. "So there is."

The wall on other side of the tiny foyer pressed a chill into Rhys's back, though he didn't remember stepping backward.

The churning in his soul must have been all over his face, because when Silas looked up, his expression went from intrigued to rattled in a heartbeat.

"Rhys, it's fine. I'm fine."

And he was. Alive and solid. Warm. But that didn't change the past, didn't change what almost took Silas. Rhys had held that sword, listened to its whispers, and rage had consumed his soul. The rough texture of the wall bit into his back.

"Rhys?"

"Anaxandros was fae." The words felt like broken glass in his mouth.

"I know." Silas stepped forward, reached for him.

Rhys flinched. He tried not to but failed. Oh, he wanted the comfort—desperately needed it. He wasn't sure he deserved it. Silas had once feared being a monster. For a moment, Rhys had been one.

Silas froze. Then he lowered his arm.

"The sword. Anaxandros's sword—"

"It was a daemon blade. That's why the scar." Silas didn't

move, but the vein in his neck ticked out a fast rhythm. "Other fae have such scars, if they live."

"It wasn't a daemon. In the sword."

Fine lines formed around Silas's eyes. "Then what—"

"It was the soul of Anaxandros's Quarter." The words tasted like sand.

Silas's breath caught. For a moment, his jaw worked, but no words came out. Then they burst forth in a rush. "The Messenger told you this?"

"Yeah." Rhys pushed himself off the wall and walked into the main part of the cabin. If he didn't sit soon, he'd fall over. His legs shook. "But I knew before that." He sank down on the edge of the bed.

Silas had followed. That he was dressed only in his ridiculous tweed pants should've made Rhys laugh, but the scar was still there. Rhys looked down at the bloodstains on the cuffs of his shirt. He'd healed his hands, healed Silas too. Wielded tremendous power, even though he wasn't supposed to.

Terrible, horrible things could be done with that power. Worse, he'd nearly done them. His heart twisted with shame. Fear compressed his lungs. How much would it take to return to that darkness? His fingers wouldn't stop trembling.

Silas knelt down before him and took his hands. "What happened?"

"When I thought you had died, I picked up the sword." He told Silas everything. The whispers, the darkness, how he'd made the trees groan.

"I wanted the whole world to burn."

"No," Silas said.

No? "I know what I felt." He would've pulled away had Silas not been gripping his hands firmly.

"I have no doubt that's what you felt. But it wasn't what

you truly wanted, or we wouldn't be having this conversation." Silas ran a thumb over Rhys's knuckles.

Because the angel would have killed him, not forgiven him.

"All this power..." Rhys stared at his hands in Silas's. "It's a little frightening." It would only get worse on land. "I don't want to become like that Quarter."

Silas kissed his hands, as some courtier from another century might. It seemed natural. "You shan't, I don't think. Anaxandros...liked to possess things. People. Power."

"That's what you feared, becoming like that."

"Yes." Silas looked up at him. "But I don't think I will."

Rhys slipped one of his hands from Silas's grasp and brushed unruly locks from Silas's forehead. "Good. Because if you ever do, I'll kick your ass."

That heart-stopping grin appeared. "I know."

"Promise me you'll kick mine too, if I start getting it into my head that I can rule the world."

"I can do better than kicking your ass." He let go of Rhys's hands, rose, and pushed him back onto the bed.

Rhys tangled his hands in Silas's hair as Silas claimed his mouth. He wrapped his legs around Silas's hips as his fae thrust the hard bulge of his erection into his rapidly hardening cock.

Silas broke the kiss. "I'll lay you out, undress you, and make love to you until you remember yourself." He ground against Rhys.

Rhys bit back a moan and gripped Silas's shoulders. "Get out of those ugly pants."

"They're fine pants." Silas stripped Rhys of the remains of his shirt and tossed it off the bed. True to Silas's word of stripping him naked, Rhys's slacks followed. Only then did Silas finally shuck the tweed.

When Silas lay on Rhys again, this time skin to skin, Rhys

couldn't swallow the moan. He tingled everywhere. Silas's deep chuckle vibrated against Rhys. "But they do get in the way."

Rhys kissed his neck, nipped at his shoulder, and stroked Silas's hair while Silas licked his way down Rhys's chest to his stomach. When he stopped to swirl his tongue around Rhys's belly button, Rhys tightened his grip and pushed Silas's head lower.

He didn't need teasing now. Warmth stirred inside Rhys. He wanted his cock inside Silas's mouth.

That's exactly what he got, hot and wet around the head. Silas licked at his tip, then engulfed him. His mouth felt like the heat of summer and warmed Rhys to his bones. He thrust into that willing mouth, needing more of Silas, more of peace, warmth, and the promise of life.

It wasn't enough. He pulled Silas off and scooted farther up the bed. "Come here."

Silas did as told. Rhys's balls tightened. He didn't want to run the world, but ruling Silas, even for a short time, felt so good. "On your back."

Though he complied, there was a touch of defiance in his expression. "I thought the plan was for me to make love to you?"

"That was your plan, not mine." Rhys snatched the bottle of lube off the nightstand. "My plan involves fucking you silly." Because he needed to feel Silas all around him, needed to know he really was alive and here with him.

He took just enough time to slick his cock and Silas's hole before he plunged into Silas, hard and fast.

Silas threw back his head and exhaled a deep groan. Rhys leaned forward as he drove himself into Silas, savoring the heat, the tight fit, and the look of rapture on Silas's face. Silas wrapped a hand around his cock and jacked himself off. Too fast.

Rhys pried Silas's hand away and forced it above Silas's head. Rhys stilled himself deep within him. "I don't want you coming yet."

Silas squirmed under him. That and his wild expression sent lightning down Rhys, and he almost came right then. He caught Silas's other hand and pushed that up near the first.

Silas said nothing, but his grin spoke volumes. Oh, this would cost him, Rhys knew. But that was also part of the plan. He wanted a good hard fucking from Silas.

Just not at the moment.

Rhys pounded into Silas, starting slow and building faster. The friction and heat made his cock ache down to his balls. His entire body felt wrapped in Silas's tight channel. Beneath him, Silas arched and met his strokes. His words were guttural. "More, Rhys."

God, how he loved the sound of Silas's voice, the feel of his body. The way the feral-fae look transformed Silas from controlled to a force of nature. Energy swirled around them—more now than ever before, as if they were still in the garden. Rhys gathered it, then pushed it into Silas as he pounded into his body. Rhys's balls tightened as element flowed through him.

Silas's whole body tensed, and he came, crying out something long and unintelligible.

As Silas tightened around his cock, all the energy slammed back into Rhys and sent him careering into his own orgasm. He thrust hard into Silas's taut body until he was utterly spent.

Breathless, he collapsed onto Silas.

"You're not going to pass out on me, are you?" Silas stroked his face.

Rhys coughed a laugh. "I should, just to spite you."

Silas wrapped his arms around Rhys, drew him in for a

quick kiss. "Impertinent and beautiful. Gods help me, but I do love you."

"Good." Rhys tangled his legs with Silas's. "Because you're stuck with me."

"And you, with me."

Rhys touched the scar on Silas's chest and then stroked his cheek. "That works. Because I love you too."

Silas was quiet for a moment, a slight smile curling his lips. "The world is full of wonders."

It was. One lay next to Rhys. "Wanna show them to me?"

Silas pulled him in close, his lips nearly touching Rhys's. "There is nothing in the world that I want more."

EPILOGUE

*V*asil Kutsera stood on the promenade deck and looked out into the New York Harbor. Early morning sun cast pale golden light onto the green hue of the Statue of Liberty. *Give me your tired, your poor, your huddled masses yearning to breathe free*, the inscription read. Well, he was one out of three. Tired. Very, very tired. He still couldn't sleep at night, even after Mr. Quint and Mr. Matherton had told him the upyr were gone. Destroyed.

He'd cleaned up the ash in the garden before anyone else had discovered it. The blood too. Disposed of the razor-sharp shards of silver. Later that day, maintenance had replaced the cracked paver. Thank the Lord no one had asked about that.

Dreams haunted him. Nothing that made any sense. Fire and sand. Wings. The achingly beautiful face of a woman with long black hair and eyes as dark as storms.

Prayer helped a little. He'd taken to clutching the tiny travel diptych his brother Jan had given him before he'd signed on to the cruise line. The Pantocrator and the Theotokos.

"You'll see such interesting things!" Jan had said.

Vasil swallowed a bitter laugh. If only he'd known.

The cruise ship moved lazily in the water, following the pilot boat. According to the logs, it had been an amazingly uneventful cruise. Except, of course, for Mr. Quint being leshii and Mr. Matherton being—whatever it was that he was. And the upyr biting him. Vasil rubbed his neck. No scar left, but for the one inside.

The one that allowed him to see what shouldn't be seen. Streaks of color wound through the sky like streamers in the air. But overwhelmingly, green ribbons fluttered and wove, tying the land to the ship. They curled around the deck, around Vasil, and slipped under the door into the ship. When Mr. Matherton and Mr. Quint pushed those double doors open in tandem, Vasil was unsurprised to see the green light wrap around them.

He was also not shocked when the pair came toward him.

Vasil rubbed his eyes. The leshii was inhumanly beautiful. Everything the stories had ever said. Most of the time, it hurt to look at him, so Vasil focused more on Mr. Matherton. There was a touch of the wild in him, but he was merely humanly gorgeous. Today he wore jeans and a black T-shirt emblazoned with some rock band's image in dark gray. Odd contrast to Mr. Quint's tan slacks and red polo shirt.

"Vasil," Mr. Matherton said. "How are you?"

"I'm well, thank you. And you?"

He liked Mr. Matherton, despite everything. Had he not been a passenger and had he not been so obviously in love with Mr. Quint… But it was what it was. Like so many other things in Vasil's life.

"Are you?" Mr. Quint asked. Another stream fluttered against the breeze. It twined around the leshii's arm.

Vasil smiled. Or tried to. "Of course."

Neither man looked convinced. Mr. Matherton glanced at the deck before speaking. "I have something for you."

"I'm not supposed to take gifts. Tips for the staff—"

"It's not from me. Or Silas."

Vasil glanced at Mr. Quint. He'd gone still in a way humans did not.

Mr. Matherton cleared his throat, his face reddening. "You asked me...that night..."

Oh. Vasil fought the urge to step back and won. But cold tendrils wrapped around his arms and legs, much as the strange light wrapped around the men in front of him. "You met an angel."

Mr. Matherton nodded. His eyes were wide with memory. Vasil could almost touch the awe. "And I asked if he'd pray for you. He said he would."

Lord have mercy. He struggled to find words in Ruthenian, let alone English. "Thank you. I don't know what to say."

"He also asked me to give you this." Mr. Matherton fished into the front pocket of his jeans, then held out a *chotkis*. The beads glinted in the light, flashing the same colors as the ribbons that danced above the harbor.

Vasil's heart felt like it stopped and then restarted. His chest hurt. Eyes watered. Breathing became difficult. His hand trembled, but he took the prayer rope from Mr. Matherton. The beads were warm. Vasil's hands tingled as he moved the beads—they were stone—through his fingers.

A chotkis from an angel. The sensation spread up his arms and haloed his scalp. *Merciful Lord.* Vasil looked up.

"I don't know what it is," Mr. Matherton said.

Vasil glanced at the leshii. "Your Mr. Quint does."

The dark-haired man nodded. "Though not the type of stone." He paused. "I don't think it's of this world."

Well, of course not. No stone shone like gold and sparkled like diamond while being dark as the empty places in the soul. It felt of peace and smelled of incense and— Vasil drew a breath. "Yes, I know."

Mr. Matherton prodded his companion with a well-placed finger to the side. "Well, what is it?"

Mr. Quint raised an eyebrow and looked—pointedly—at Vasil.

"It's a chotkis. A prayer rope. Like a rosary."

"Oh."

Vasil's chest tightened again. "Thank you." He held out his hand to Mr. Matherton. It was safer than the strange urge he had to hug both men. Kiss them like brothers.

Mr. Matherton took his hand and pulled Vasil into an embrace anyway. It was warm and quick. Exactly right. "Take care," Mr. Matherton said.

Mr. Quint held out a business card to Vasil. "If you ever need anything." His voice was soft, full of remorse.

This time Vasil ignored his better judgment. He wrapped Mr. Quint in a fierce hug. "Thank you."

"You have nothing to thank me for."

He let Mr. Quint go. Vasil's head swam, whether from all of the light flowing around these two men or from the warmth of the chotkis on his arm, he couldn't tell. But the weariness that had plagued him was gone. "No, I do."

Mr. Quint was an exquisite picture of skepticism.

"You showed me the world as it is."

"A curse."

"A gift, Mr. Quint." Vasil slid the beads down into his hand. Counted one off. "I need only to discover what to do with it."

ABOUT THE AUTHOR

Anna Zabo writes contemporary and paranormal romance for all colors of the rainbow and lives in Pittsburgh, Pennsylvania, which isn't nearly as boring as most people think.

Anna has an MFA in Writing Popular Fiction from Seton Hill University, where they fell in with a roving band of romance writers and never looked back. They also have a BA in Creative Writing from Carnegie Mellon University.

www.annazabo.com
annazaboauthor@gmail.com

ALSO BY ANNA ZABO

The Takeover Series

Takeover

Just Business (Takeover #2)

Due Diligence (Takeover #3)

Daily Grind (Takeover #4)

Coming Soon

Outside the Lines, A Bluewater Bay Book